VOLTRON FORCE
TOURNAMENT OF LIONS

D1472358

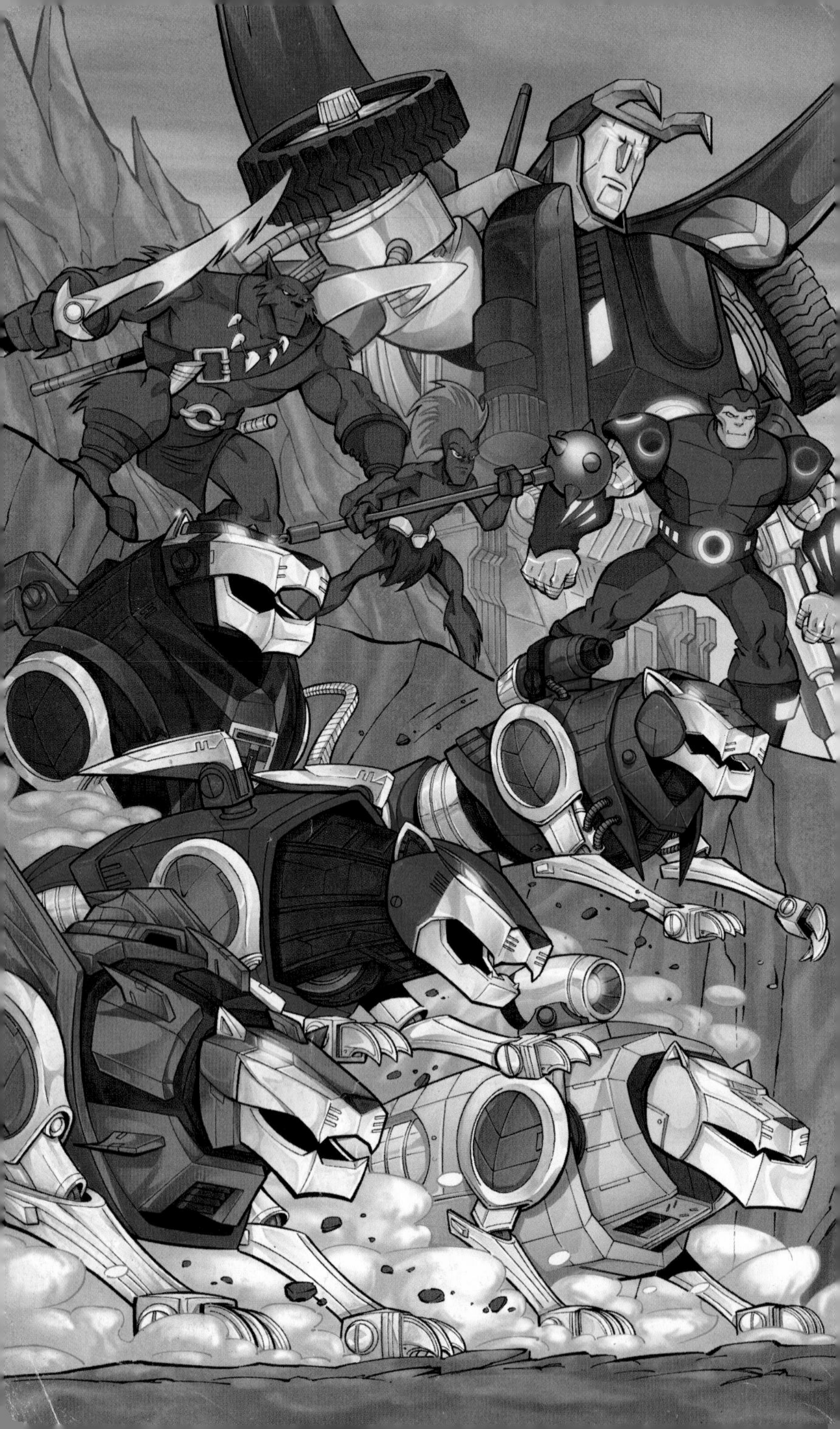

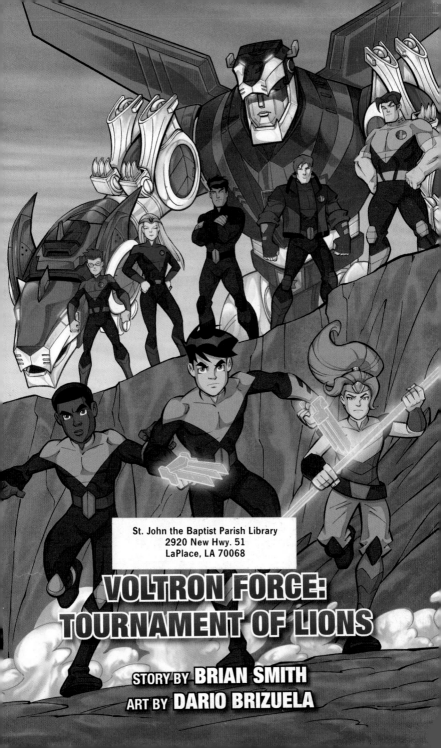

St. John the Baptist Parish Library
2920 New Hwy. 51
LaPlace, LA 70068

VOLTRON FORCE: TOURNAMENT OF LIONS

STORY BY **BRIAN SMITH**

ART BY **DARIO BRIZUELA**

Voltron Force vol. 2: Tournament of Lions
Story/Brian Smith
Artist/Dario Brizuela
Ink/Marlo Alquiza, Walden Wong
Colorist/Hi-Fi Colour Design
Letterer/Deron Bennett

Cover Art/Dario Brizuela
Graphics and Cover Design/Sam Elzway
Series Editor/Traci N. Todd
Editor/Mike Montesa

Voltron Force ™ & © World Events Productions
under license to Classic Media.

The stories, characters and incidents mentioned in this
publication are entirely fictional.

No portion of this book may be reproduced without written
permission from the copyright holders.

Printed in the U.S.A.

Published by VIZ Media, LLC
P.O. Box 77010
San Francisco, CA 94107

10 9 8 7 6 5 4 3 2 1
First printing, June 2012

RATED **A** FOR ALL AGES

PARENTAL ADVISORY
VOLTRON FORCE: TOURNAMENT OF
LIONS is rated A and is suitable for
readers of all ages.
ratings.viz.com

vizkids
www.vizkids.com

VIZ media
www.viz.com

With the combined might of five robot lions and the combined skill of five highly trained pilots, Voltron is the most powerful force for good in the universe.

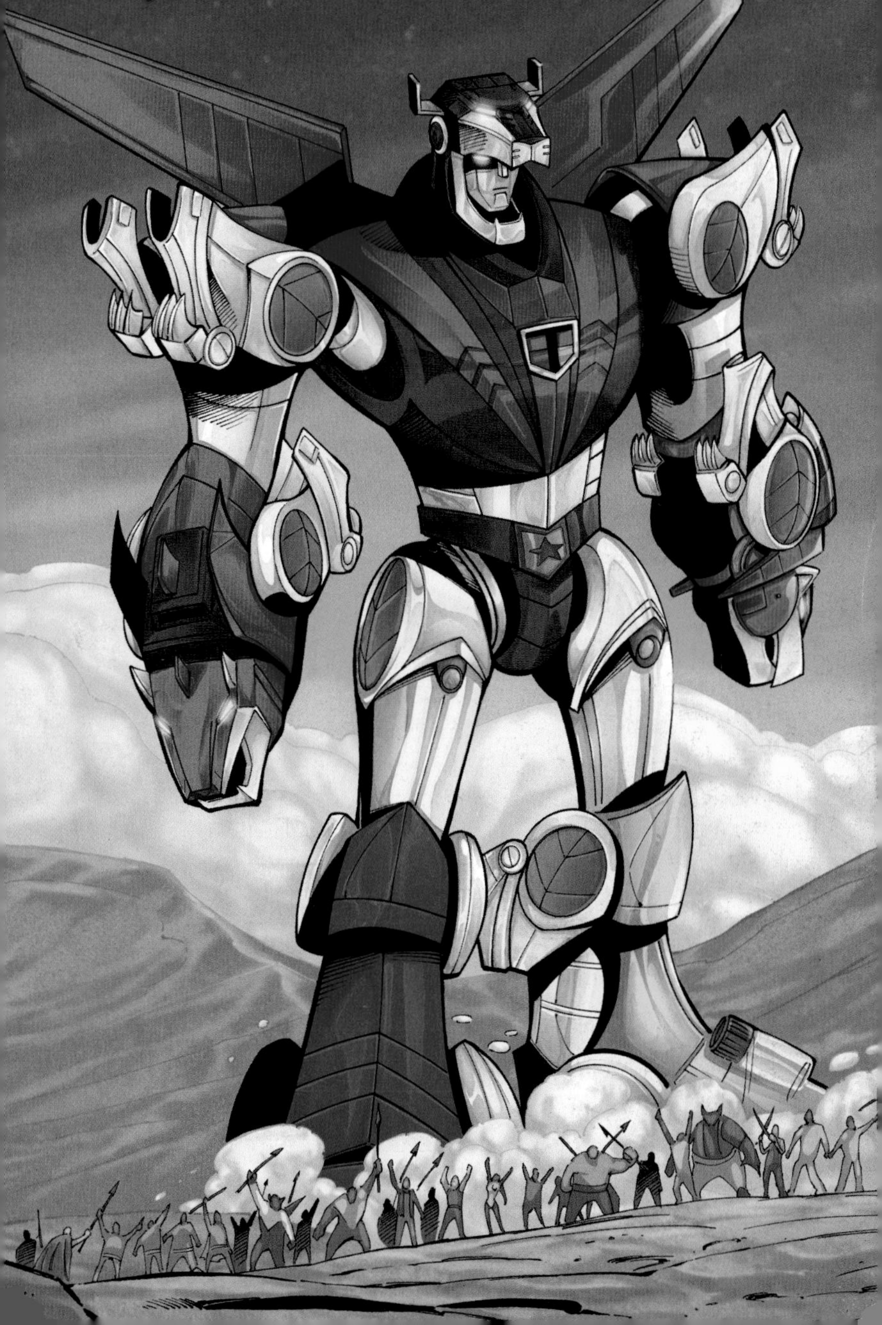

VOLTRON FORCE PILOTS AND CADETS

Keith is the Voltron Force commander. He pilots Black Lion.

Lance pilots Red Lion. He's quick with the one-liners and willing to bend the rules.

Hunk works with Pidge to update and repair the lions. Hunk is the Yellow Lion pilot.

Pidge is the resident tech genius. Pidge pilots Green Lion.

Allura is the princess of Arus, the planet that is home to the Voltron lions. Allura pilots Blue Lion.

Larmina is Allura's niece. She wants to be where the action is—and that's anywhere she can show off her martial arts training.

Daniel grew up dreaming of piloting Black Lion and is impulsive and fearless.

Vince possesses the same ancient, mysterious power locked inside Voltron.

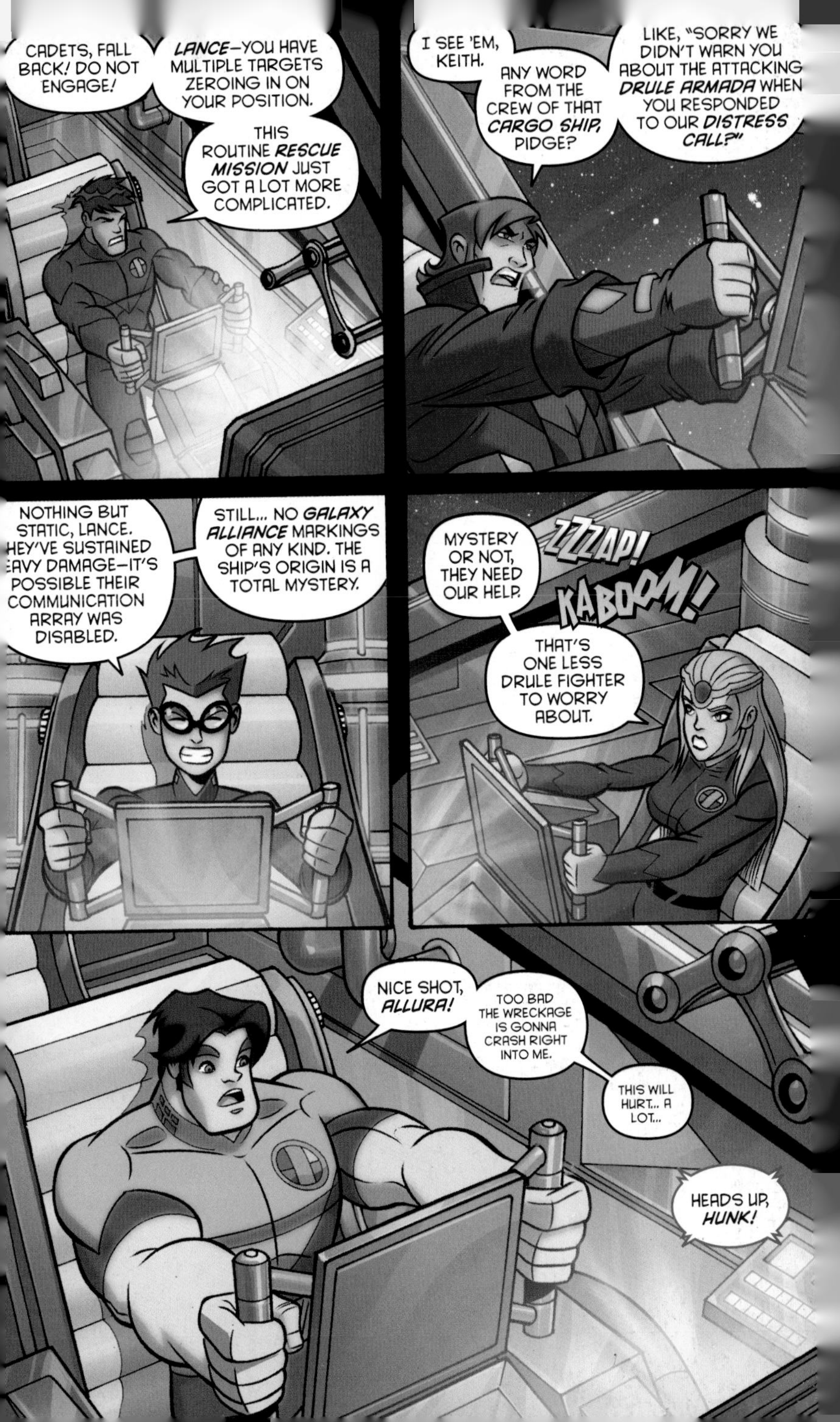
CADETS, FALL BACK! DO NOT ENGAGE!
LANCE—YOU HAVE MULTIPLE TARGETS ZEROING IN ON YOUR POSITION.
THIS ROUTINE RESCUE MISSION JUST GOT A LOT MORE COMPLICATED.
I SEE 'EM, KEITH.
ANY WORD FROM THE CREW OF THAT CARGO SHIP, PIDGE?
LIKE, "SORRY WE DIDN'T WARN YOU ABOUT THE ATTACKING DRULE ARMADA WHEN YOU RESPONDED TO OUR DISTRESS CALL?"
NOTHING BUT STATIC, LANCE. HEY'VE SUSTAINED EAVY DAMAGE—IT'S POSSIBLE THEIR COMMUNICATION ARRAY WAS DISABLED.
STILL... NO GALAXY ALLIANCE MARKINGS OF ANY KIND. THE SHIP'S ORIGIN IS A TOTAL MYSTERY.
MYSTERY OR NOT, THEY NEED OUR HELP.
ZZZAP!
KABOOM!
THAT'S ONE LESS DRULE FIGHTER TO WORRY ABOUT.
NICE SHOT, ALLURA!
TOO BAD THE WRECKAGE IS GONNA CRASH RIGHT INTO ME.
THIS WILL HURT... A LOT...
HEADS UP, HUNK!

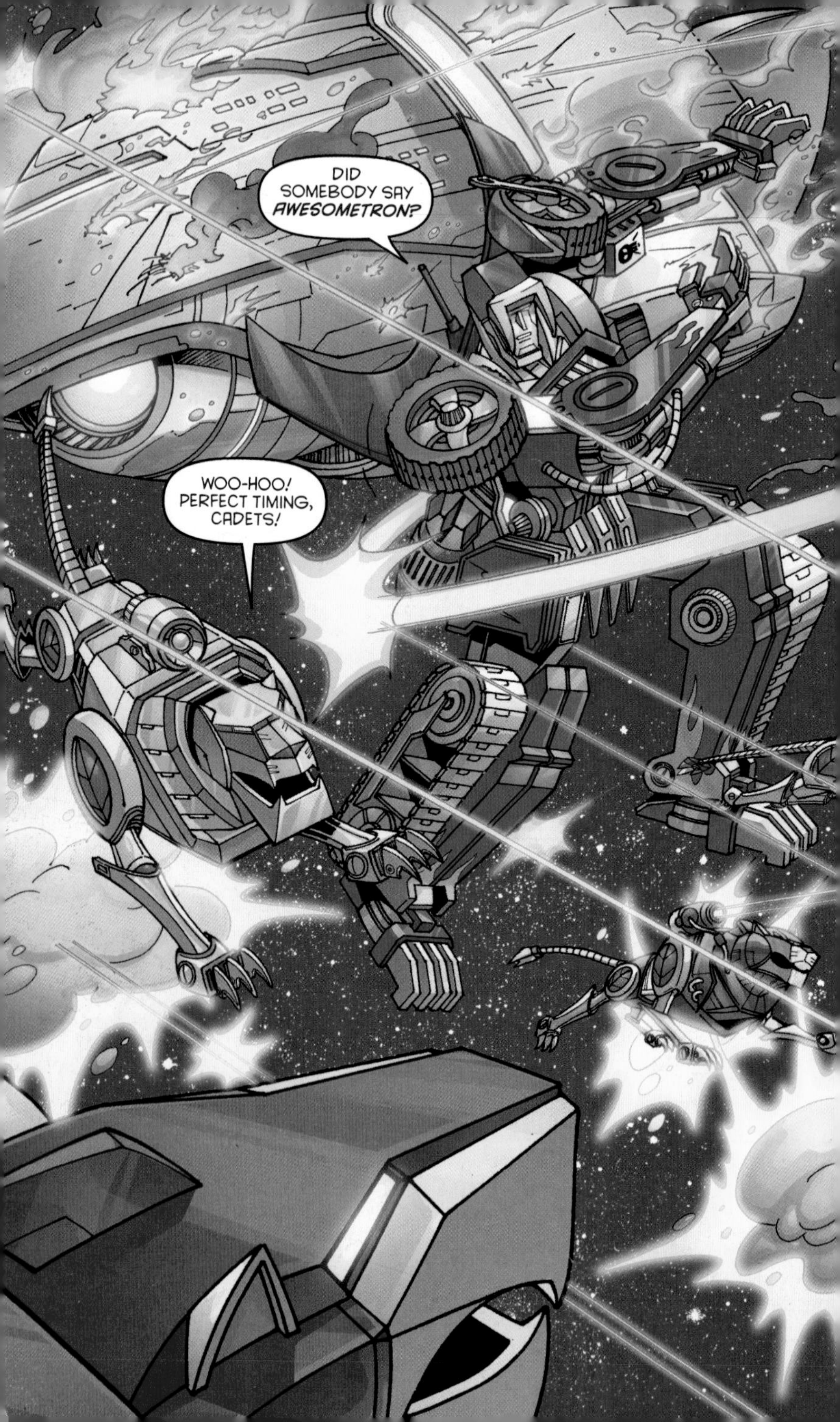
DID SOMEBODY SAY *AWESOMETRON?*
WOO-HOO! PERFECT TIMING, CADETS!

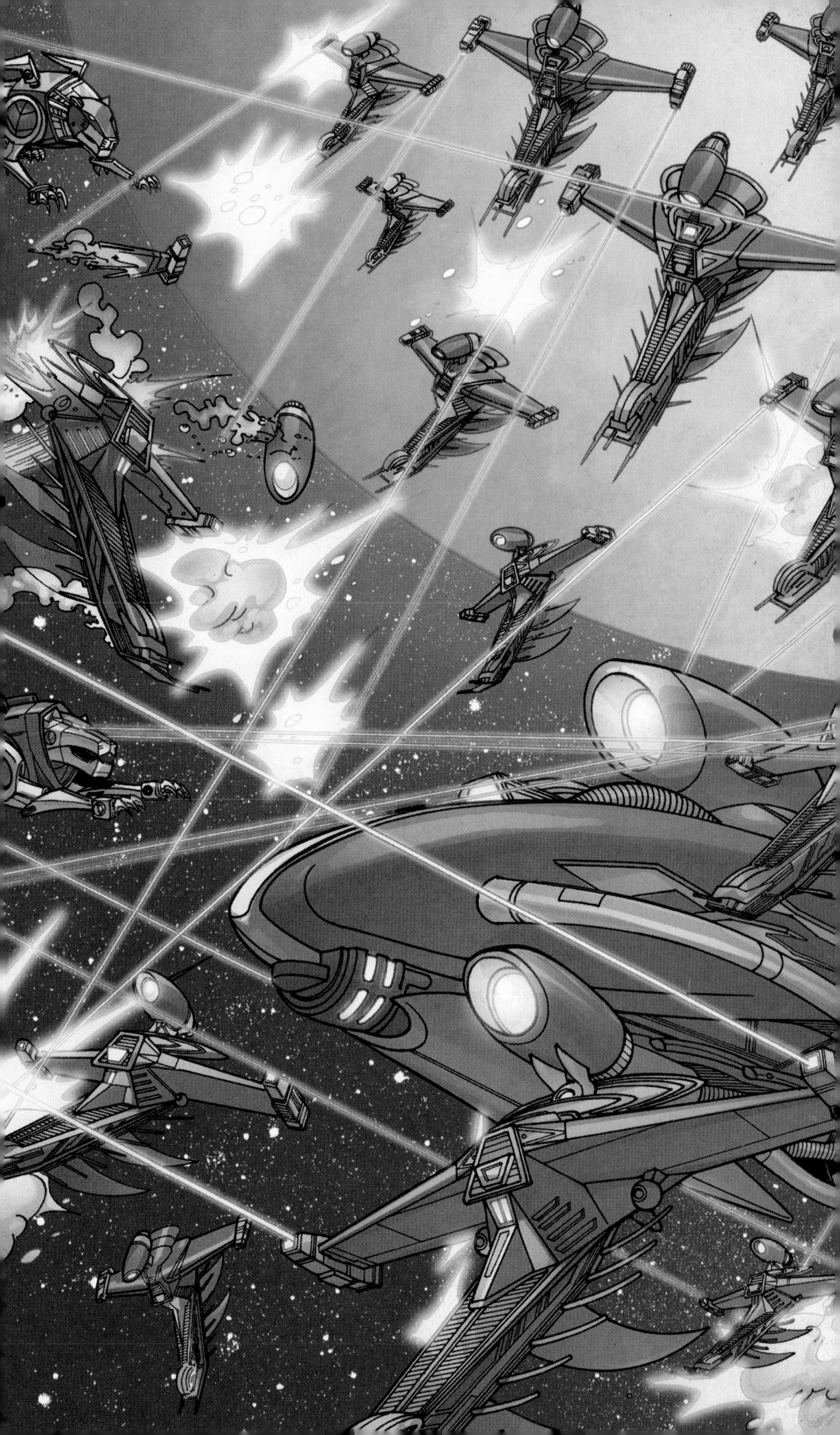

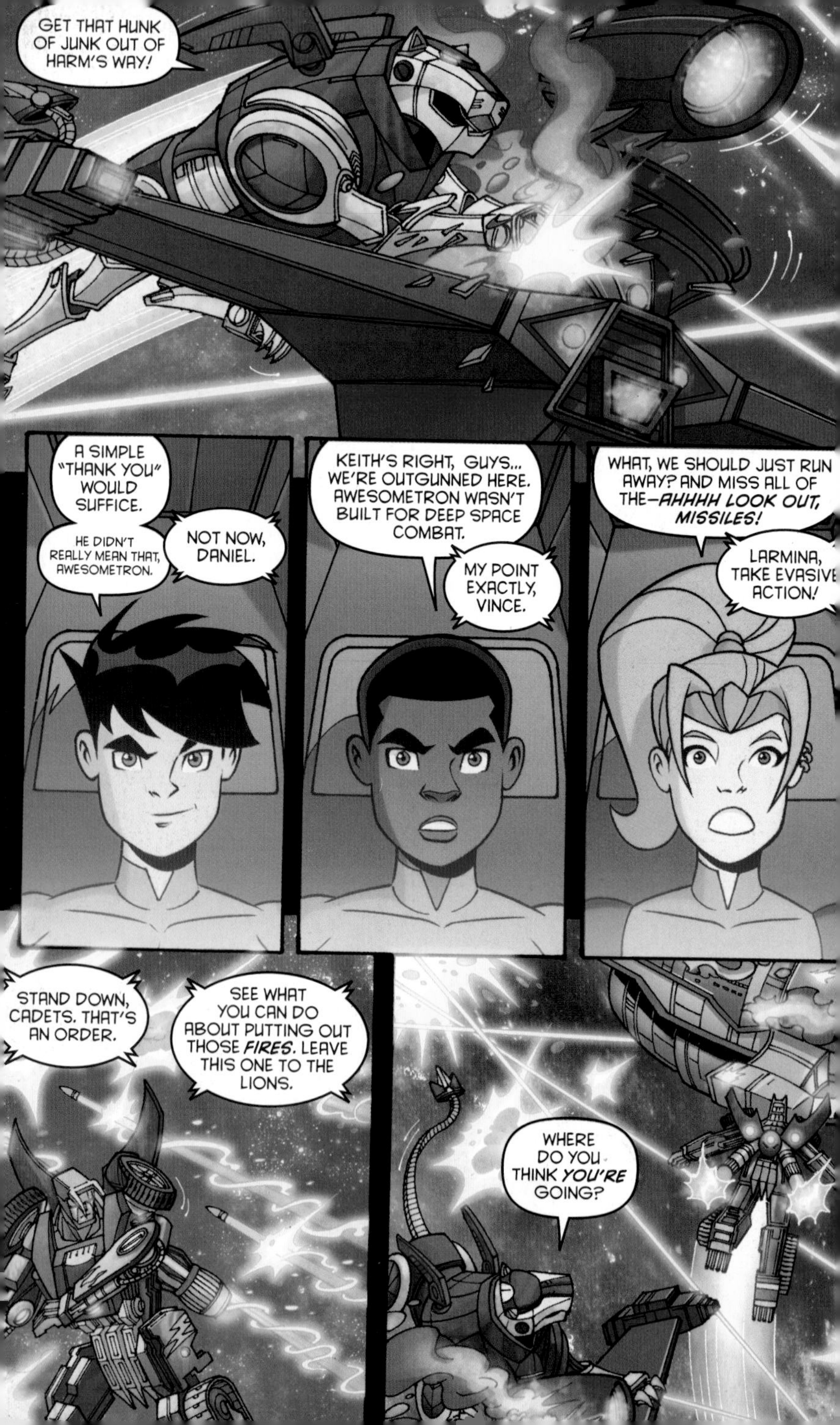
GET THAT HUNK OF JUNK OUT OF HARM'S WAY!
A SIMPLE "THANK YOU" WOULD SUFFICE.
HE DIDN'T REALLY MEAN THAT, AWESOMETRON.
NOT NOW, DANIEL.
KEITH'S RIGHT, GUYS... WE'RE OUTGUNNED HERE. AWESOMETRON WASN'T BUILT FOR DEEP SPACE COMBAT.
MY POINT EXACTLY, VINCE.
WHAT, WE SHOULD JUST RUN AWAY? AND MISS ALL OF THE—AHHHH LOOK OUT, MISSILES!
LARMINA, TAKE EVASIVE ACTION!
STAND DOWN, CADETS. THAT'S AN ORDER.
SEE WHAT YOU CAN DO ABOUT PUTTING OUT THOSE FIRES. LEAVE THIS ONE TO THE LIONS.
WHERE DO YOU THINK YOU'RE GOING?

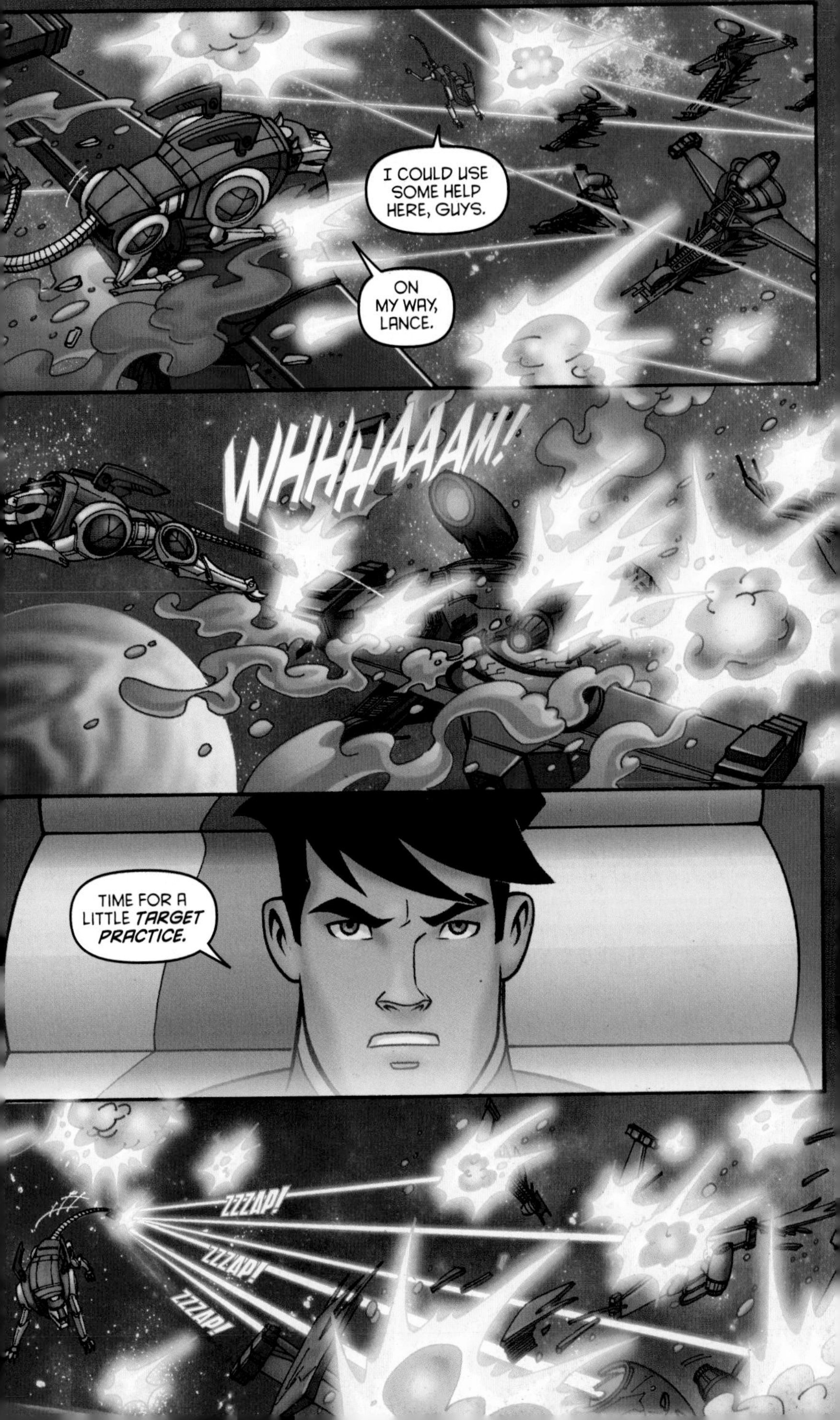
I COULD USE SOME HELP HERE, GUYS.
ON MY WAY, LANCE.
WHHHAAAM!
TIME FOR A LITTLE *TARGET PRACTICE.*
ZZZAP!
ZZZAP!
ZZZAP!

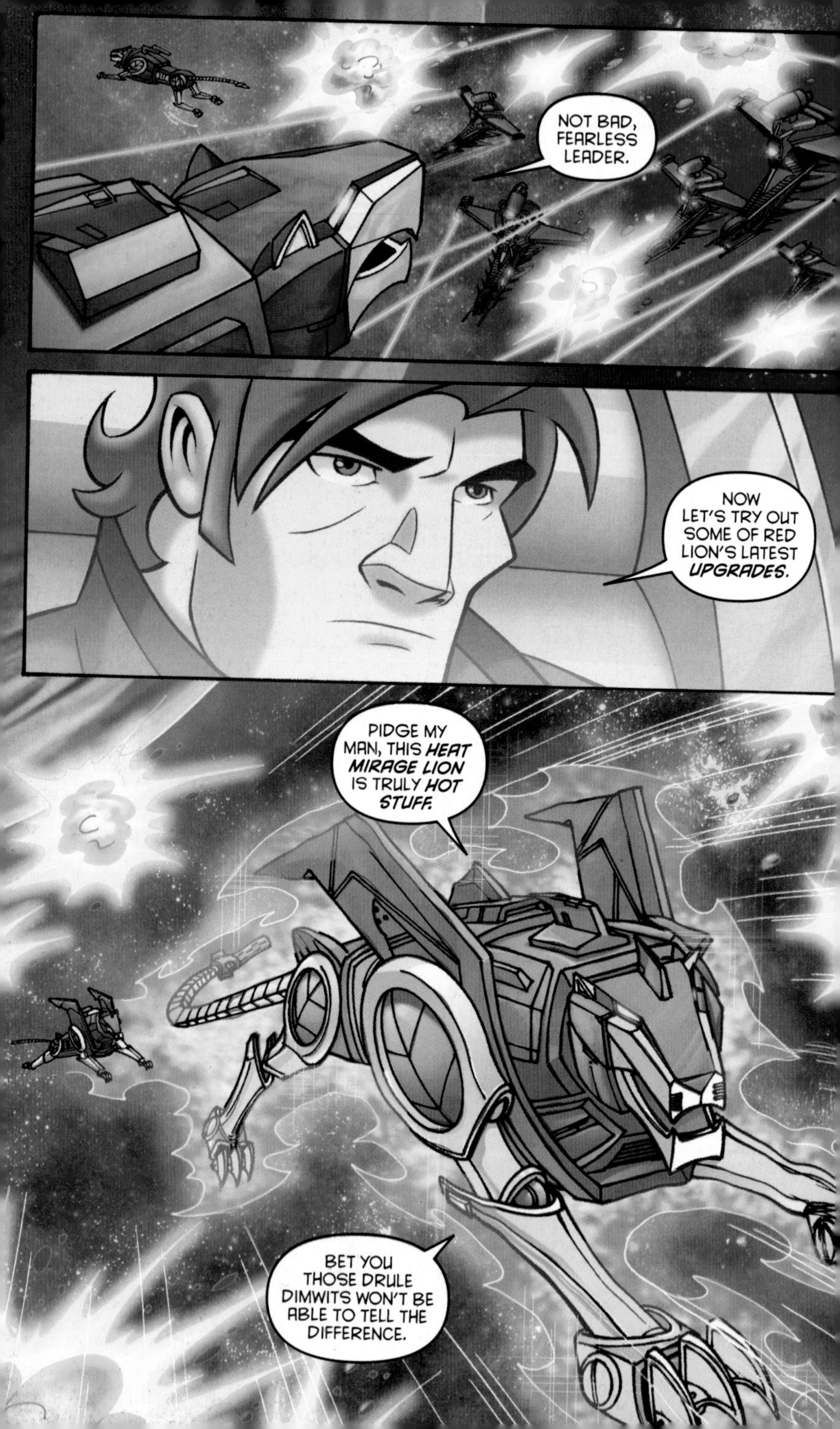
NOT BAD, FEARLESS LEADER.
NOW LET'S TRY OUT SOME OF RED LION'S LATEST *UPGRADES.*
PIDGE MY MAN, THIS *HEAT MIRAGE LION* IS TRULY *HOT STUFF.*
BET YOU THOSE DRULE DIMWITS WON'T BE ABLE TO TELL THE DIFFERENCE.

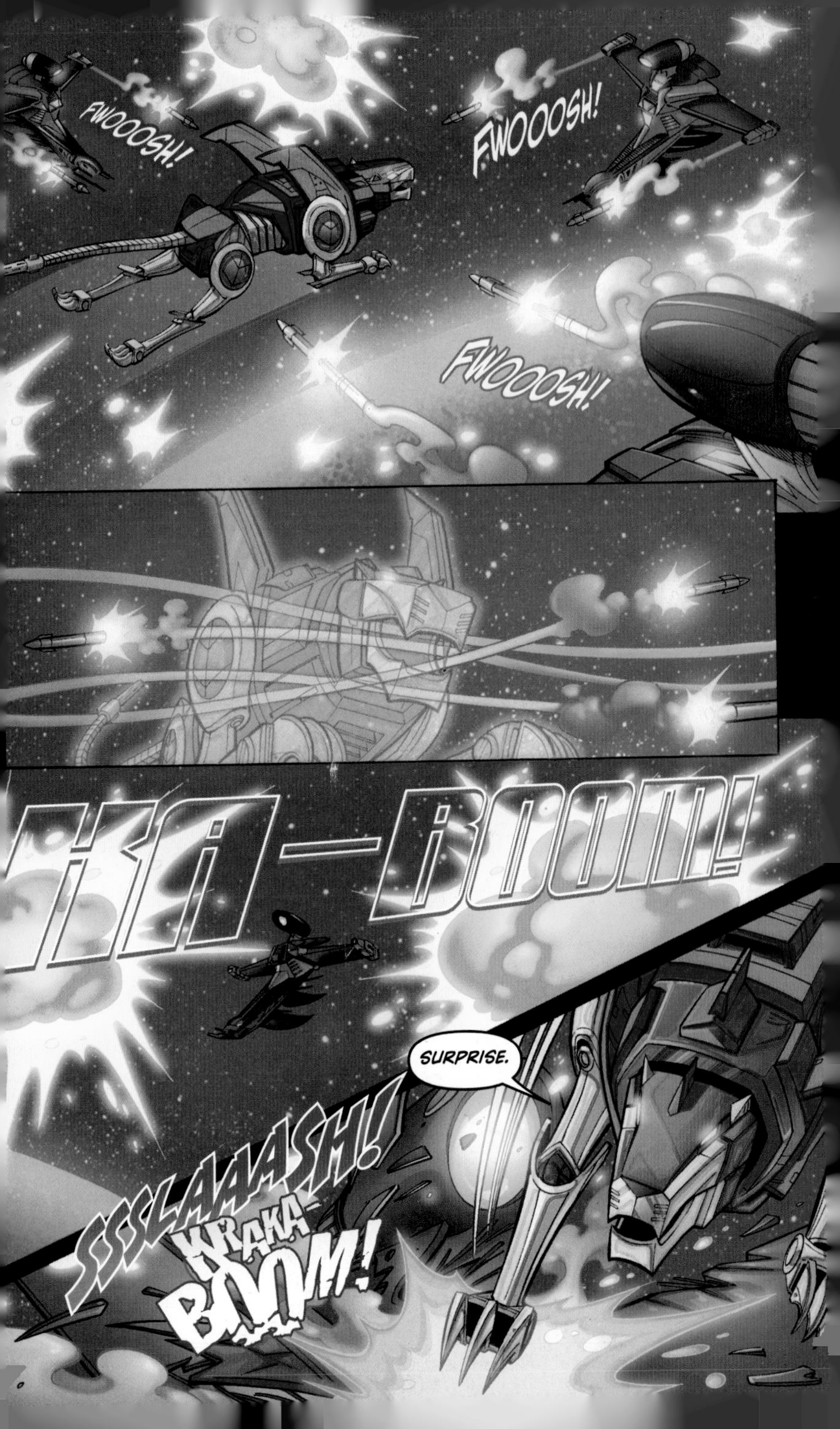
FWOOOSH!
FWOOOSH!
FWOOOSH!
KA-BOOM!
SURPRISE.
SSSLAAAASH!
KRAKA-BOOM!

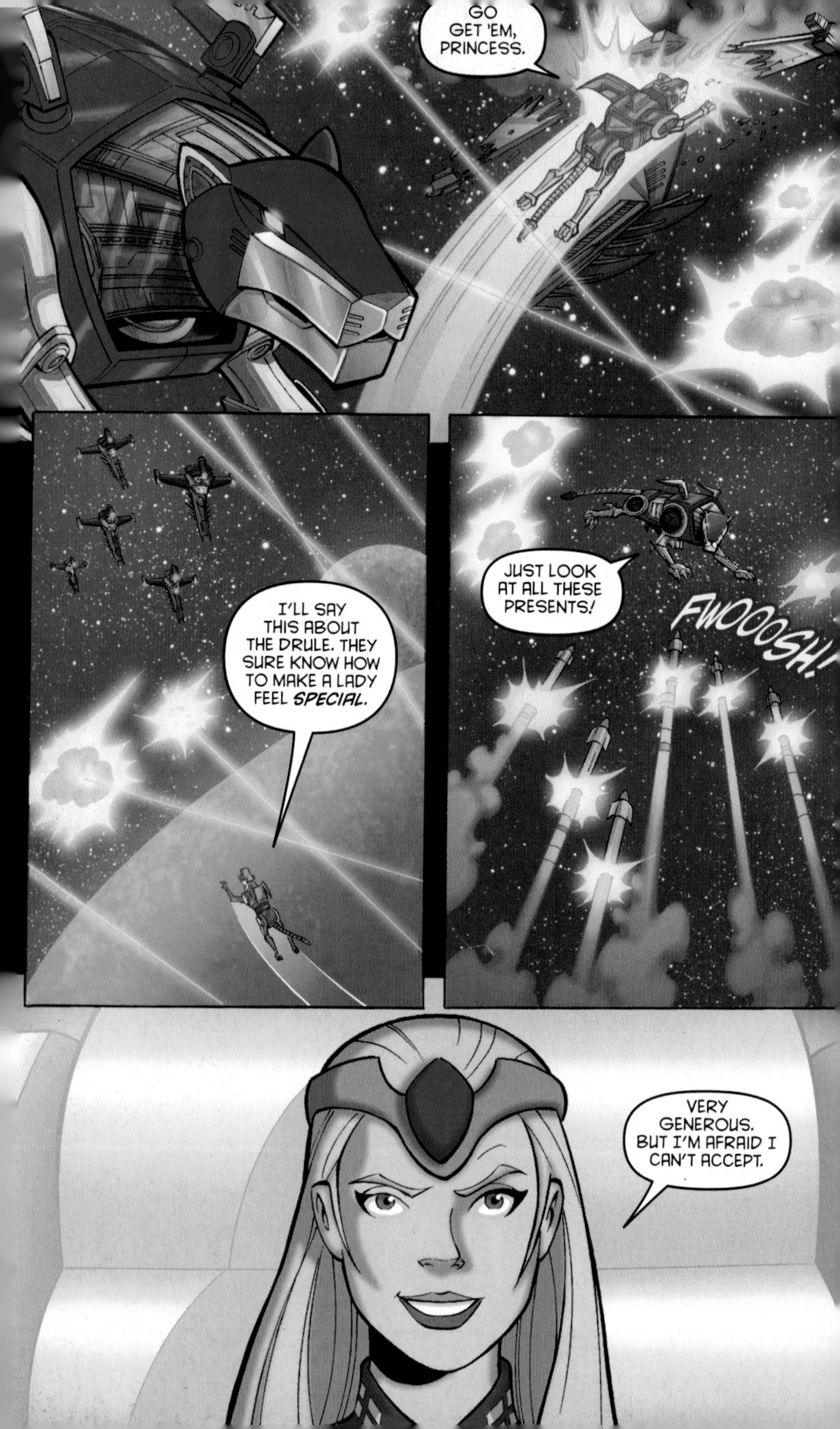
GO GET 'EM, PRINCESS.
I'LL SAY THIS ABOUT THE DRULE. THEY SURE KNOW HOW TO MAKE A LADY FEEL *SPECIAL*.
JUST LOOK AT ALL THESE PRESENTS!
FWOOOSH!
VERY GENEROUS. BUT I'M AFRAID I CAN'T ACCEPT.

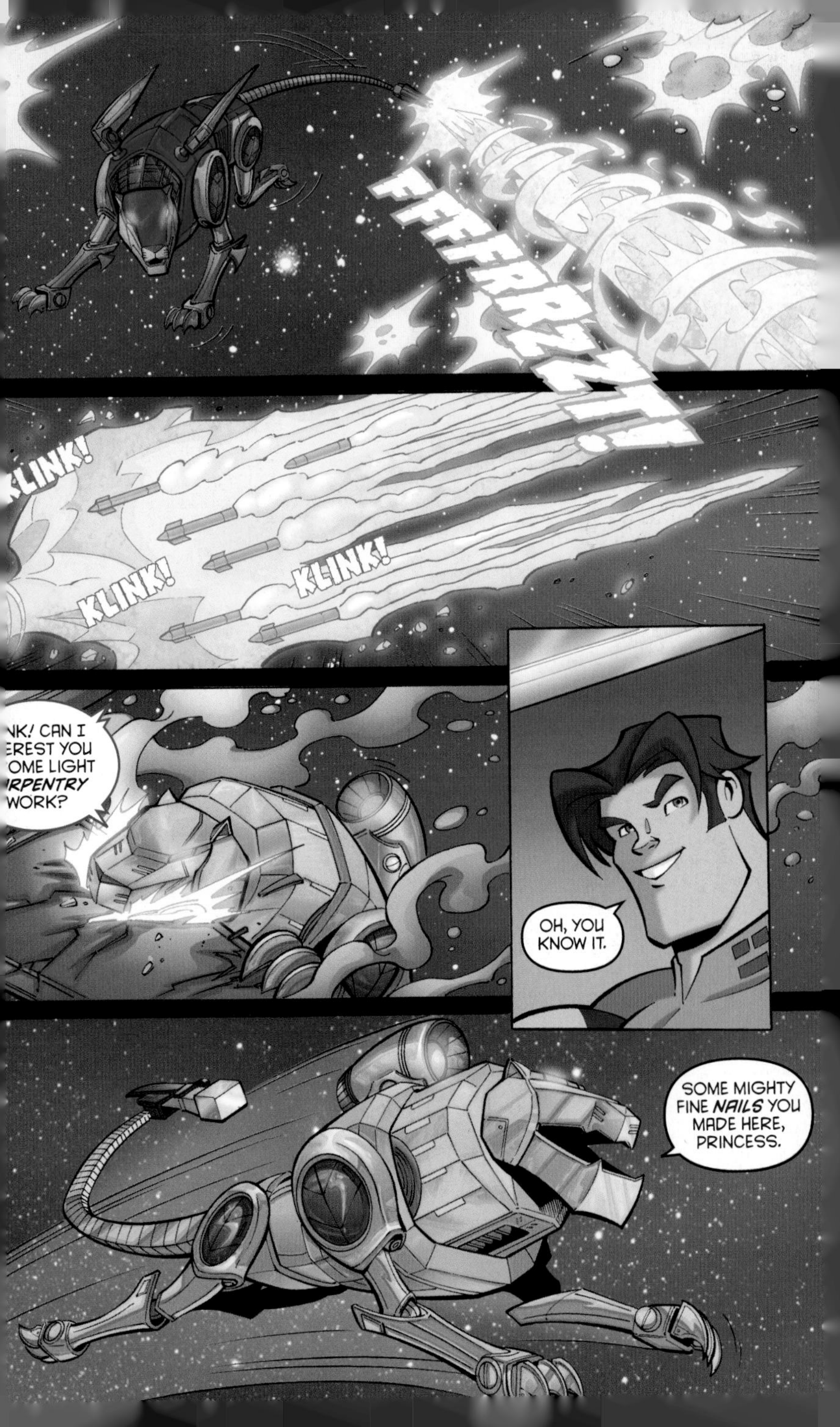
FFFFRAZZT!!
KLINK!
KLINK!
KLINK!
NK! CAN I
EREST YOU
OME LIGHT
RPENTRY
WORK?
OH, YOU KNOW IT.
SOME MIGHTY FINE NAILS YOU MADE HERE, PRINCESS.

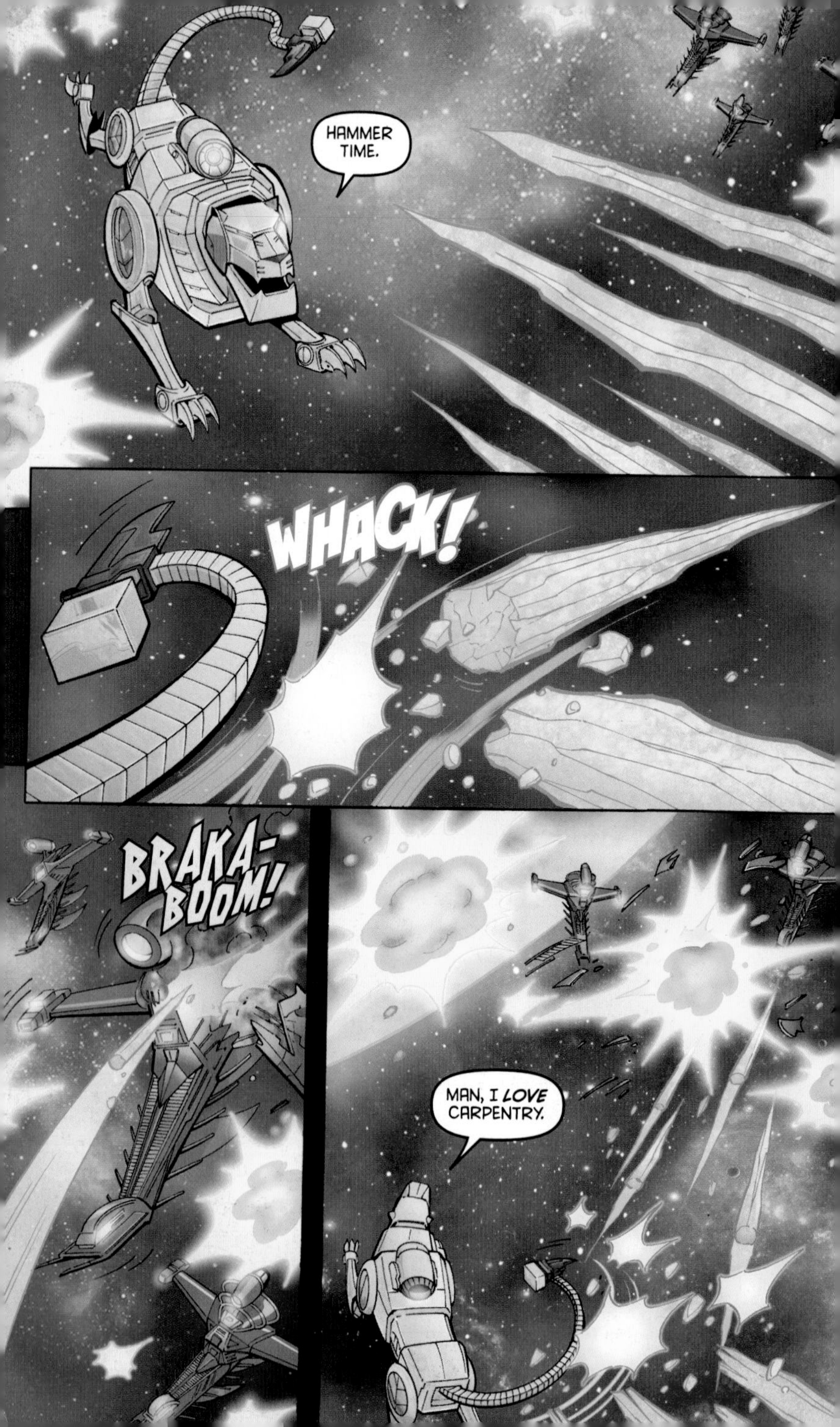
HAMMER TIME.
WHACK!
BRAKA-BOOM!
MAN, I *LOVE* CARPENTRY.

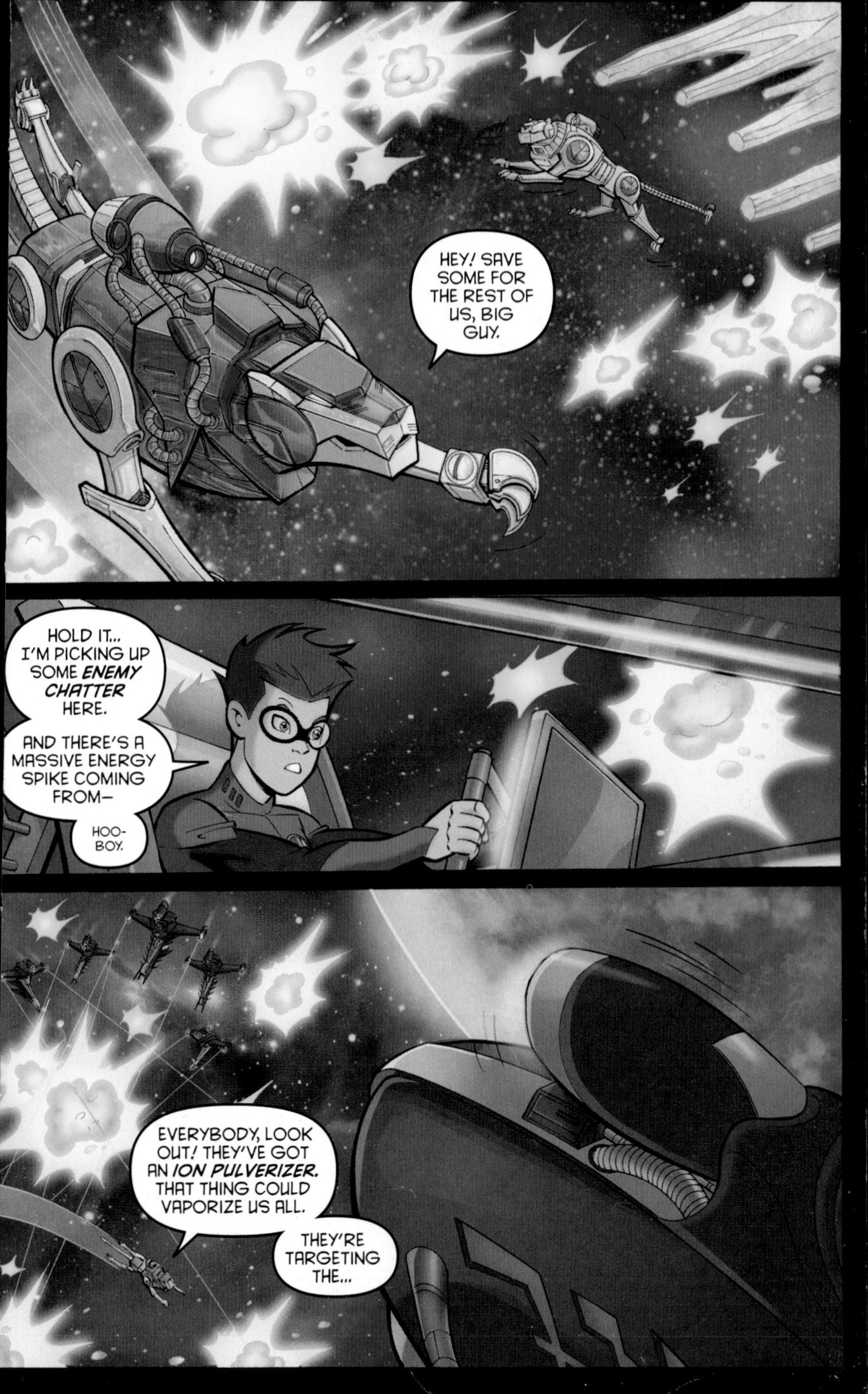
HEY! SAVE SOME FOR THE REST OF US, BIG GUY.
HOLD IT... I'M PICKING UP SOME ENEMY CHATTER HERE.
AND THERE'S A MASSIVE ENERGY SPIKE COMING FROM—
HOO-BOY.
EVERYBODY, LOOK OUT! THEY'VE GOT AN ION PULVERIZER. THAT THING COULD VAPORIZE US ALL.
THEY'RE TARGETING THE...

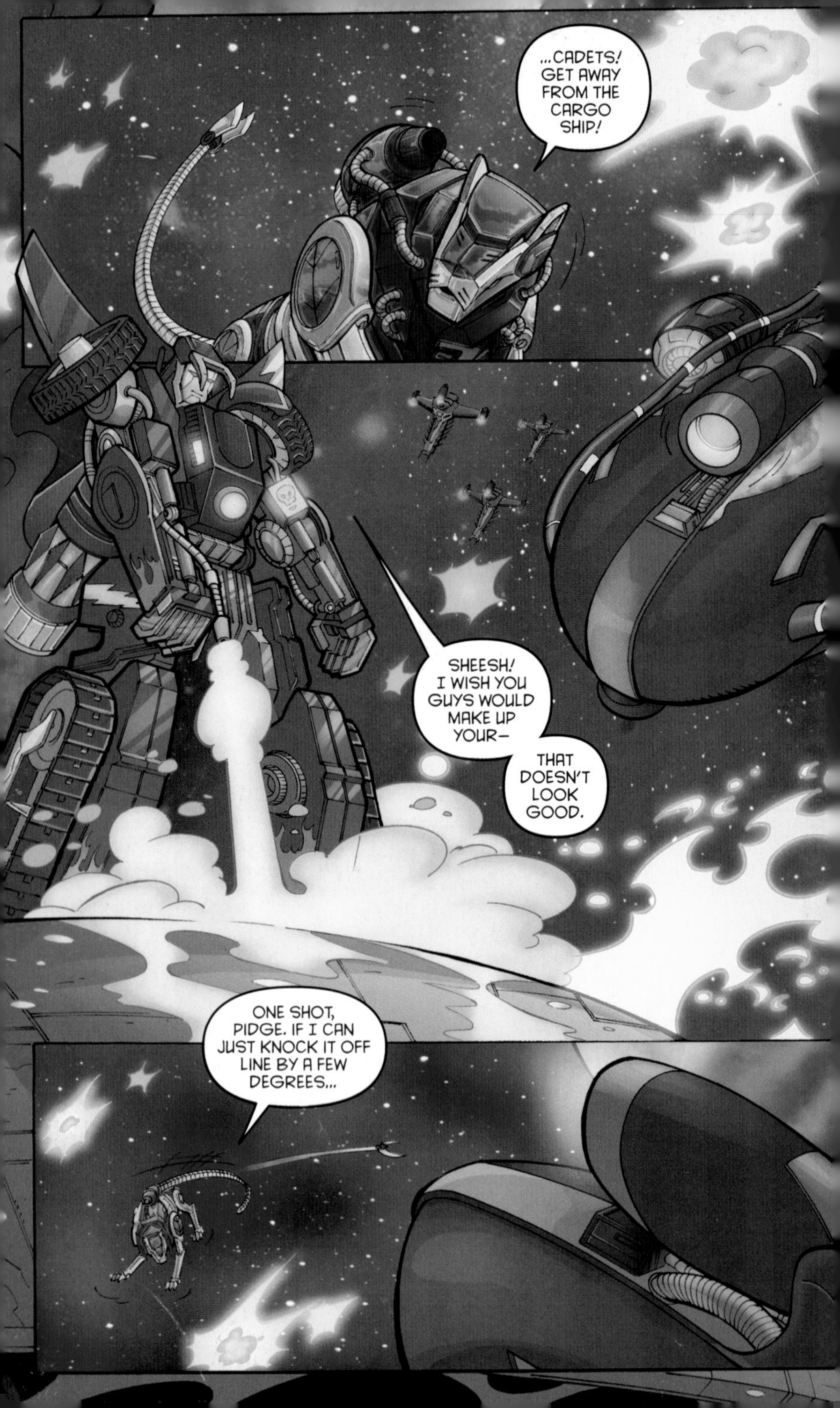
...CADETS! GET AWAY FROM THE CARGO SHIP!
SHEESH! I WISH YOU GUYS WOULD MAKE UP YOUR—
THAT DOESN'T LOOK GOOD.
ONE SHOT, PIDGE. IF I CAN JUST KNOCK IT OFF LINE BY A FEW DEGREES...

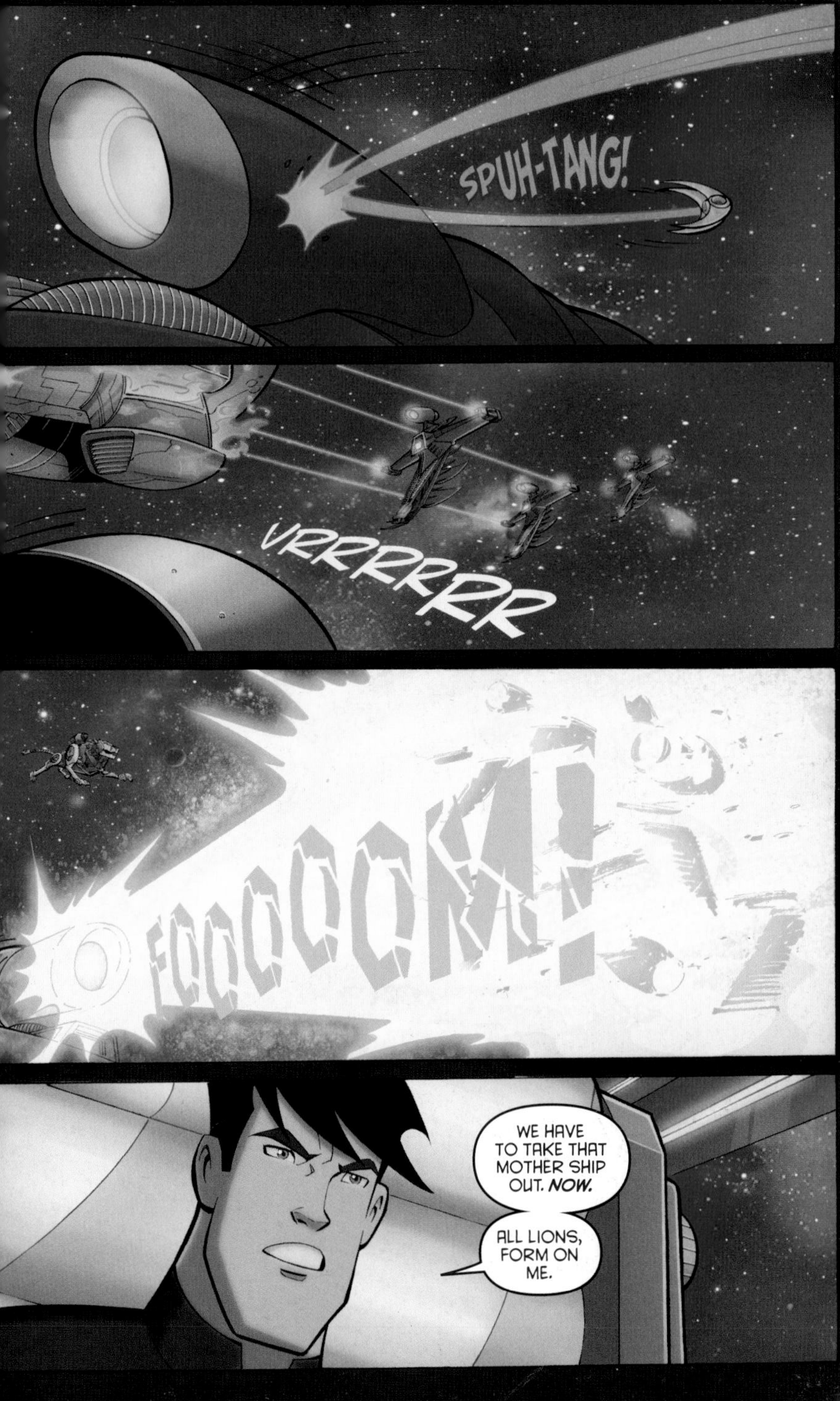
SPUH-TANG!
VRRRRRRR
FOOOOOOM!
WE HAVE TO TAKE THAT MOTHER SHIP OUT. *NOW.*
ALL LIONS, FORM ON ME.

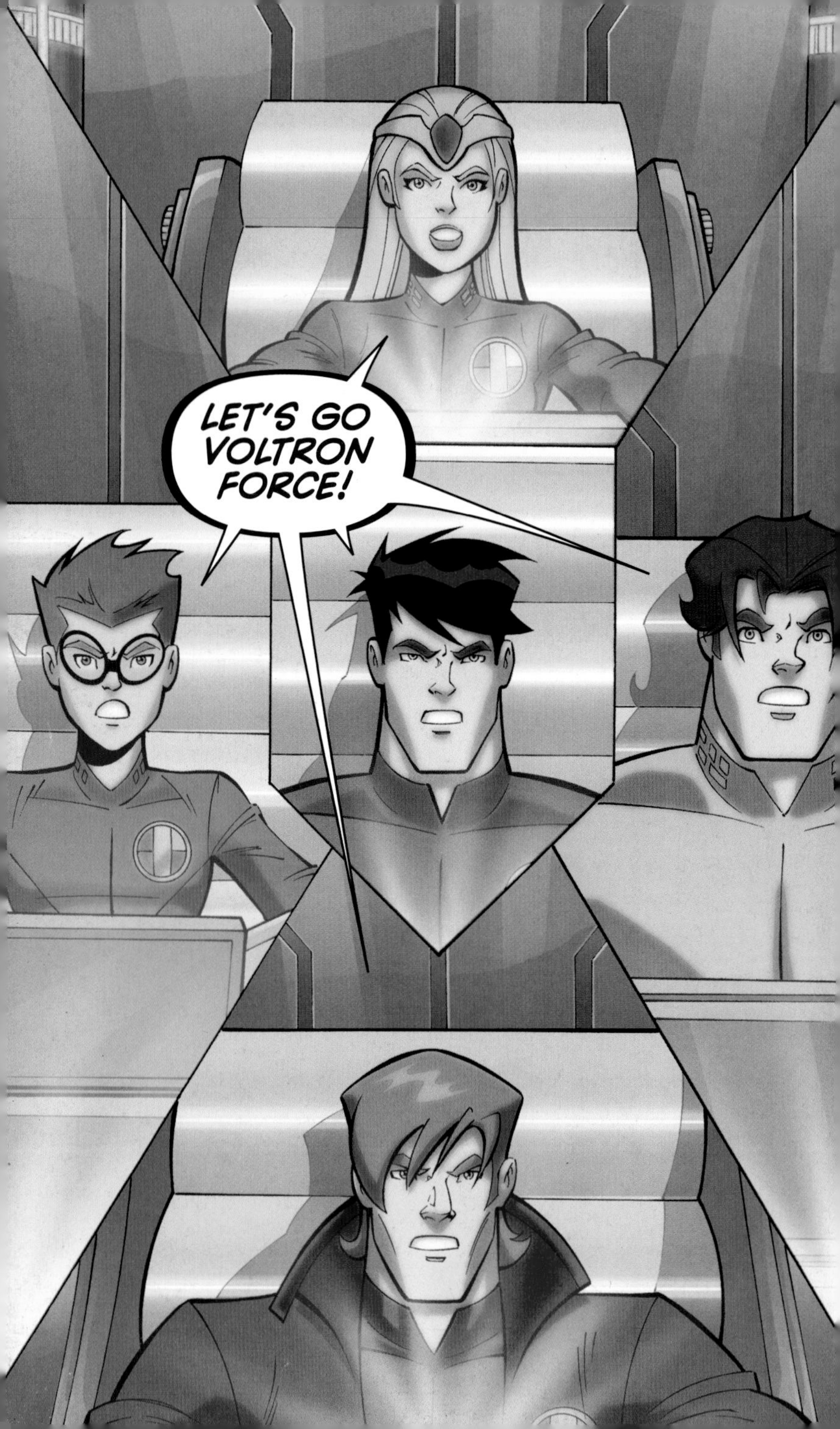
LET'S GO VOLTRON FORCE!

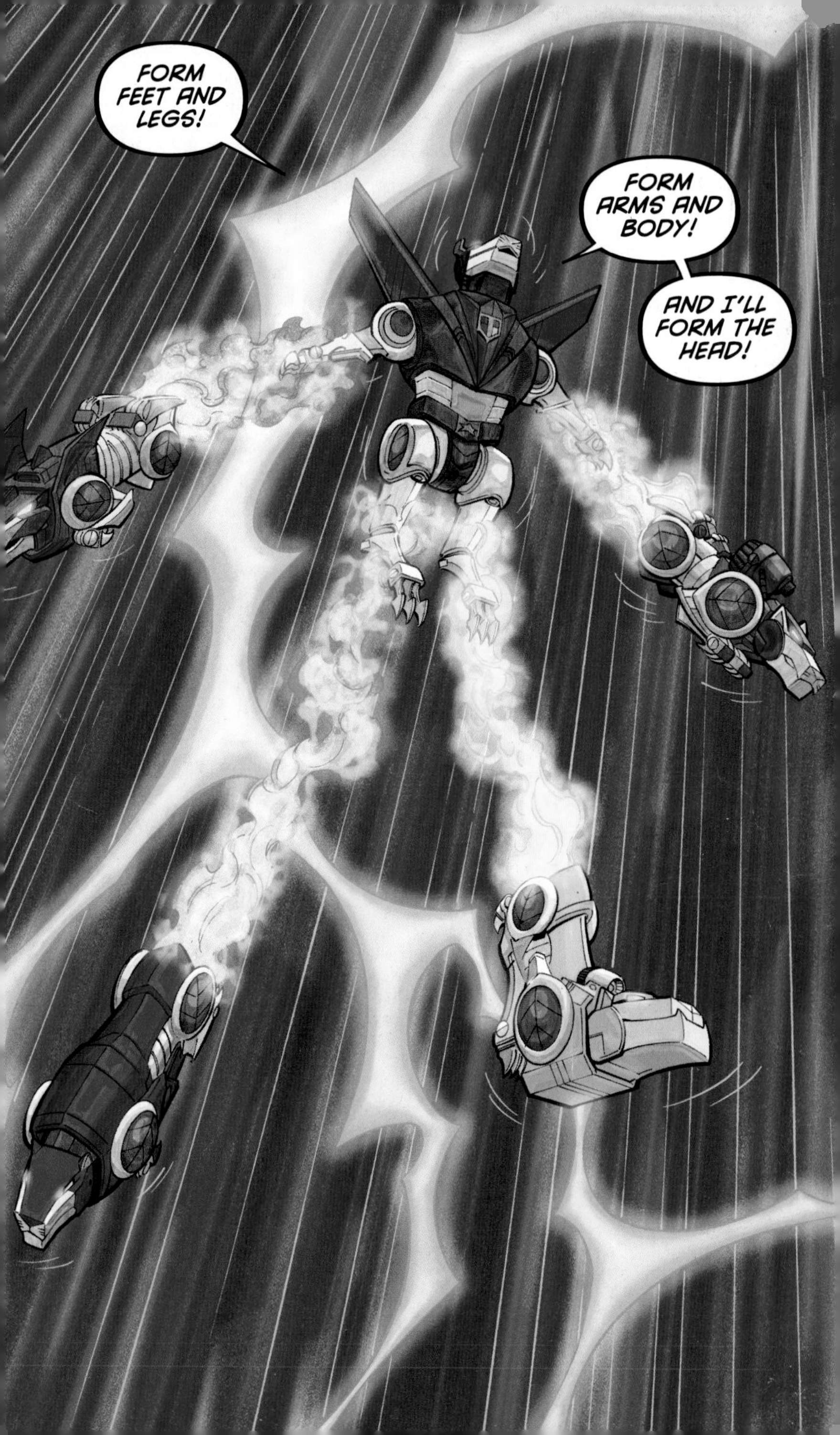
FORM FEET AND LEGS!
FORM ARMS AND BODY!
AND I'LL FORM THE HEAD!

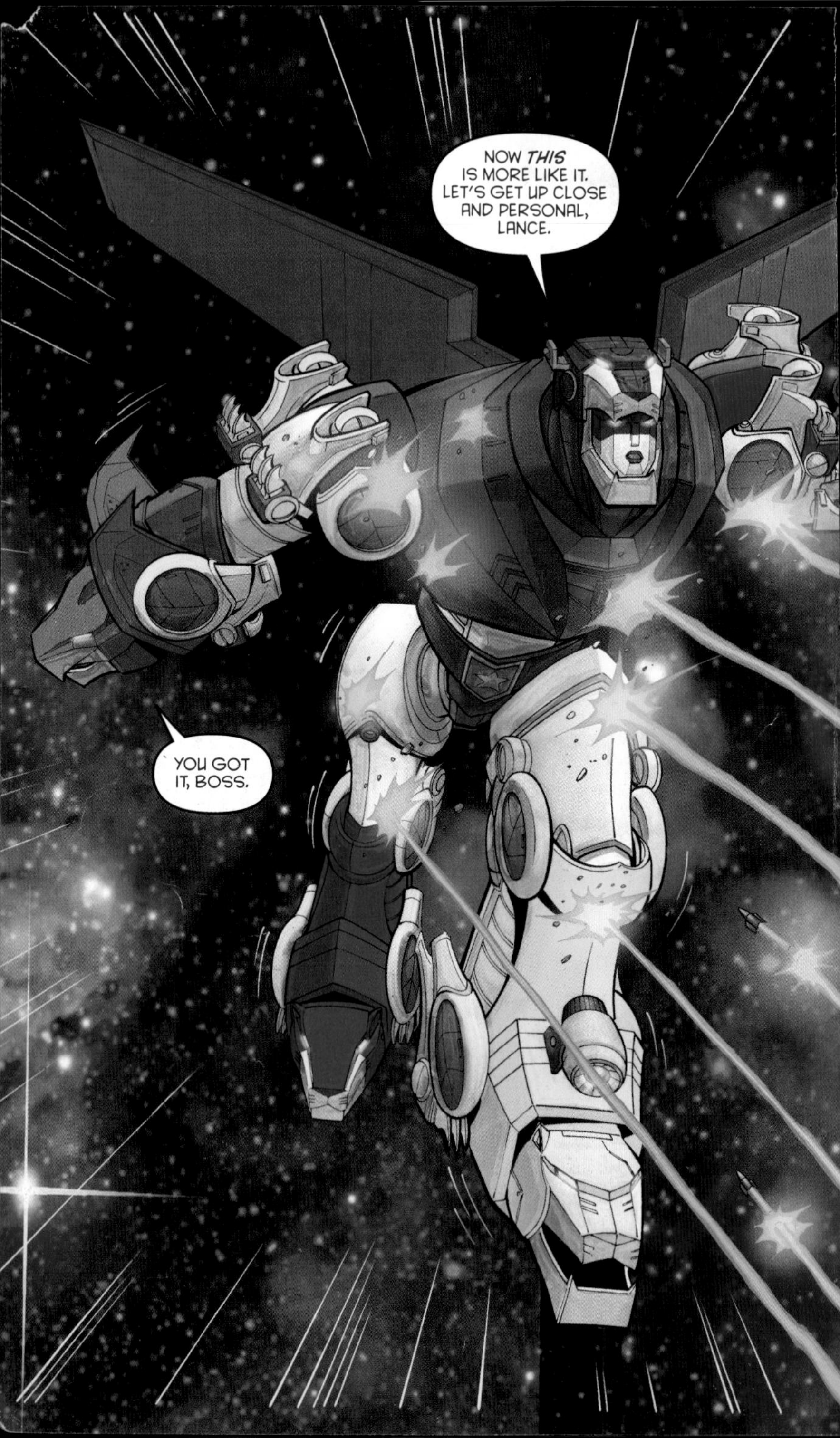
NOW *THIS* IS MORE LIKE IT. LET'S GET UP CLOSE AND PERSONAL, LANCE.
YOU GOT IT, BOSS.

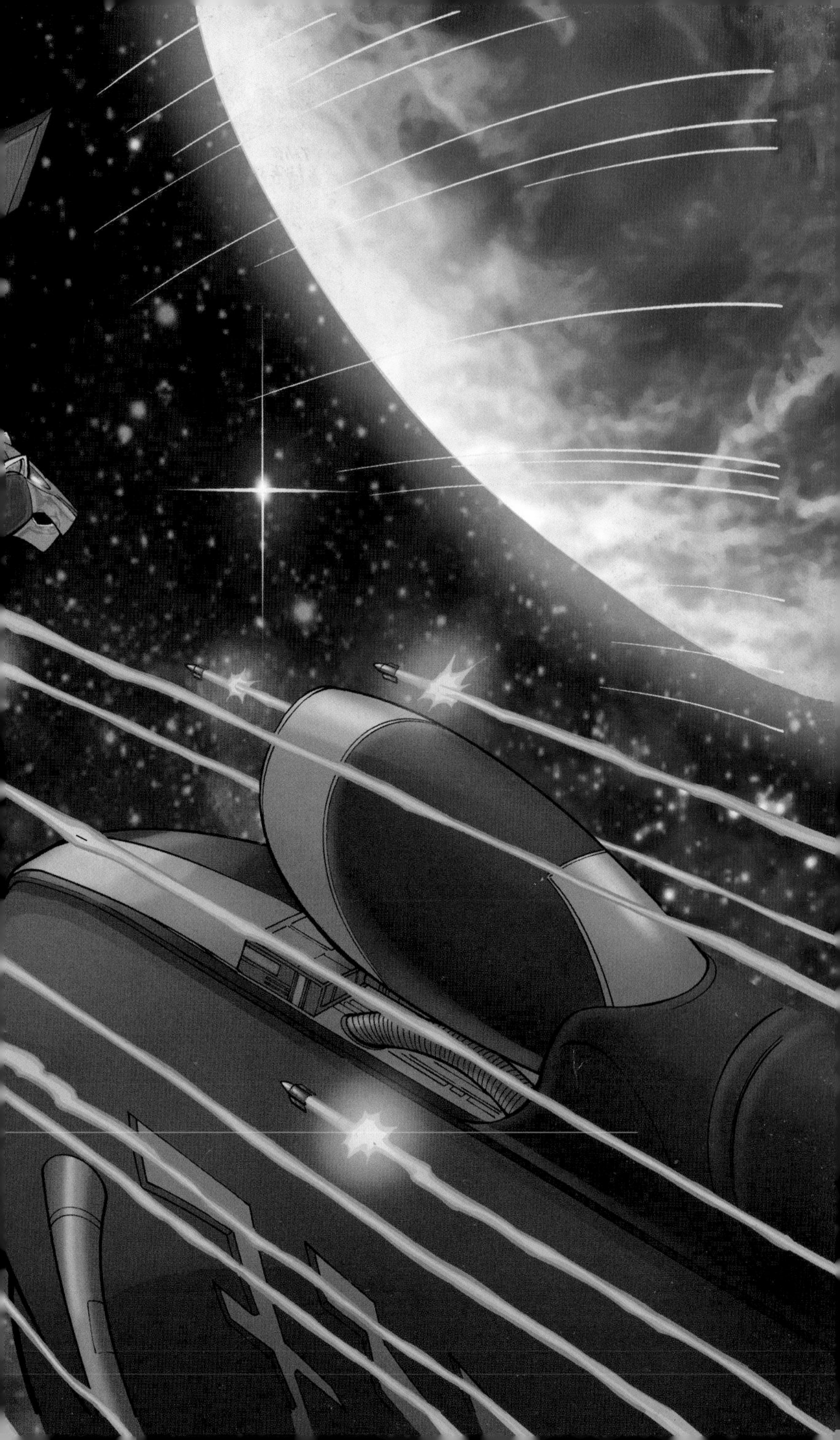

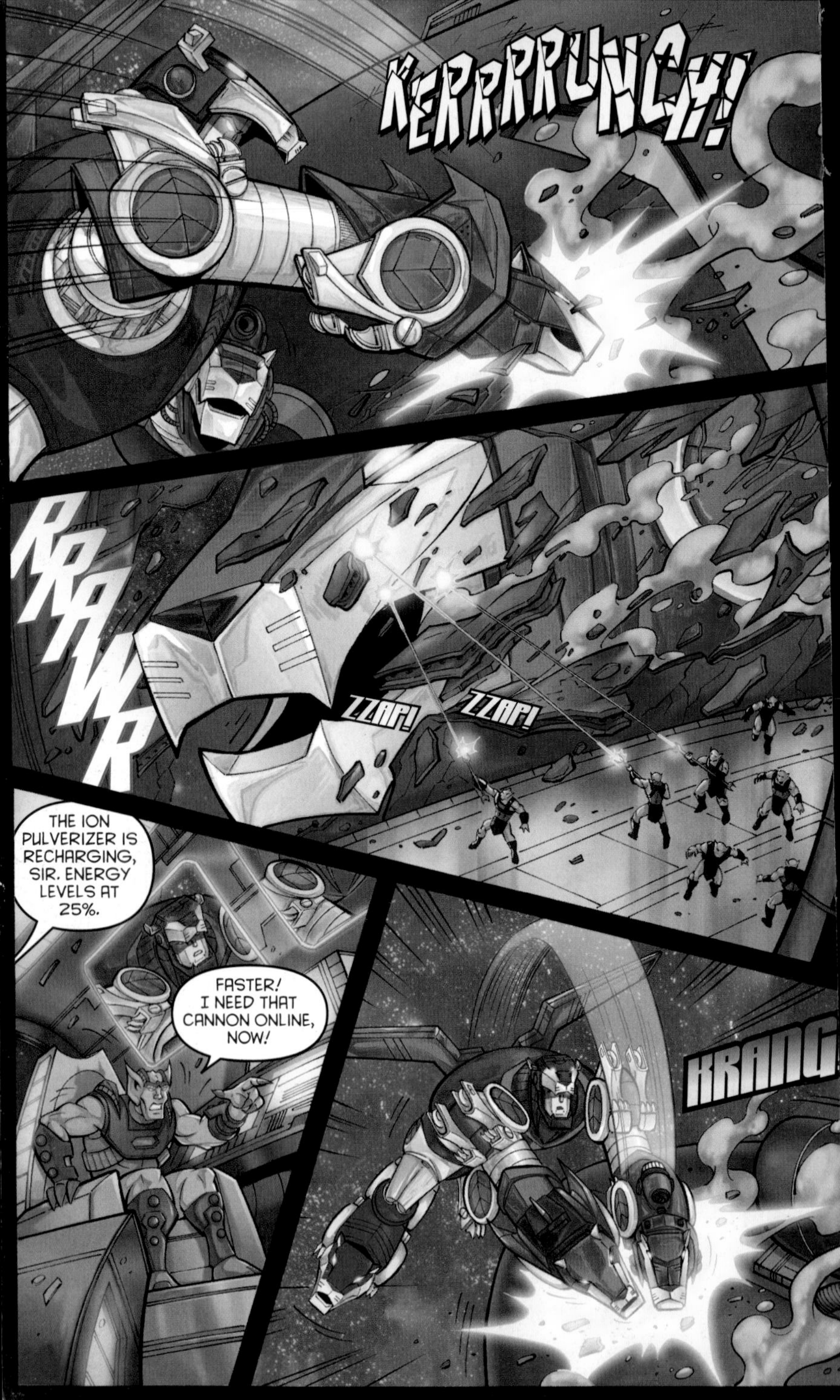
KERRRRUNCH!
RRAWR
ZZAP!
ZZAP!
THE ION PULVERIZER IS RECHARGING, SIR. ENERGY LEVELS AT 25%.
FASTER! I NEED THAT CANNON ONLINE, NOW!
KRANG!

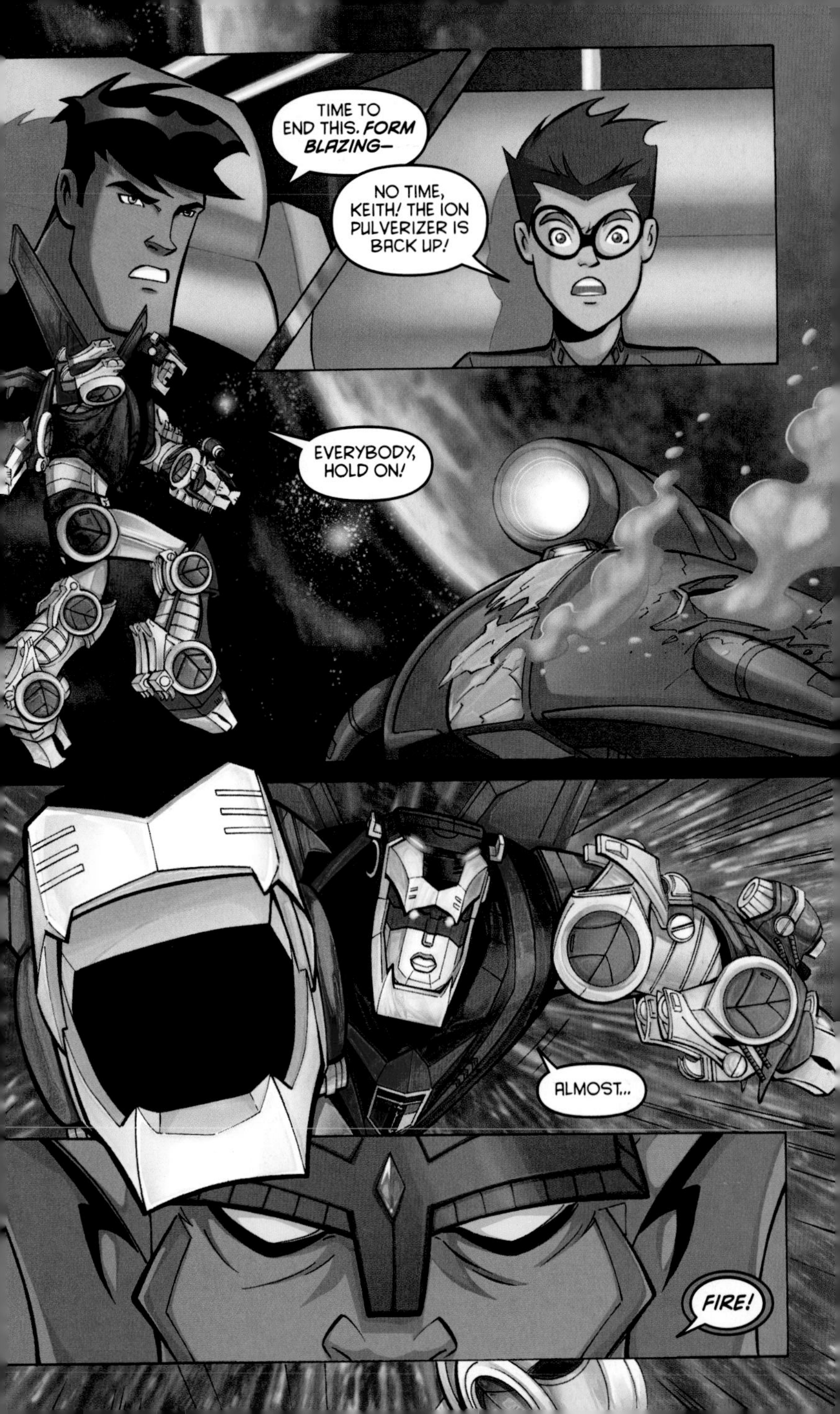
TIME TO END THIS. *FORM BLAZING—*
NO TIME, KEITH! THE ION PULVERIZER IS BACK UP!
EVERYBODY, HOLD ON!
ALMOST...
FIRE!

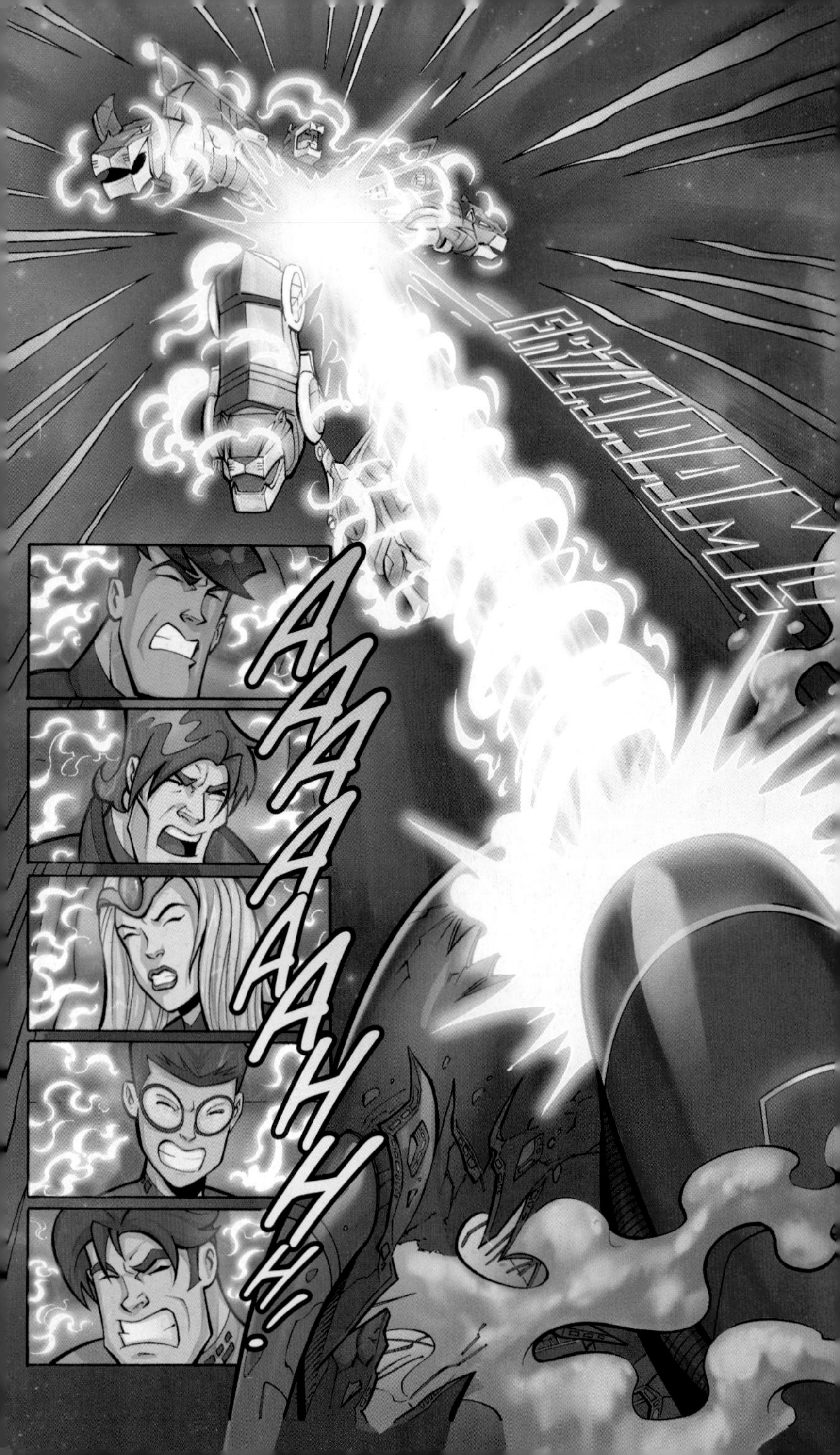
AAAAAAAAHHHH!

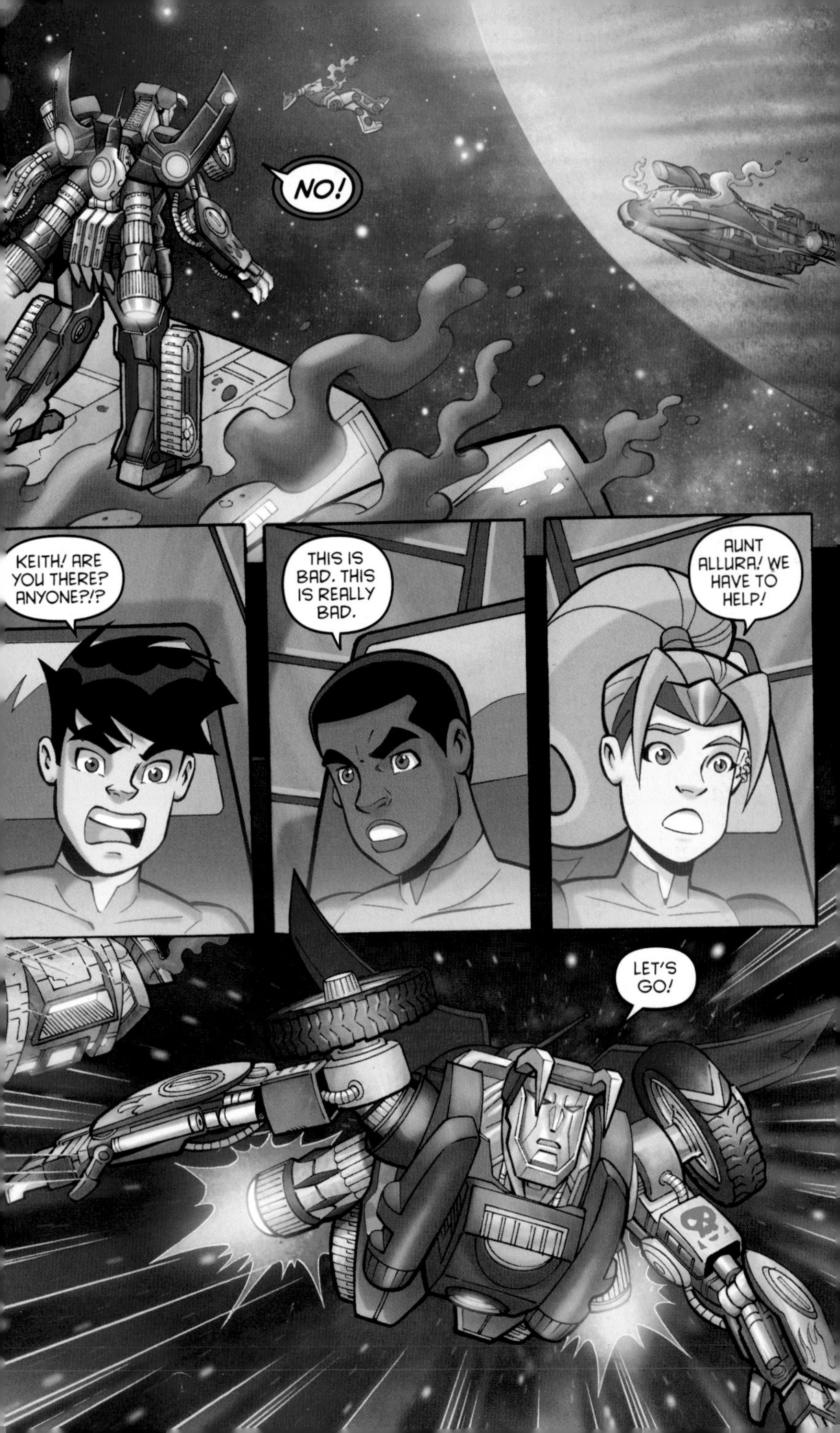
NO!
KEITH! ARE YOU THERE? ANYONE?!?
THIS IS BAD. THIS IS REALLY BAD.
AUNT ALLURA! WE HAVE TO HELP!
LET'S GO!

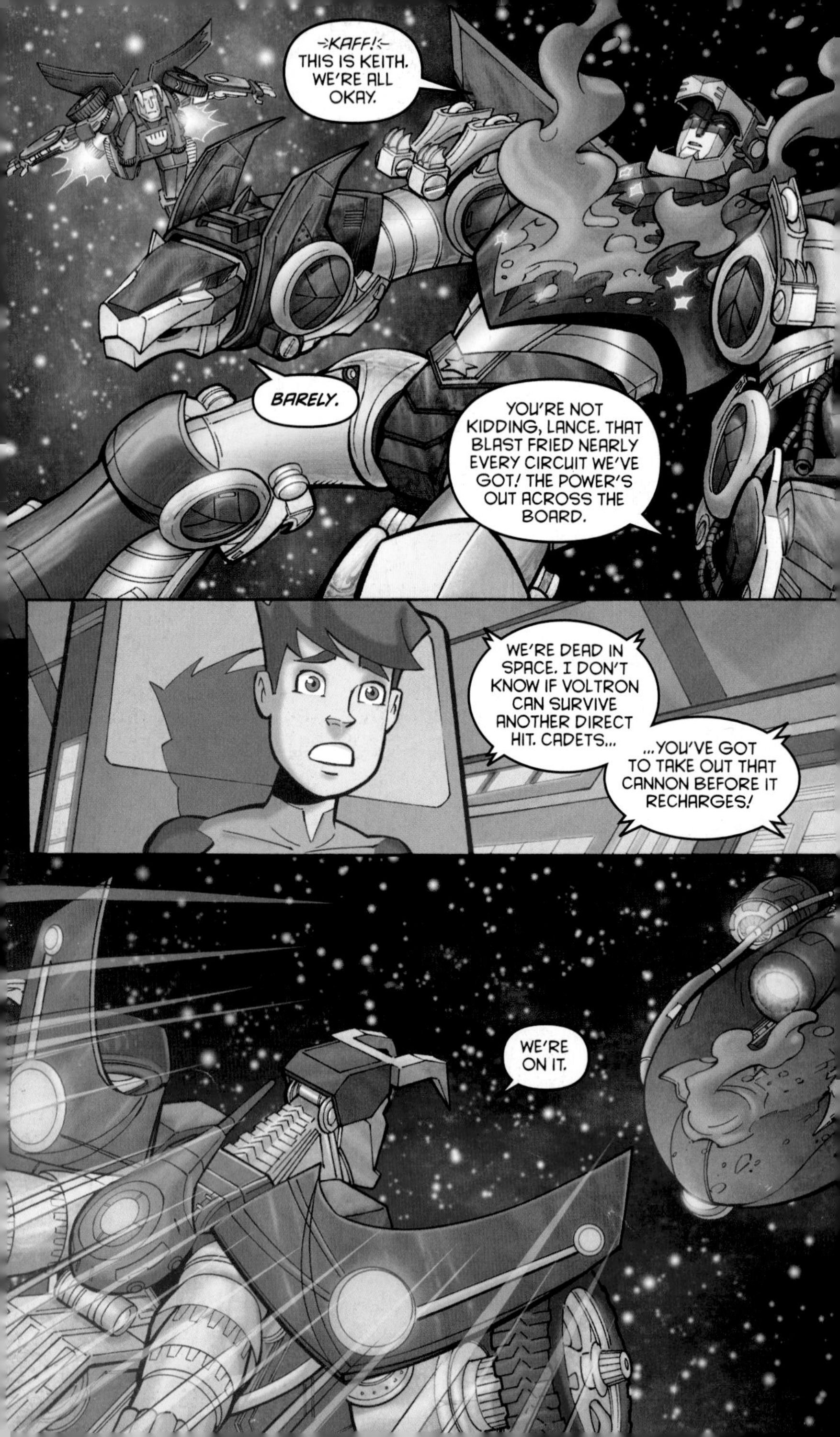
KAFF! THIS IS KEITH. WE'RE ALL OKAY.
BARELY.
YOU'RE NOT KIDDING, LANCE. THAT BLAST FRIED NEARLY EVERY CIRCUIT WE'VE GOT! THE POWER'S OUT ACROSS THE BOARD.
WE'RE DEAD IN SPACE. I DON'T KNOW IF VOLTRON CAN SURVIVE ANOTHER DIRECT HIT. CADETS...
...YOU'VE GOT TO TAKE OUT THAT CANNON BEFORE IT RECHARGES!
WE'RE ON IT.

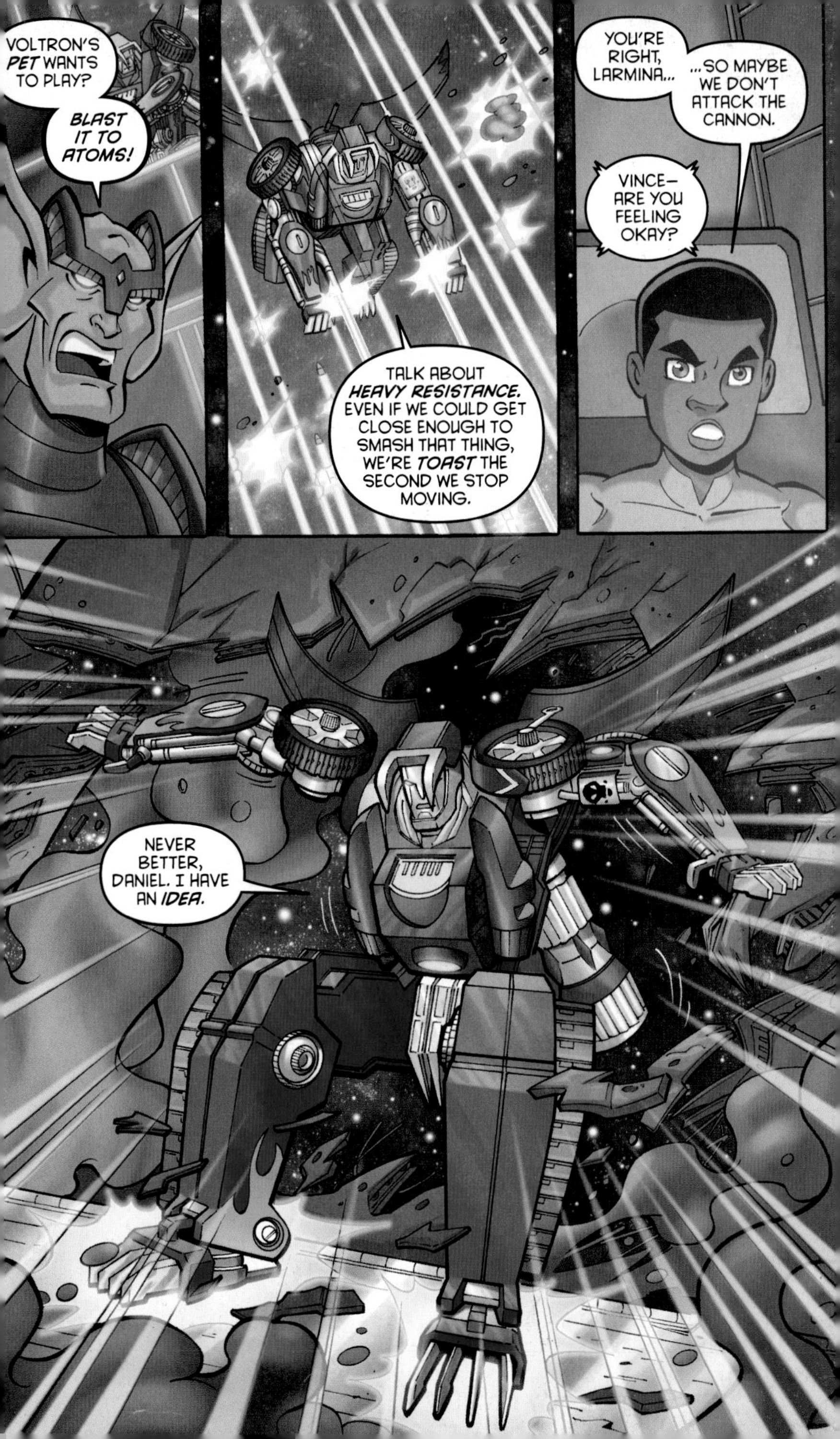
VOLTRON'S *PET* WANTS TO PLAY?
BLAST IT TO ATOMS!
TALK ABOUT *HEAVY RESISTANCE.* EVEN IF WE COULD GET CLOSE ENOUGH TO SMASH THAT THING, WE'RE *TOAST* THE SECOND WE STOP MOVING.
YOU'RE RIGHT, LARMINA...
...SO MAYBE WE DON'T ATTACK THE CANNON.
VINCE— ARE YOU FEELING OKAY?
NEVER BETTER, DANIEL. I HAVE AN *IDEA*.

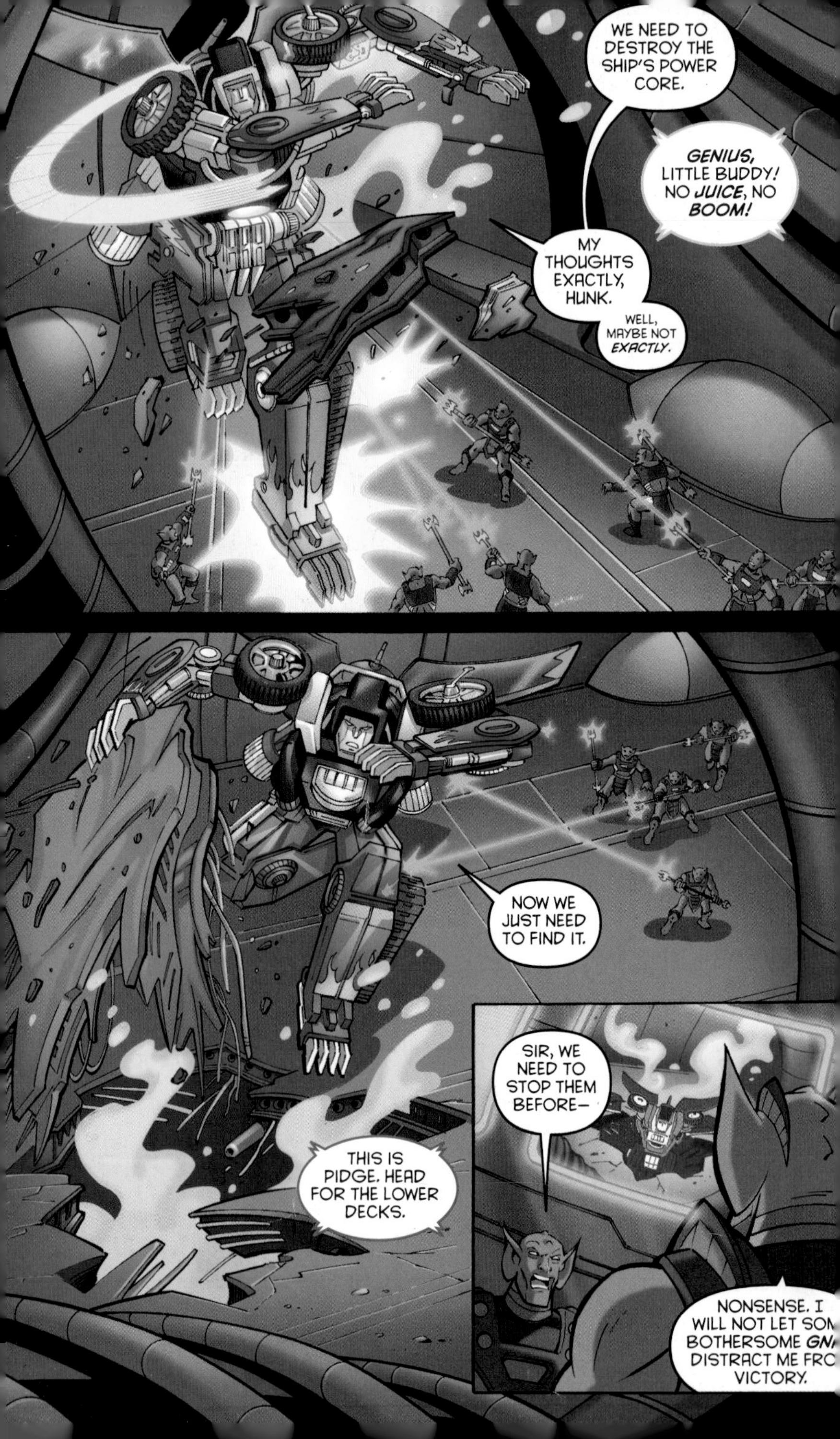
WE NEED TO DESTROY THE SHIP'S POWER CORE.
MY THOUGHTS EXACTLY, HUNK.
WELL, MAYBE NOT *EXACTLY*.
GENIUS, LITTLE BUDDY! NO *JUICE*, NO *BOOM!*
NOW WE JUST NEED TO FIND IT.
THIS IS PIDGE. HEAD FOR THE LOWER DECKS.
SIR, WE NEED TO STOP THEM BEFORE–
NONSENSE. I WILL NOT LET SOM BOTHERSOME *GN* DISTRACT ME FRO VICTORY.

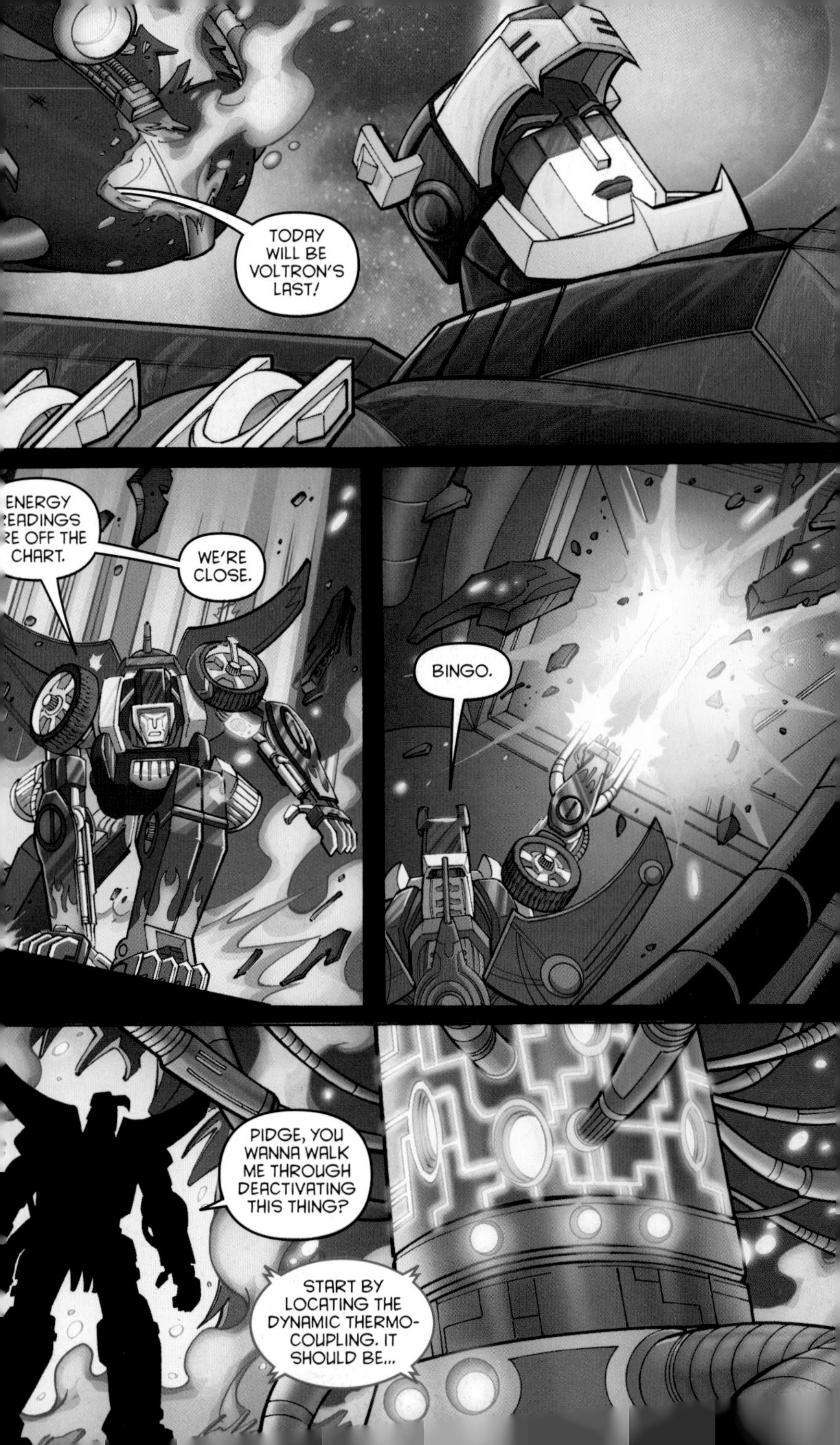
TODAY WILL BE VOLTRON'S LAST!
ENERGY READINGS ARE OFF THE CHART.
WE'RE CLOSE.
BINGO.
PIDGE, YOU WANNA WALK ME THROUGH DEACTIVATING THIS THING?
START BY LOCATING THE DYNAMIC THERMO-COUPLING. IT SHOULD BE...

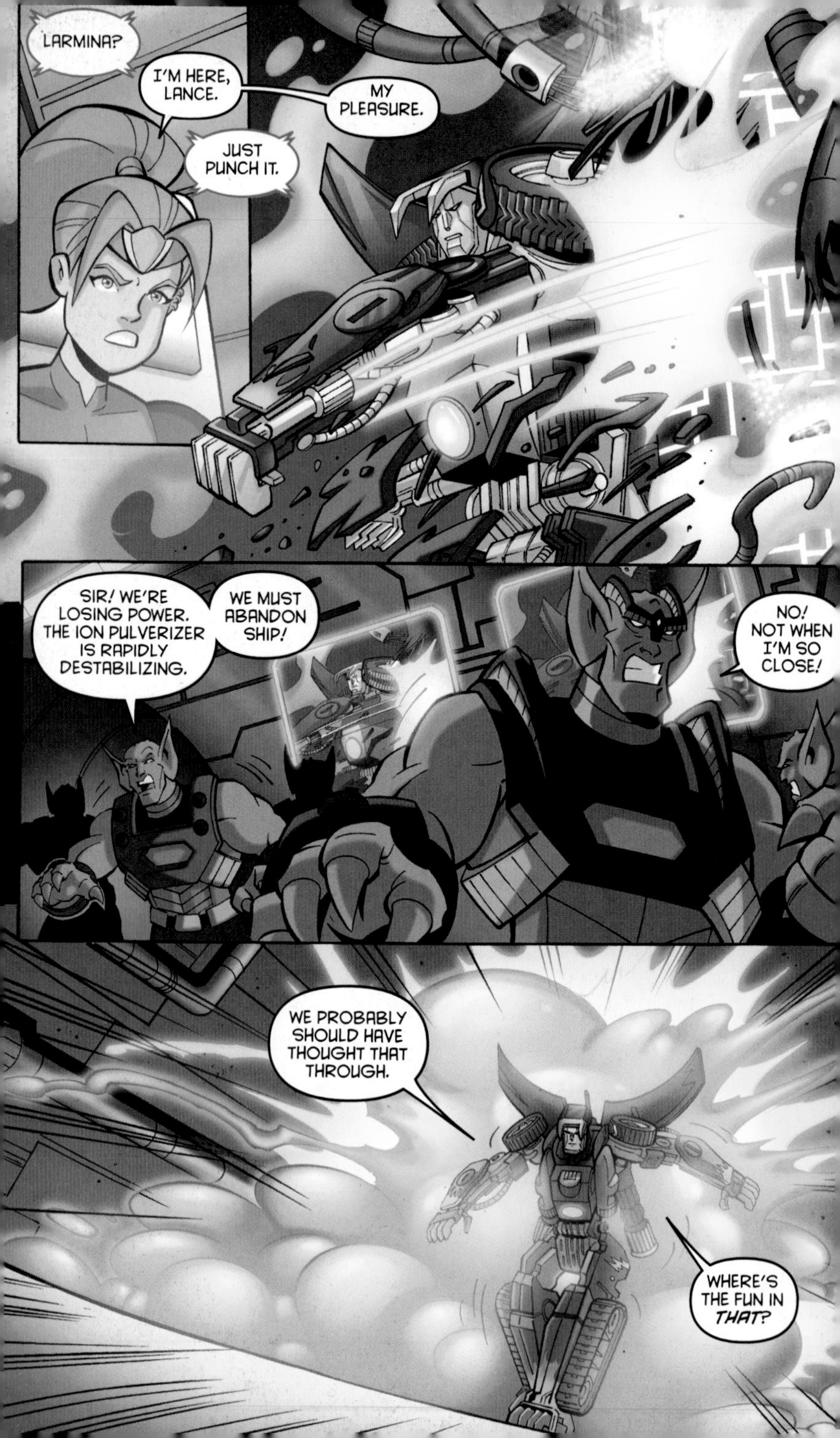
LARMINA?
I'M HERE, LANCE.
MY PLEASURE.
JUST PUNCH IT.
SIR! WE'RE LOSING POWER. THE ION PULVERIZER IS RAPIDLY DESTABILIZING.
WE MUST ABANDON SHIP!
NO! NOT WHEN I'M SO CLOSE!
WE PROBABLY SHOULD HAVE THOUGHT THAT THROUGH.
WHERE'S THE FUN IN *THAT*?

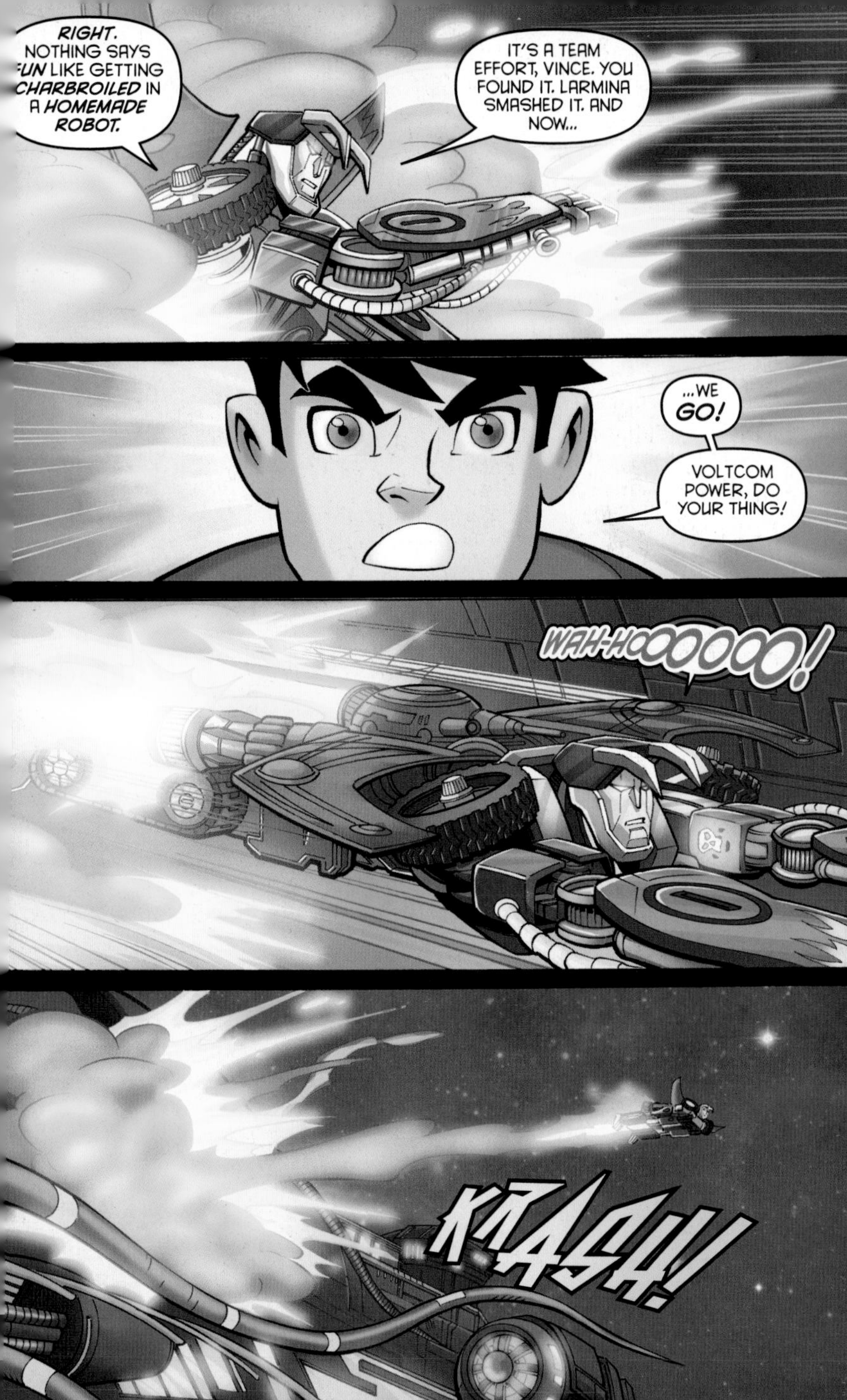
RIGHT. NOTHING SAYS FUN LIKE GETTING CHARBROILED IN A HOMEMADE ROBOT.
IT'S A TEAM EFFORT, VINCE. YOU FOUND IT. LARMINA SMASHED IT. AND NOW...
...WE GO!
VOLTCOM POWER, DO YOUR THING!
WAH-HOOOOOOO!
KRASH!

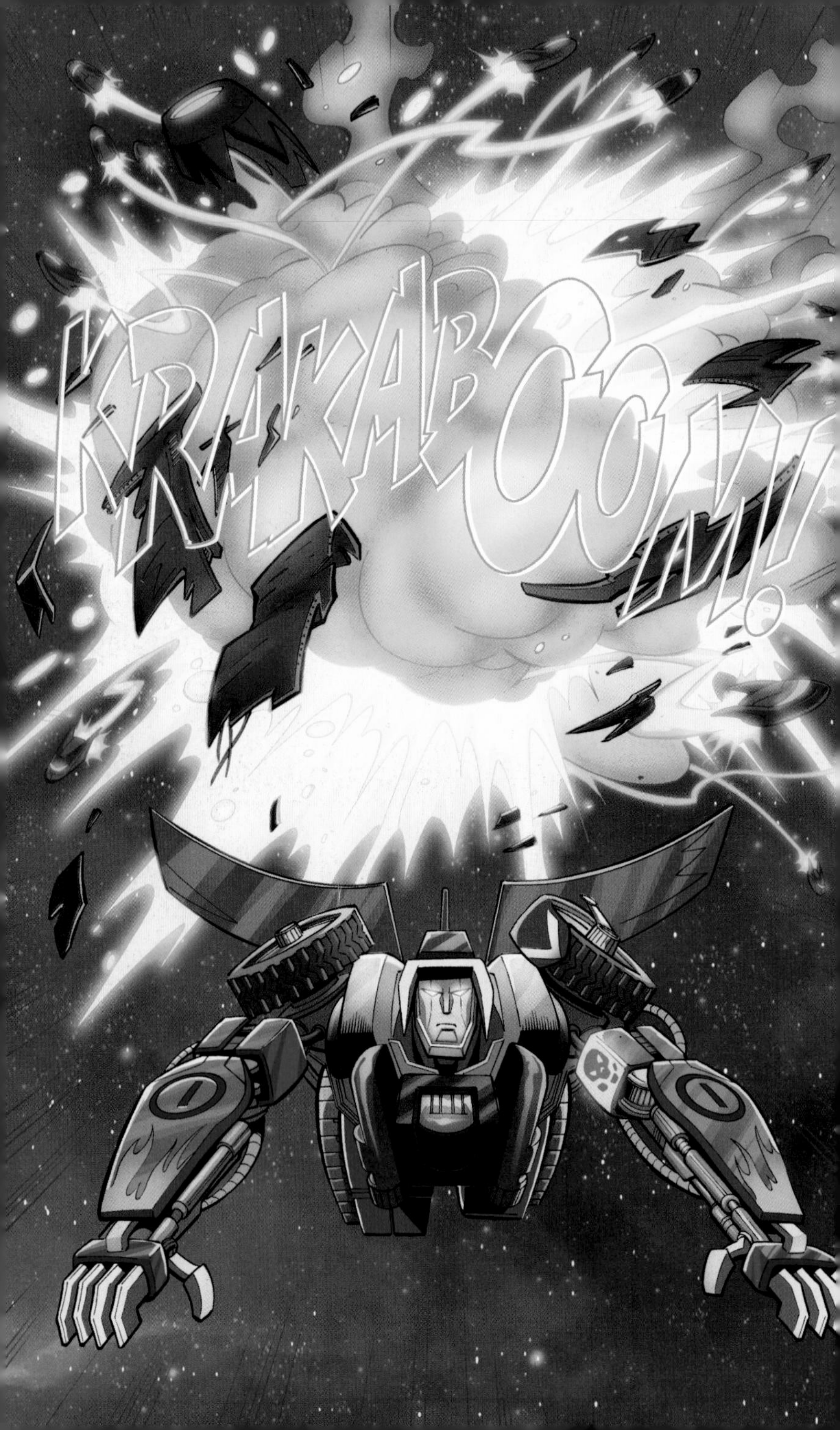
KRAKABOOM!

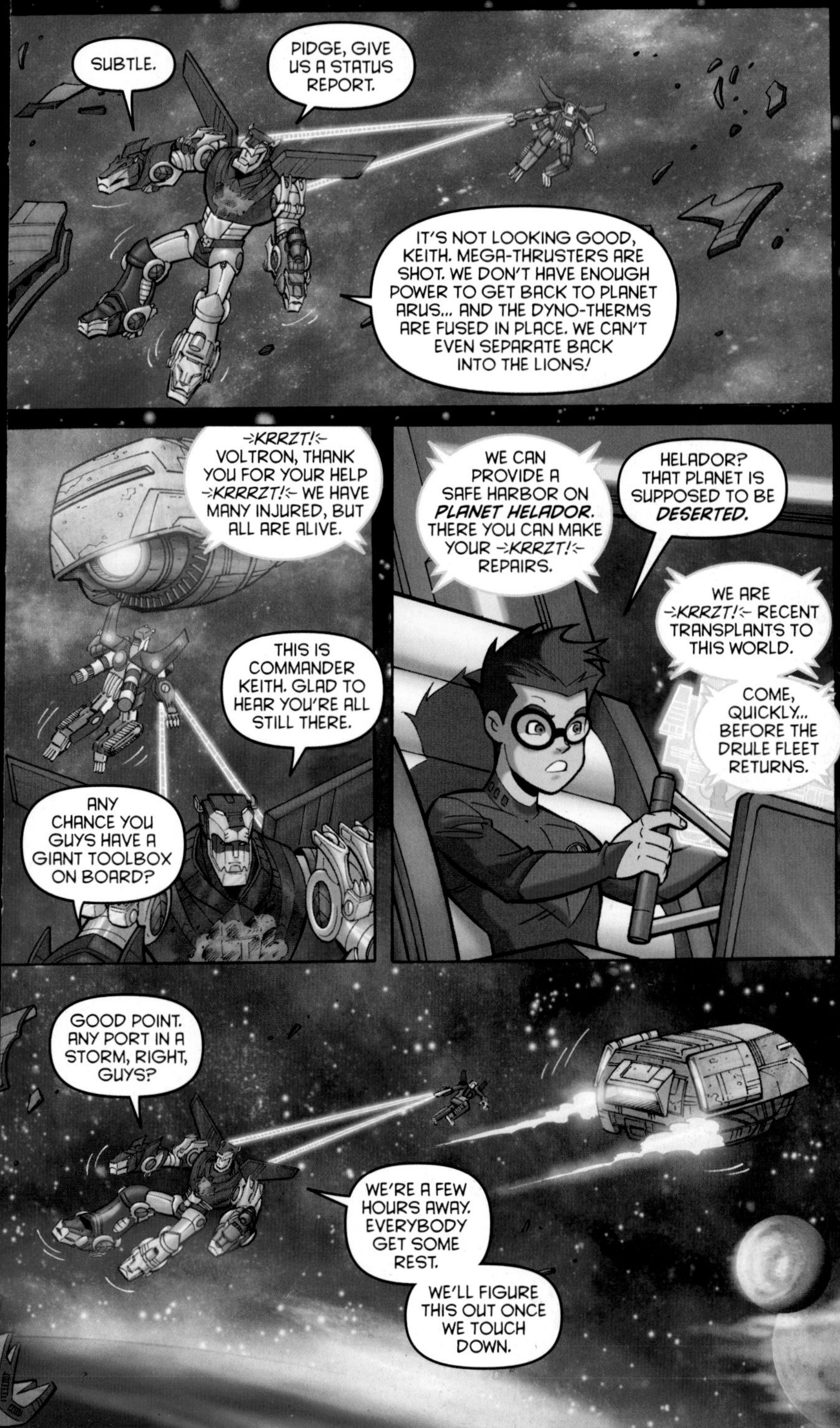
SUBTLE.
PIDGE, GIVE US A STATUS REPORT.
IT'S NOT LOOKING GOOD, KEITH. MEGA-THRUSTERS ARE SHOT. WE DON'T HAVE ENOUGH POWER TO GET BACK TO PLANET ARUS... AND THE DYNO-THERMS ARE FUSED IN PLACE. WE CAN'T EVEN SEPARATE BACK INTO THE LIONS!
-KRRZT!- VOLTRON, THANK YOU FOR YOUR HELP -KRRRZT!- WE HAVE MANY INJURED, BUT ALL ARE ALIVE.
THIS IS COMMANDER KEITH. GLAD TO HEAR YOU'RE ALL STILL THERE.
ANY CHANCE YOU GUYS HAVE A GIANT TOOLBOX ON BOARD?
WE CAN PROVIDE A SAFE HARBOR ON *PLANET HELADOR*. THERE YOU CAN MAKE YOUR -KRRZT!- REPAIRS.
HELADOR? THAT PLANET IS SUPPOSED TO BE *DESERTED.*
WE ARE -KRRZT!- RECENT TRANSPLANTS TO THIS WORLD.
COME, QUICKLY... BEFORE THE DRULE FLEET RETURNS.
GOOD POINT. ANY PORT IN A STORM, RIGHT, GUYS?
WE'RE A FEW HOURS AWAY. EVERYBODY GET SOME REST.
WE'LL FIGURE THIS OUT ONCE WE TOUCH DOWN.

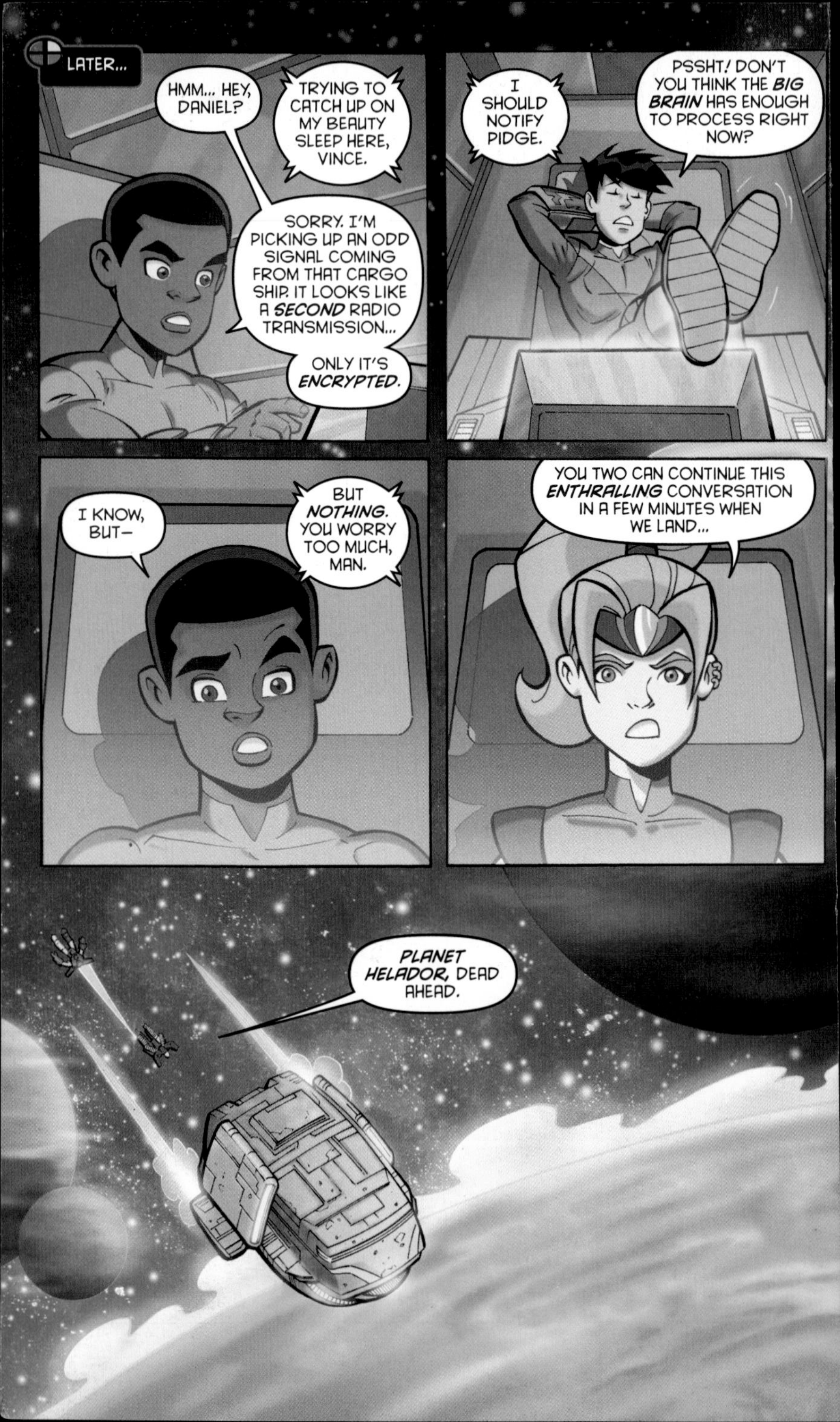
LATER...
HMM... HEY, DANIEL?
TRYING TO CATCH UP ON MY BEAUTY SLEEP HERE, VINCE.
SORRY. I'M PICKING UP AN ODD SIGNAL COMING FROM THAT CARGO SHIP. IT LOOKS LIKE A *SECOND* RADIO TRANSMISSION...
ONLY IT'S *ENCRYPTED*.
I SHOULD NOTIFY PIDGE.
PSSHT! DON'T YOU THINK THE *BIG BRAIN* HAS ENOUGH TO PROCESS RIGHT NOW?
I KNOW, BUT—
BUT *NOTHING*. YOU WORRY TOO MUCH, MAN.
YOU TWO CAN CONTINUE THIS *ENTHRALLING* CONVERSATION IN A FEW MINUTES WHEN WE LAND...
PLANET HELADOR, DEAD AHEAD.

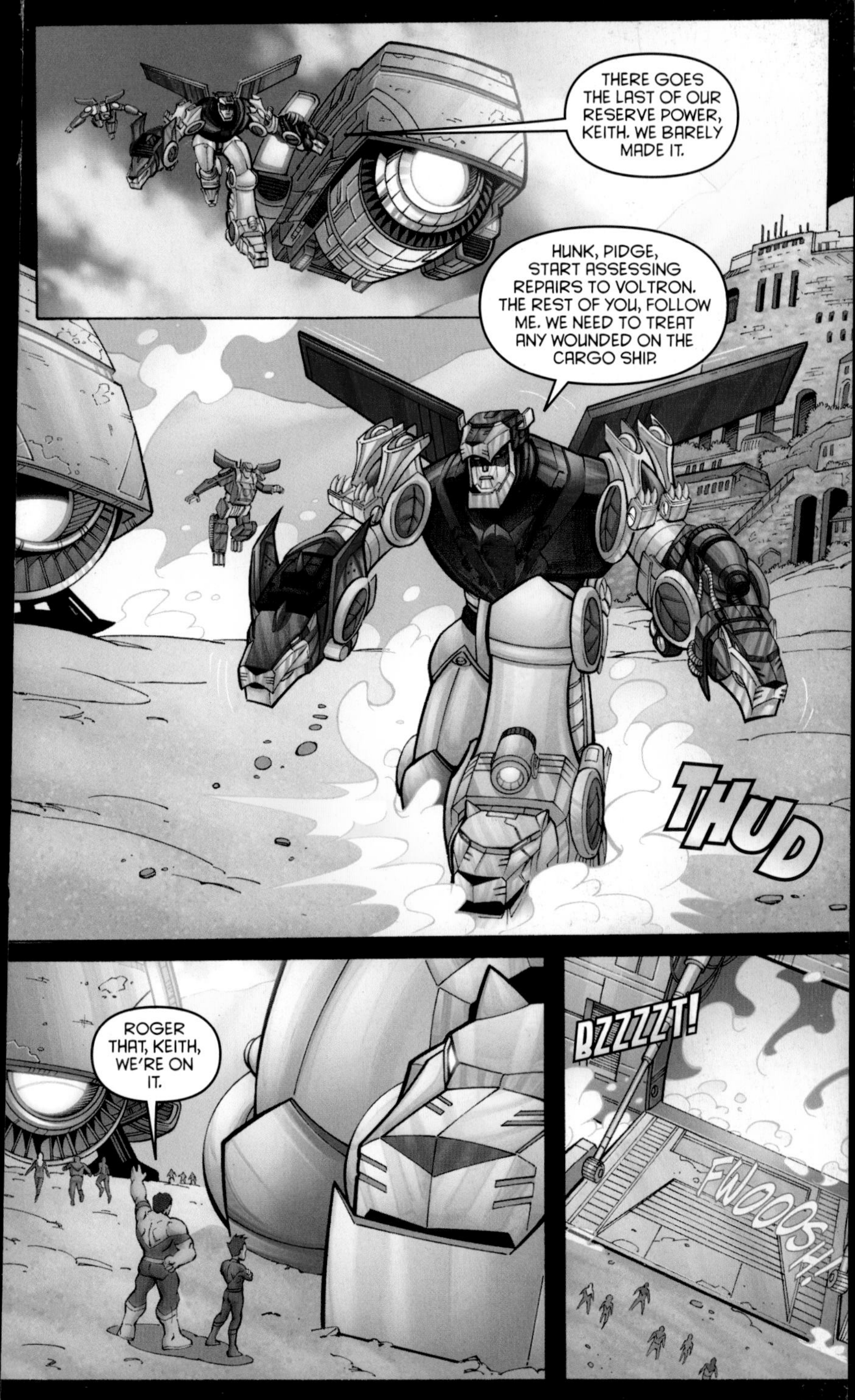
THERE GOES THE LAST OF OUR RESERVE POWER, KEITH. WE BARELY MADE IT.
HUNK, PIDGE, START ASSESSING REPAIRS TO VOLTRON. THE REST OF YOU, FOLLOW ME. WE NEED TO TREAT ANY WOUNDED ON THE CARGO SHIP.
THUD
ROGER THAT, KEITH, WE'RE ON IT.
BZZZZT!
FWOOOSH!

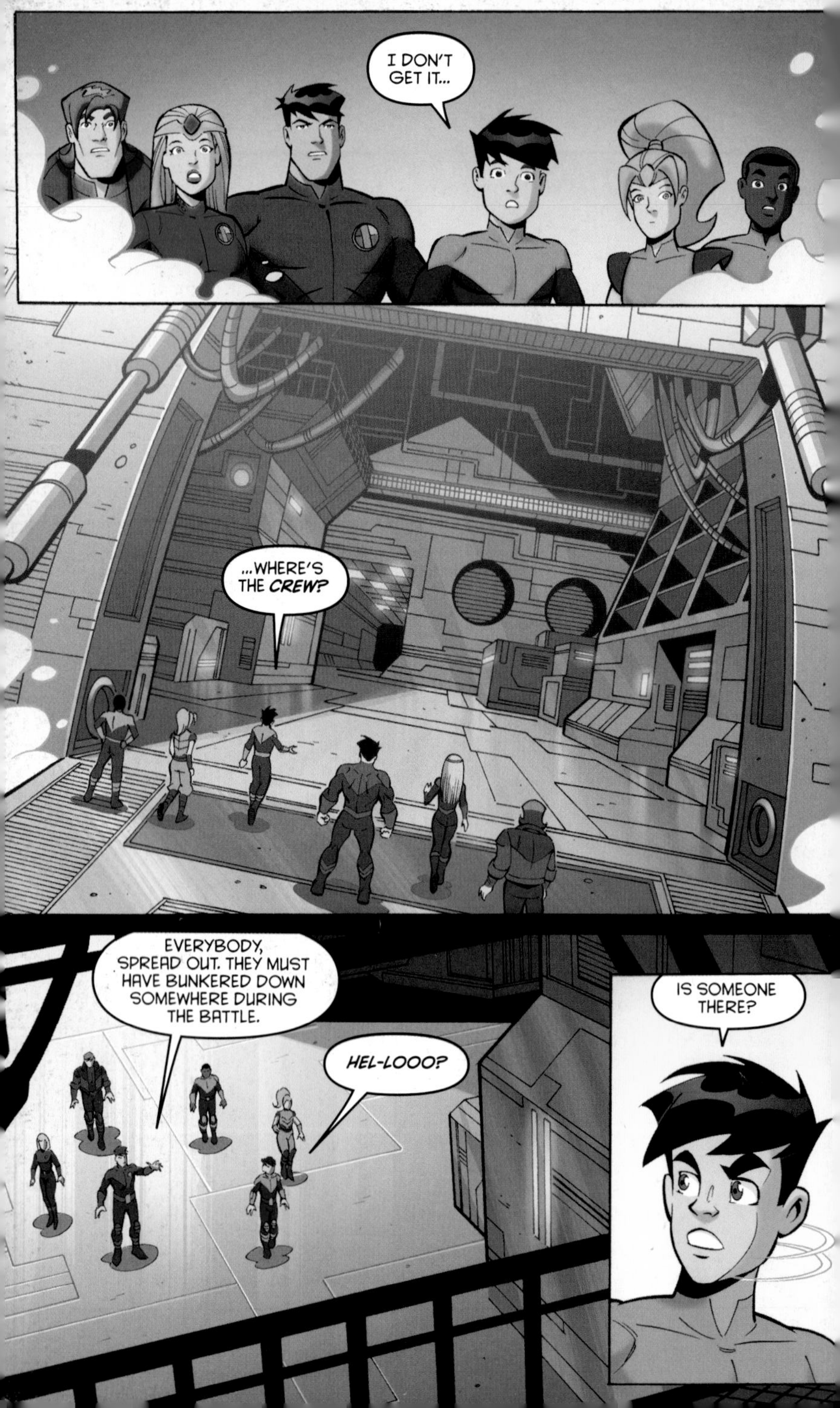

I DON'T GET IT...
...WHERE'S THE *CREW?*
EVERYBODY, SPREAD OUT. THEY MUST HAVE BUNKERED DOWN SOMEWHERE DURING THE BATTLE.
HEL-LOOO?
IS SOMEONE THERE?

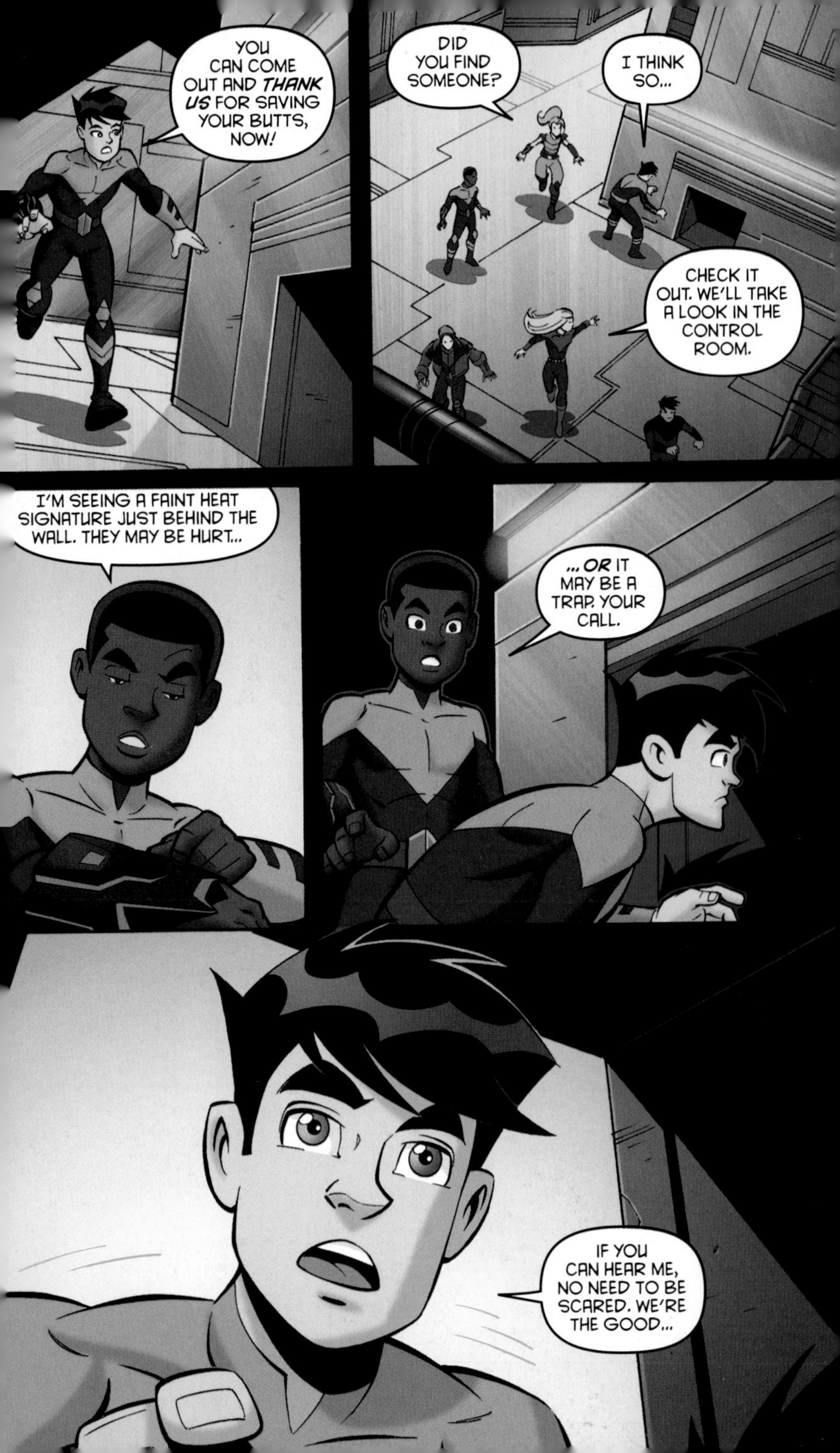
YOU CAN COME OUT AND *THANK US* FOR SAVING YOUR BUTTS, NOW!
DID YOU FIND SOMEONE?
I THINK SO...
CHECK IT OUT. WE'LL TAKE A LOOK IN THE CONTROL ROOM.
I'M SEEING A FAINT HEAT SIGNATURE JUST BEHIND THE WALL. THEY MAY BE HURT...
...OR IT MAY BE A TRAP. YOUR CALL.
IF YOU CAN HEAR ME, NO NEED TO BE SCARED. WE'RE THE GOOD...

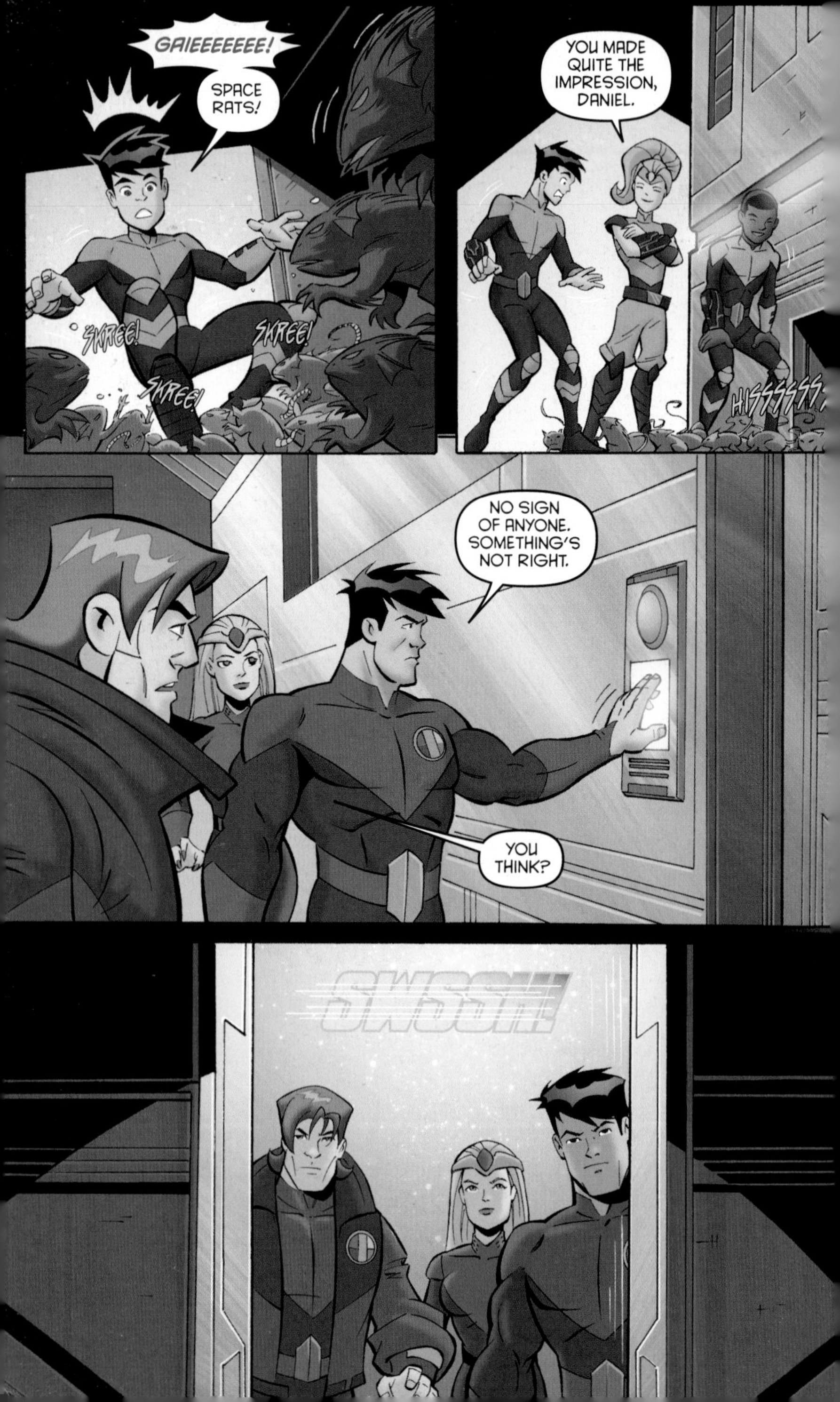

GAIEEEEEEE!
SPACE RATS!
SKREE!
SKREE!
SKREE!
YOU MADE QUITE THE IMPRESSION, DANIEL.
HISSSSSS
NO SIGN OF ANYONE. SOMETHING'S NOT RIGHT.
YOU THINK?
SWSSH!

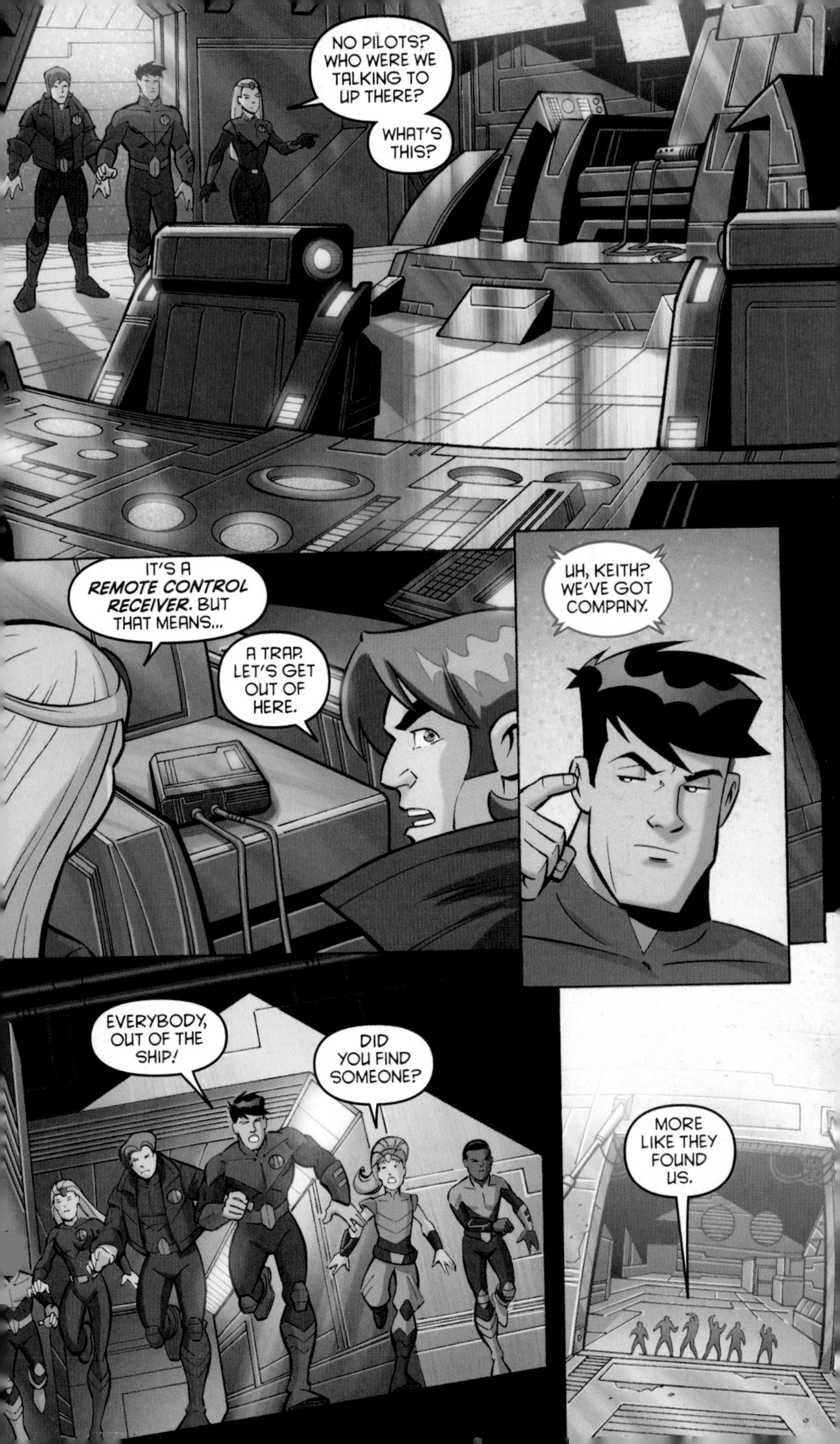
NO PILOTS? WHO WERE WE TALKING TO UP THERE?
WHAT'S THIS?
IT'S A *REMOTE CONTROL RECEIVER*. BUT THAT MEANS...
A TRAP. LET'S GET OUT OF HERE.
UH, KEITH? WE'VE GOT COMPANY.
EVERYBODY, OUT OF THE SHIP!
DID YOU FIND SOMEONE?
MORE LIKE THEY FOUND US.

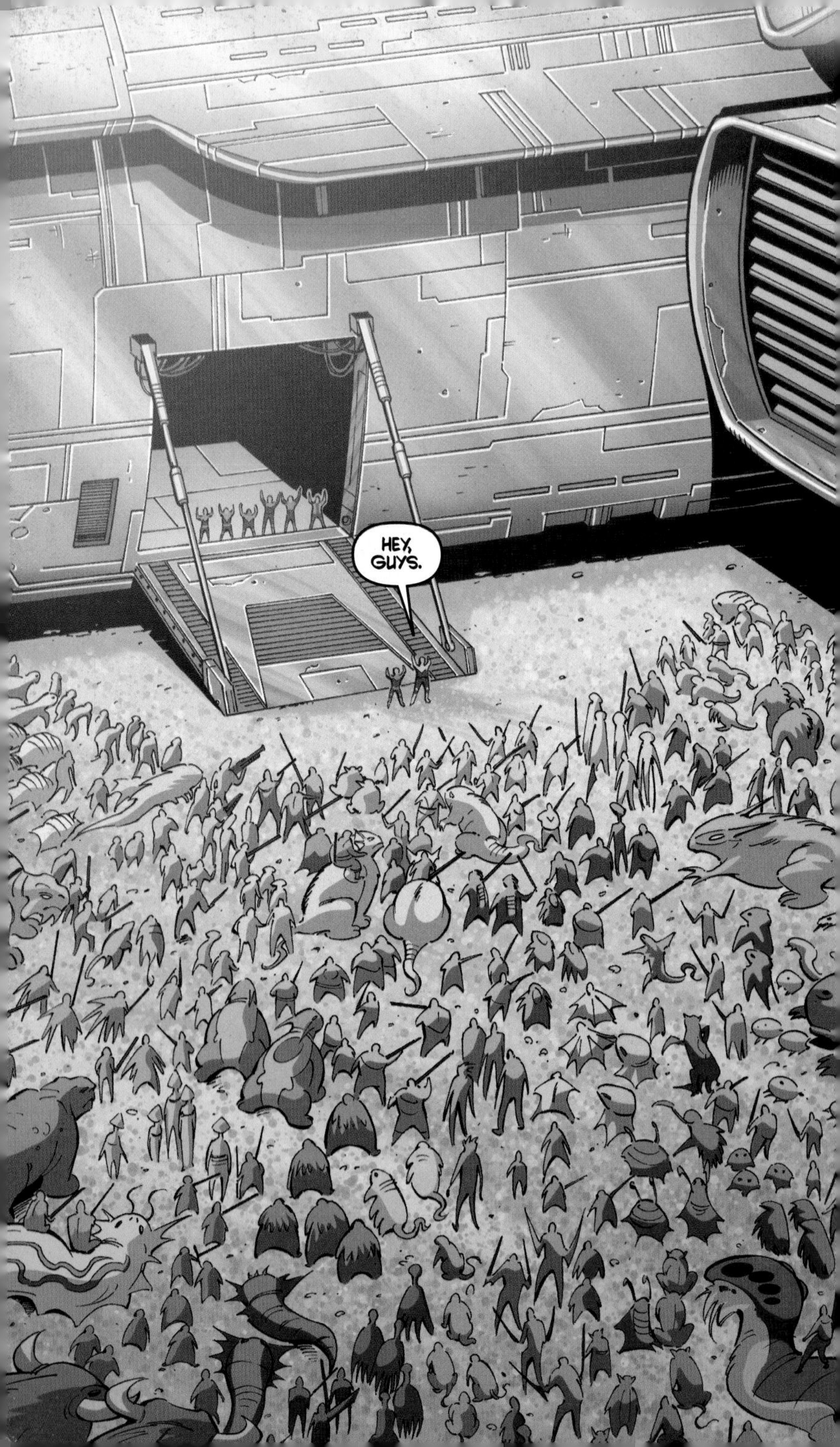
HEY, GUYS.

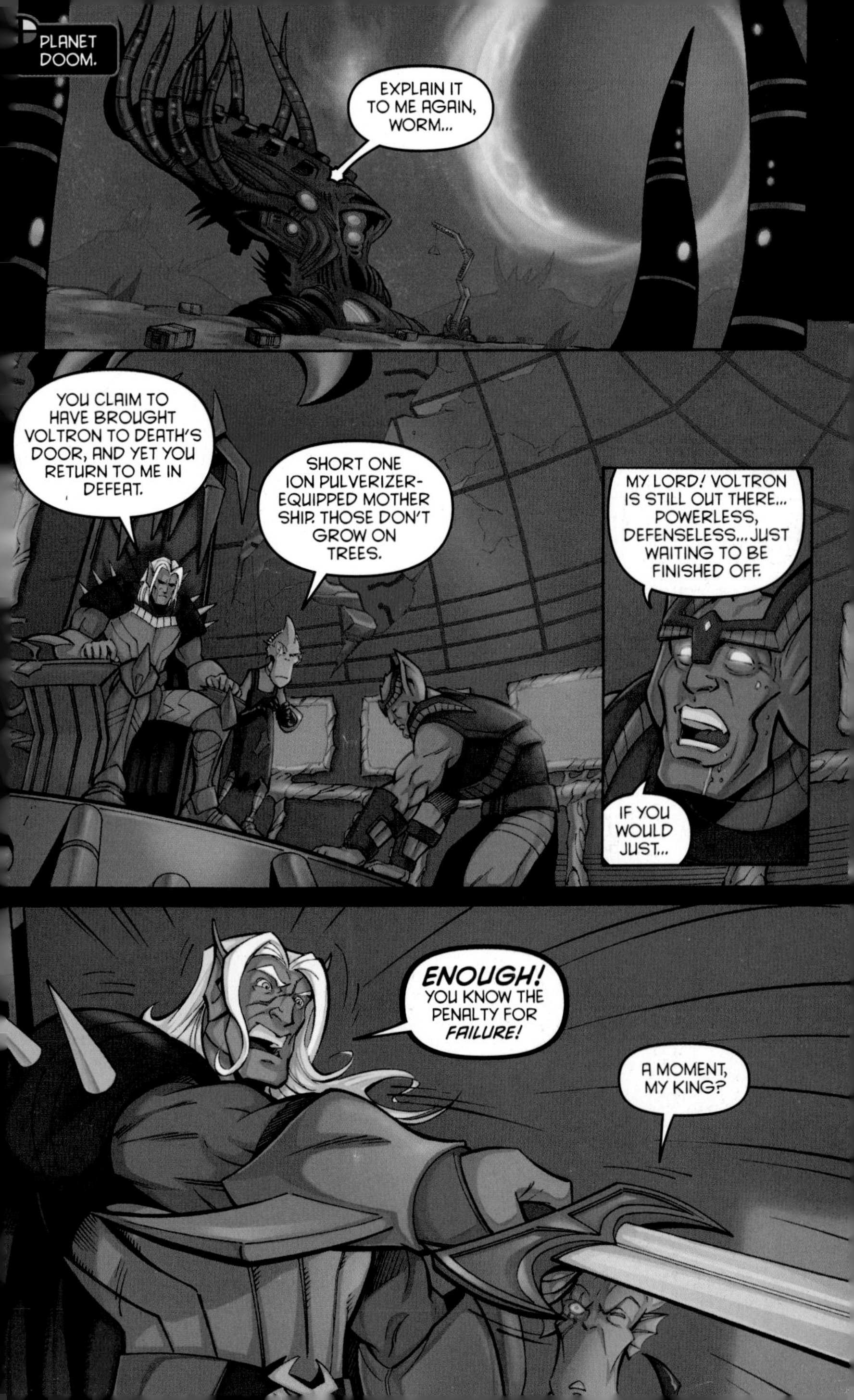
PLANET DOOM.
EXPLAIN IT TO ME AGAIN, WORM...
YOU CLAIM TO HAVE BROUGHT VOLTRON TO DEATH'S DOOR, AND YET YOU RETURN TO ME IN DEFEAT.
SHORT ONE ION PULVERIZER-EQUIPPED MOTHER SHIP. THOSE DON'T GROW ON TREES.
MY LORD! VOLTRON IS STILL OUT THERE... POWERLESS, DEFENSELESS... JUST WAITING TO BE FINISHED OFF.
IF YOU WOULD JUST...
ENOUGH! YOU KNOW THE PENALTY FOR FAILURE!
A MOMENT, MY KING?

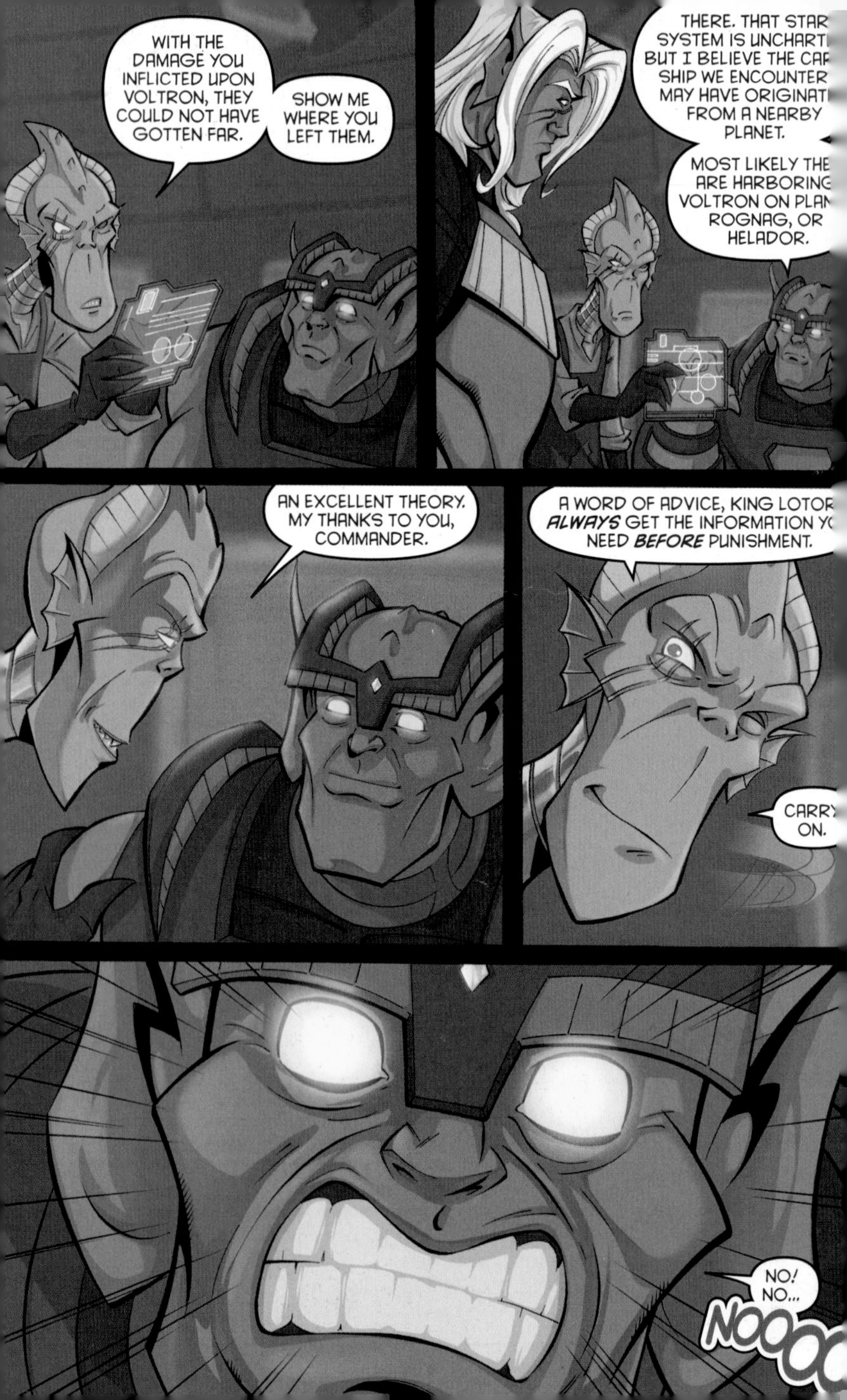
WITH THE DAMAGE YOU INFLICTED UPON VOLTRON, THEY COULD NOT HAVE GOTTEN FAR.
SHOW ME WHERE YOU LEFT THEM.
THERE. THAT STAR SYSTEM IS UNCHART BUT I BELIEVE THE CAR SHIP WE ENCOUNTER MAY HAVE ORIGINAT FROM A NEARBY PLANET.
MOST LIKELY THE ARE HARBORING VOLTRON ON PLAN ROGNAG, OR HELADOR.
AN EXCELLENT THEORY. MY THANKS TO YOU, COMMANDER.
A WORD OF ADVICE, KING LOTOR *ALWAYS* GET THE INFORMATION YO NEED *BEFORE* PUNISHMENT.
CARRY ON.
NO! NO...
NOOO

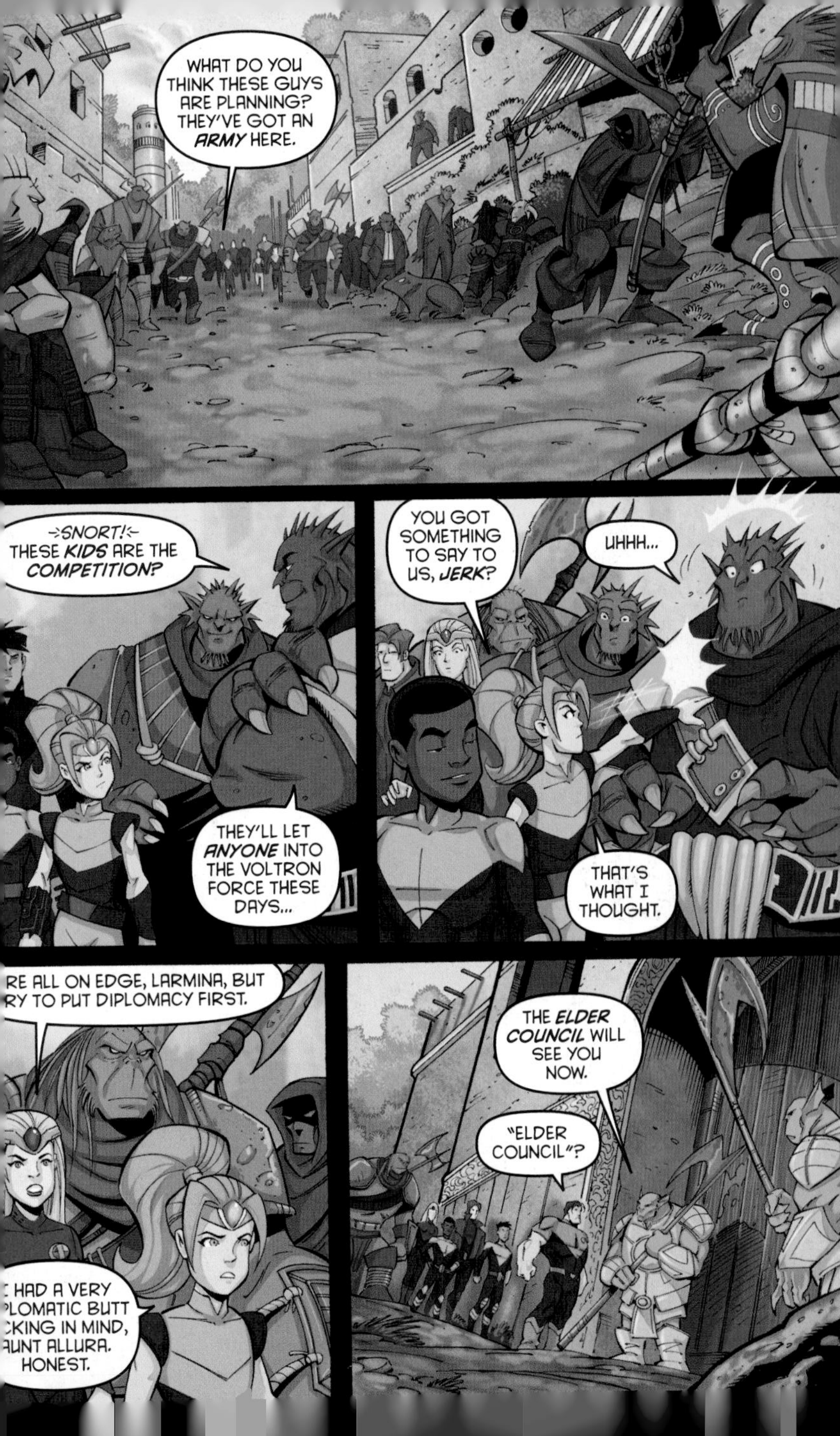
WHAT DO YOU THINK THESE GUYS ARE PLANNING? THEY'VE GOT AN ARMY HERE.
-SNORT!- THESE KIDS ARE THE COMPETITION?
THEY'LL LET ANYONE INTO THE VOLTRON FORCE THESE DAYS...
YOU GOT SOMETHING TO SAY TO US, JERK?
UHHH...
THAT'S WHAT I THOUGHT.
RE ALL ON EDGE, LARMINA, BUT RY TO PUT DIPLOMACY FIRST.
HAD A VERY PLOMATIC BUTT CKING IN MIND, AUNT ALLURA. HONEST.
THE ELDER COUNCIL WILL SEE YOU NOW.
"ELDER COUNCIL"?

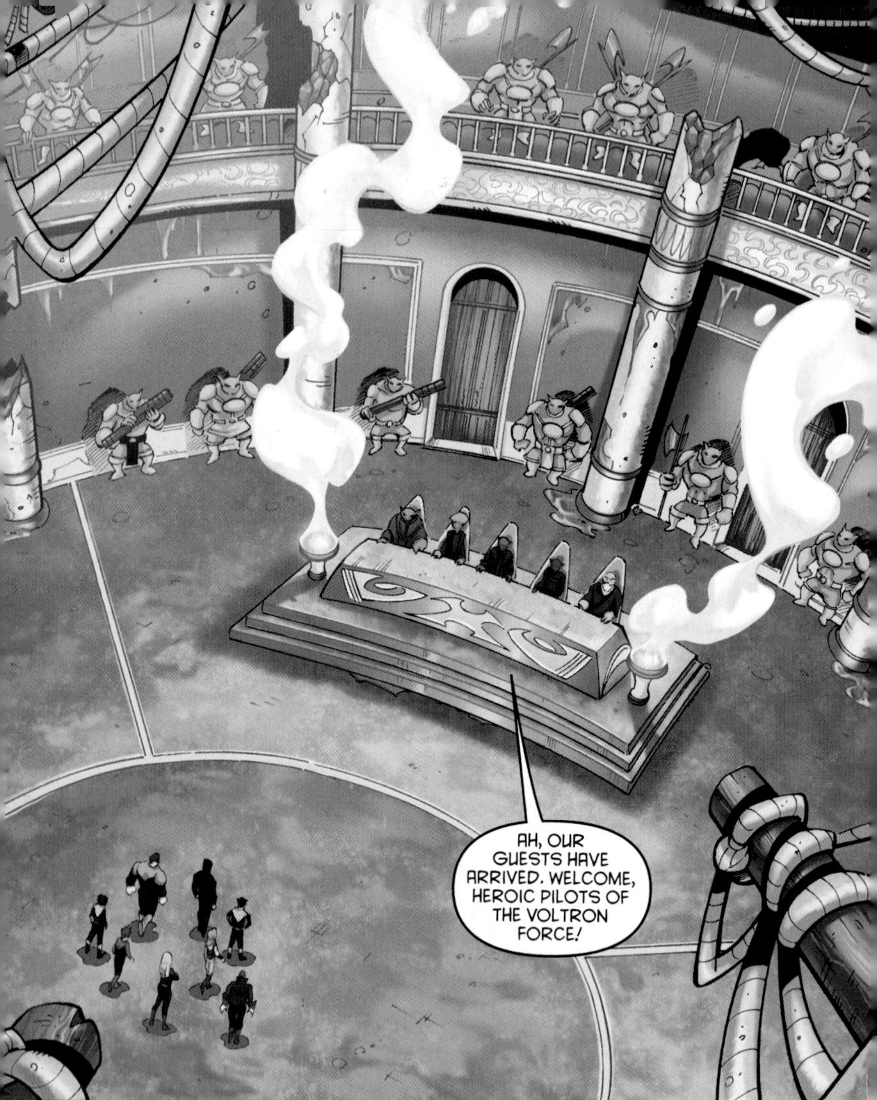
AH, OUR GUESTS HAVE ARRIVED. WELCOME, HEROIC PILOTS OF THE VOLTRON FORCE!

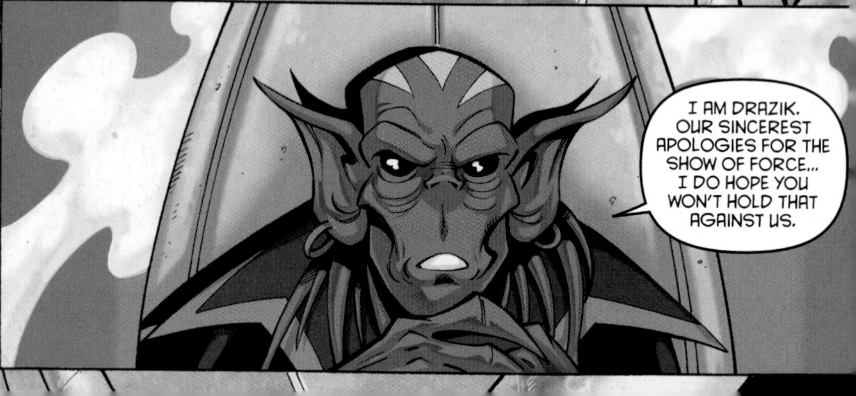
I AM DRAZIK. OUR SINCEREST APOLOGIES FOR THE SHOW OF FORCE... I DO HOPE YOU WON'T HOLD THAT AGAINST US.

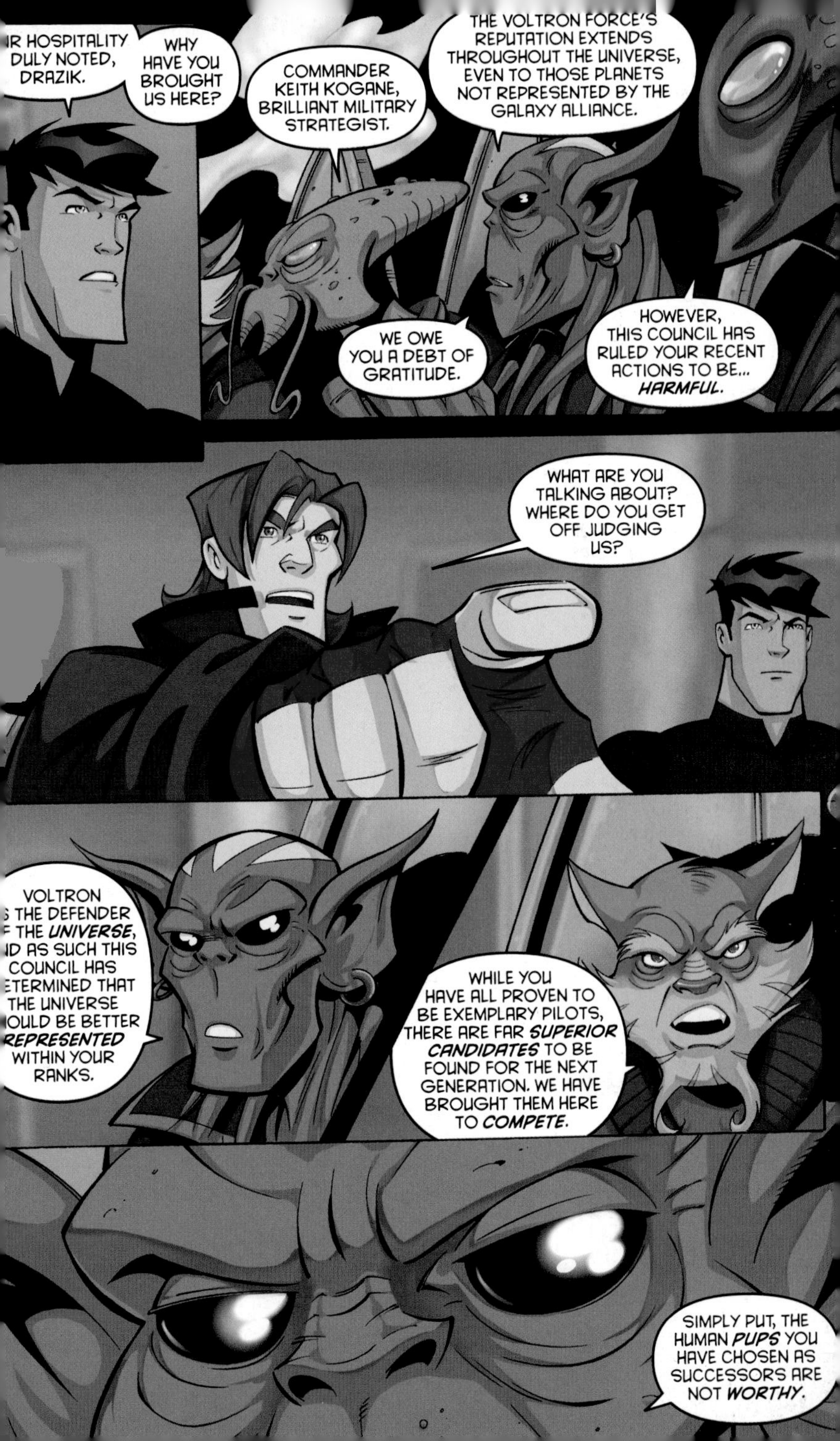

R HOSPITALITY DULY NOTED, DRAZIK.
WHY HAVE YOU BROUGHT US HERE?
COMMANDER KEITH KOGANE, BRILLIANT MILITARY STRATEGIST.
THE VOLTRON FORCE'S REPUTATION EXTENDS THROUGHOUT THE UNIVERSE, EVEN TO THOSE PLANETS NOT REPRESENTED BY THE GALAXY ALLIANCE.
WE OWE YOU A DEBT OF GRATITUDE.
HOWEVER, THIS COUNCIL HAS RULED YOUR RECENT ACTIONS TO BE... *HARMFUL*.
WHAT ARE YOU TALKING ABOUT? WHERE DO YOU GET OFF JUDGING US?
VOLTRON S THE DEFENDER F THE *UNIVERSE*, D AS SUCH THIS COUNCIL HAS ETERMINED THAT THE UNIVERSE OULD BE BETTER *REPRESENTED* WITHIN YOUR RANKS.
WHILE YOU HAVE ALL PROVEN TO BE EXEMPLARY PILOTS, THERE ARE FAR *SUPERIOR CANDIDATES* TO BE FOUND FOR THE NEXT GENERATION. WE HAVE BROUGHT THEM HERE TO *COMPETE*.
SIMPLY PUT, THE HUMAN *PUPS* YOU HAVE CHOSEN AS SUCCESSORS ARE NOT *WORTHY*.

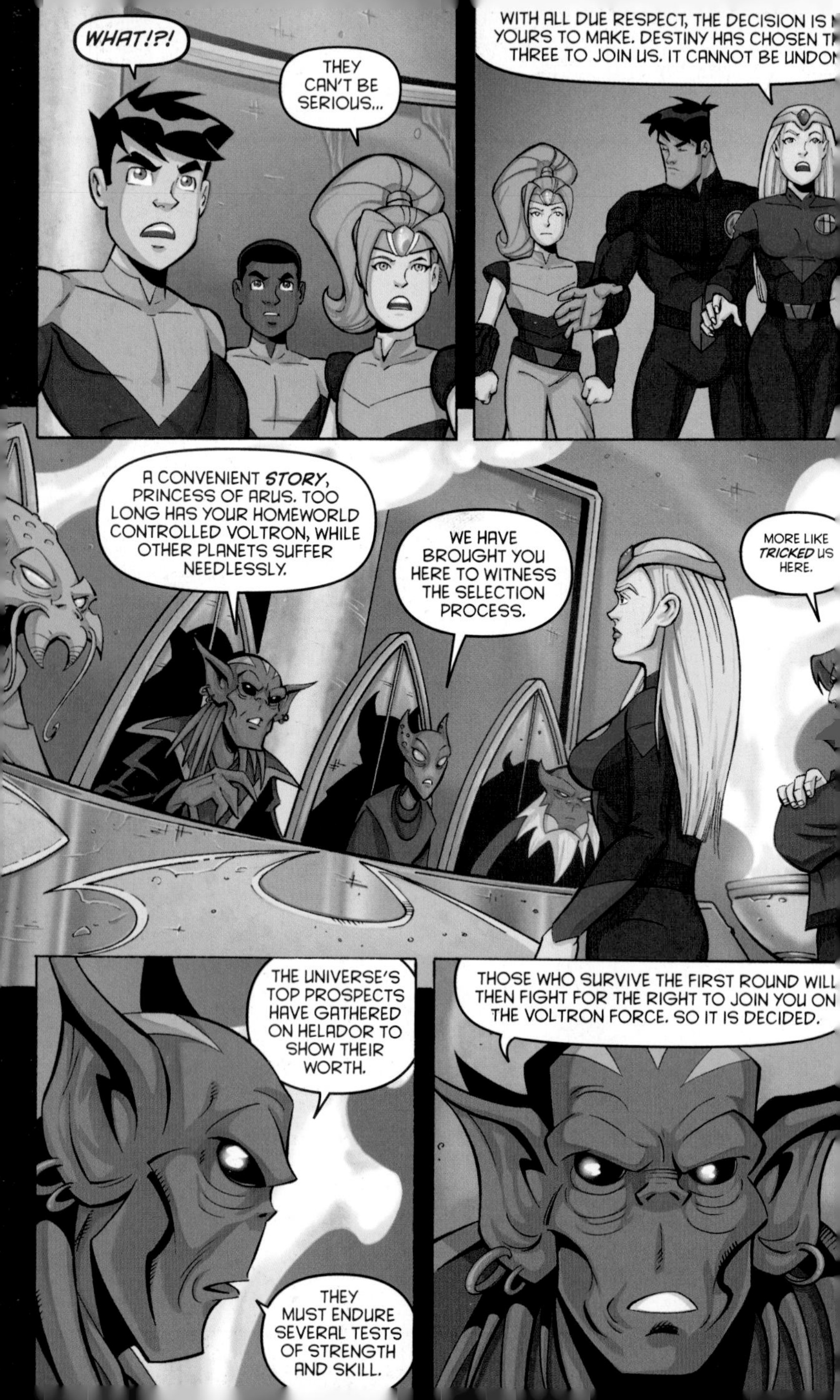

WHAT!?!
THEY CAN'T BE SERIOUS...
WITH ALL DUE RESPECT, THE DECISION IS YOURS TO MAKE. DESTINY HAS CHOSEN THREE TO JOIN US. IT CANNOT BE
A CONVENIENT STORY, PRINCESS OF ARUS. TOO LONG HAS YOUR HOMEWORLD CONTROLLED VOLTRON, WHILE OTHER PLANETS SUFFER NEEDLESSLY.
WE HAVE BROUGHT YOU HERE TO WITNESS THE SELECTION PROCESS.
MORE LIKE TRICKED US HERE.
THE UNIVERSE'S TOP PROSPECTS HAVE GATHERED ON HELADOR TO SHOW THEIR WORTH.
THEY MUST ENDURE SEVERAL TESTS OF STRENGTH AND SKILL.
THOSE WHO SURVIVE THE FIRST ROUND WILL THEN FIGHT FOR THE RIGHT TO JOIN YOU ON THE VOLTRON FORCE. SO IT IS DECIDED.

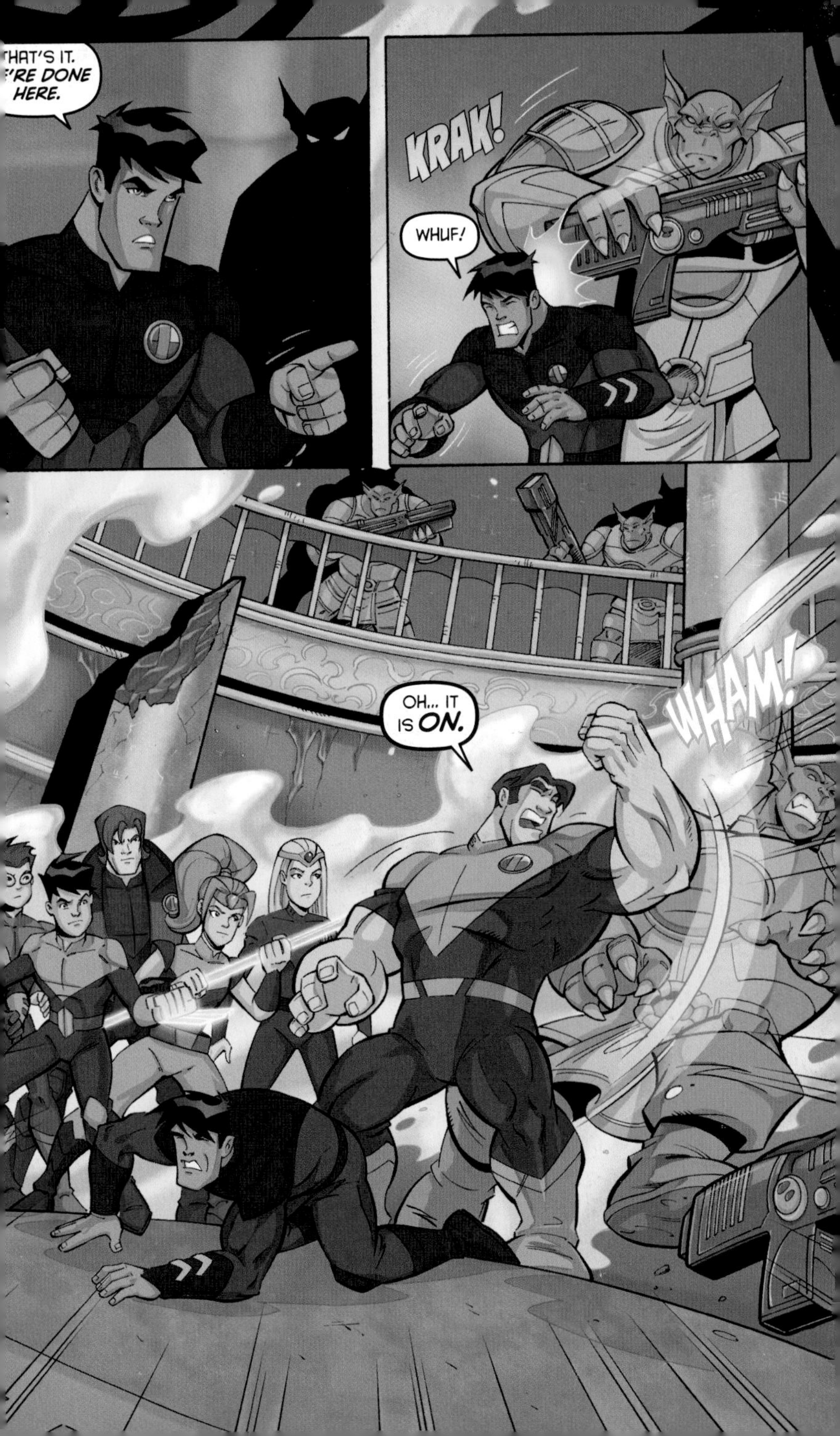
THAT'S IT. 'RE DONE HERE.
KRAK!
WHUF!
OH... IT IS ON.
WHAM!

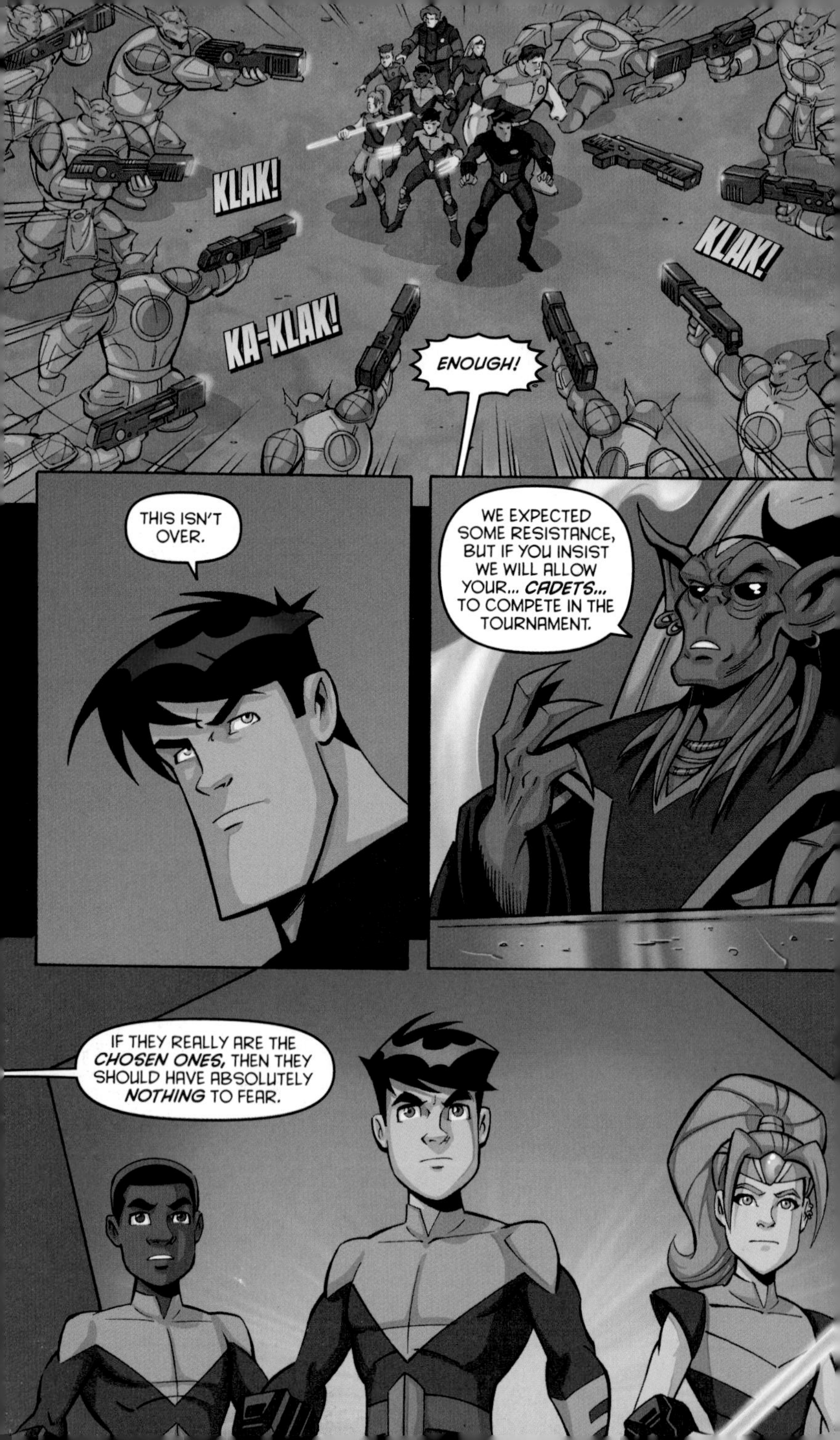
KLAK!
KLAK!
KA-KLAK!
ENOUGH!
THIS ISN'T OVER.
WE EXPECTED SOME RESISTANCE, BUT IF YOU INSIST WE WILL ALLOW YOUR... CADETS... TO COMPETE IN THE TOURNAMENT.
IF THEY REALLY ARE THE CHOSEN ONES, THEN THEY SHOULD HAVE ABSOLUTELY NOTHING TO FEAR.

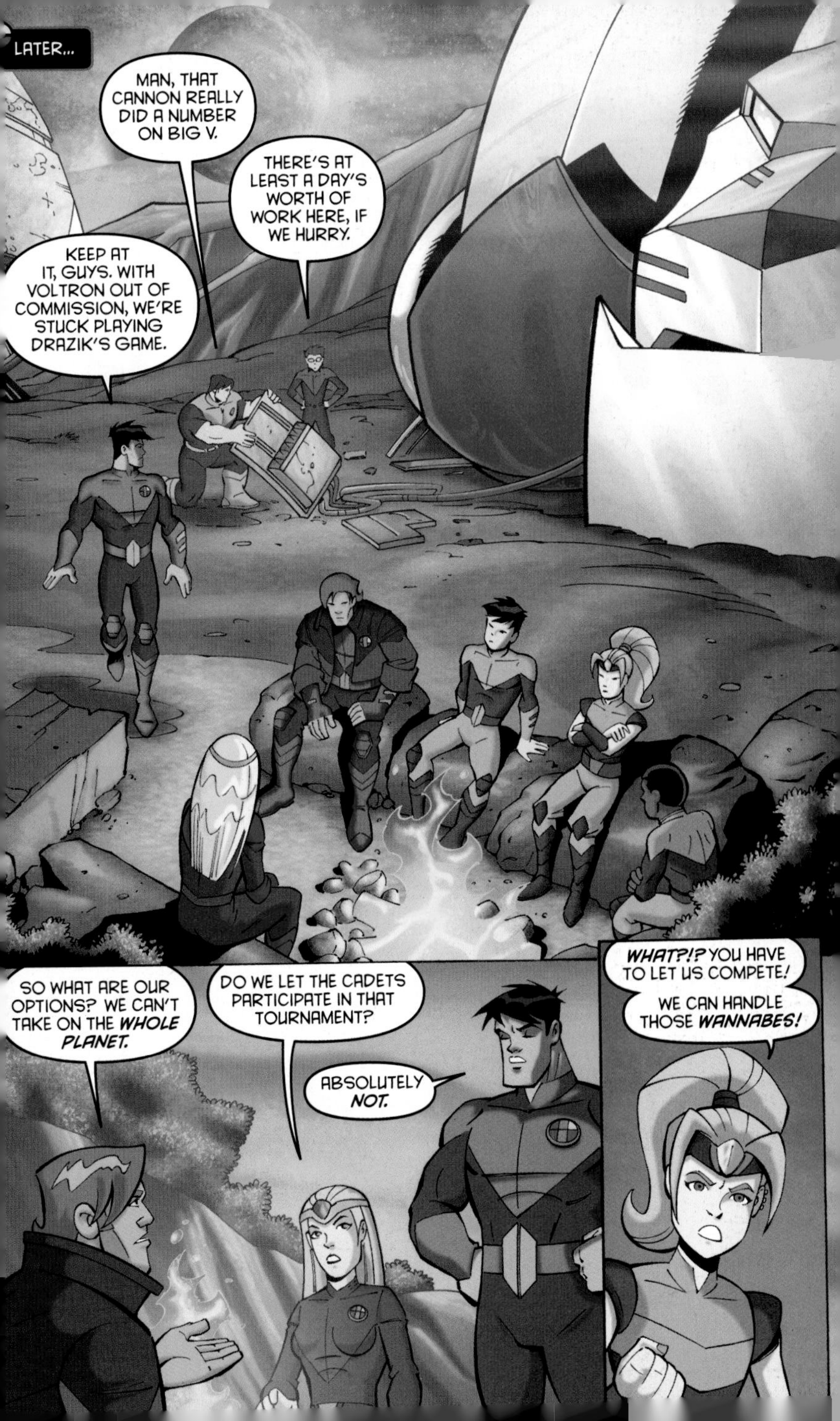
LATER...
MAN, THAT CANNON REALLY DID A NUMBER ON BIG V.
THERE'S AT LEAST A DAY'S WORTH OF WORK HERE, IF WE HURRY.
KEEP AT IT, GUYS. WITH VOLTRON OUT OF COMMISSION, WE'RE STUCK PLAYING DRAZIK'S GAME.
SO WHAT ARE OUR OPTIONS? WE CAN'T TAKE ON THE WHOLE PLANET.
DO WE LET THE CADETS PARTICIPATE IN THAT TOURNAMENT?
ABSOLUTELY NOT.
WHAT?!? YOU HAVE TO LET US COMPETE!
WE CAN HANDLE THOSE WANNABES!

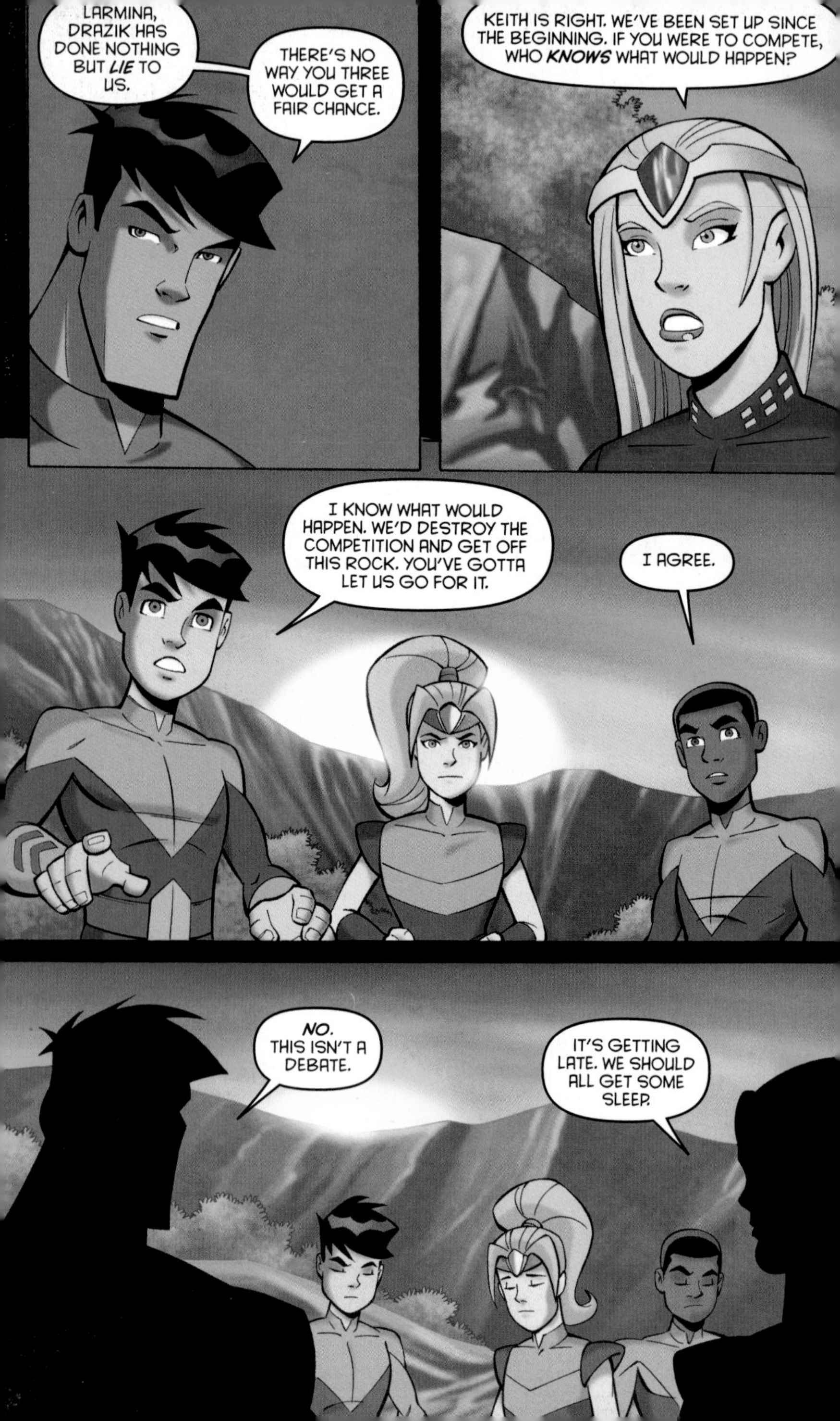
LARMINA, DRAZIK HAS DONE NOTHING BUT *LIE* TO US.
THERE'S NO WAY YOU THREE WOULD GET A FAIR CHANCE.
KEITH IS RIGHT. WE'VE BEEN SET UP SINCE THE BEGINNING. IF YOU WERE TO COMPETE, WHO ***KNOWS*** WHAT WOULD HAPPEN?
I KNOW WHAT WOULD HAPPEN. WE'D DESTROY THE COMPETITION AND GET OFF THIS ROCK. YOU'VE GOTTA LET US GO FOR IT.
I AGREE.
NO. THIS ISN'T A DEBATE.
IT'S GETTING LATE. WE SHOULD ALL GET SOME SLEEP.

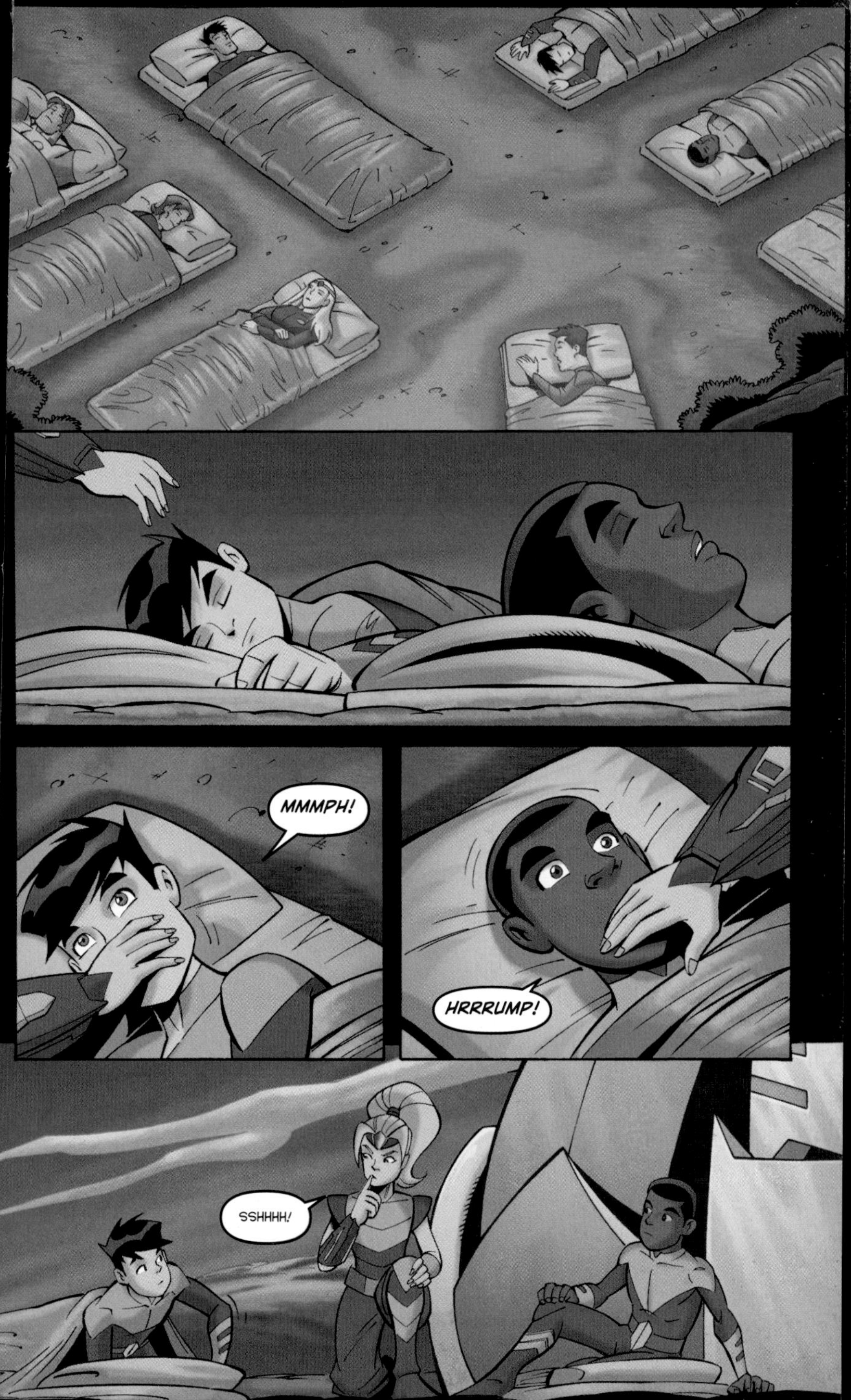
MMMPH!
HRRRUMP!
SSHHHH!

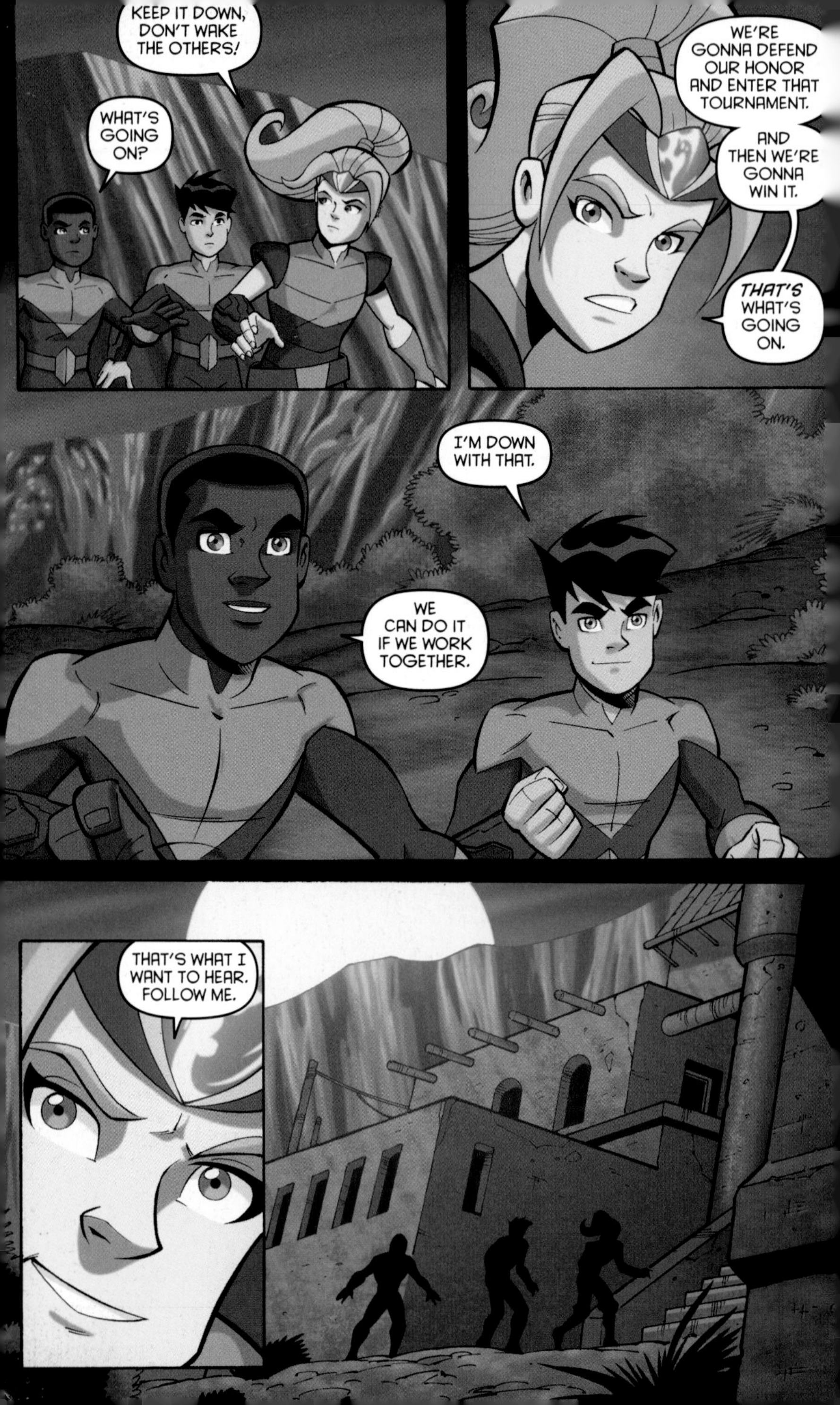
KEEP IT DOWN, DON'T WAKE THE OTHERS!
WHAT'S GOING ON?
WE'RE GONNA DEFEND OUR HONOR AND ENTER THAT TOURNAMENT.
AND THEN WE'RE GONNA WIN IT.
THAT'S WHAT'S GOING ON.
I'M DOWN WITH THAT.
WE CAN DO IT IF WE WORK TOGETHER.
THAT'S WHAT I WANT TO HEAR. FOLLOW ME.

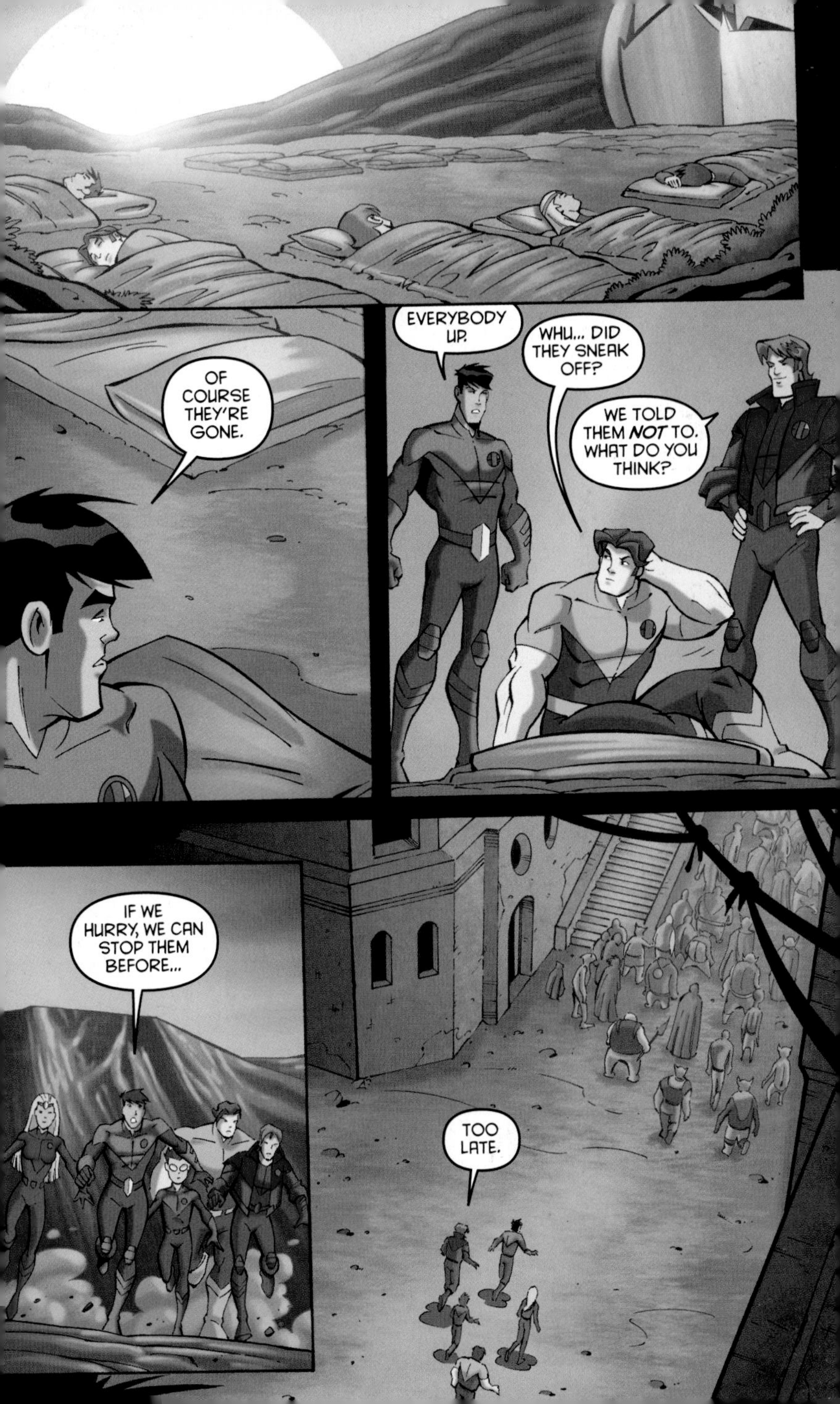
OF COURSE THEY'RE GONE.
EVERYBODY UP.
WHU... DID THEY SNEAK OFF?
WE TOLD THEM NOT TO. WHAT DO YOU THINK?
IF WE HURRY, WE CAN STOP THEM BEFORE...
TOO LATE.

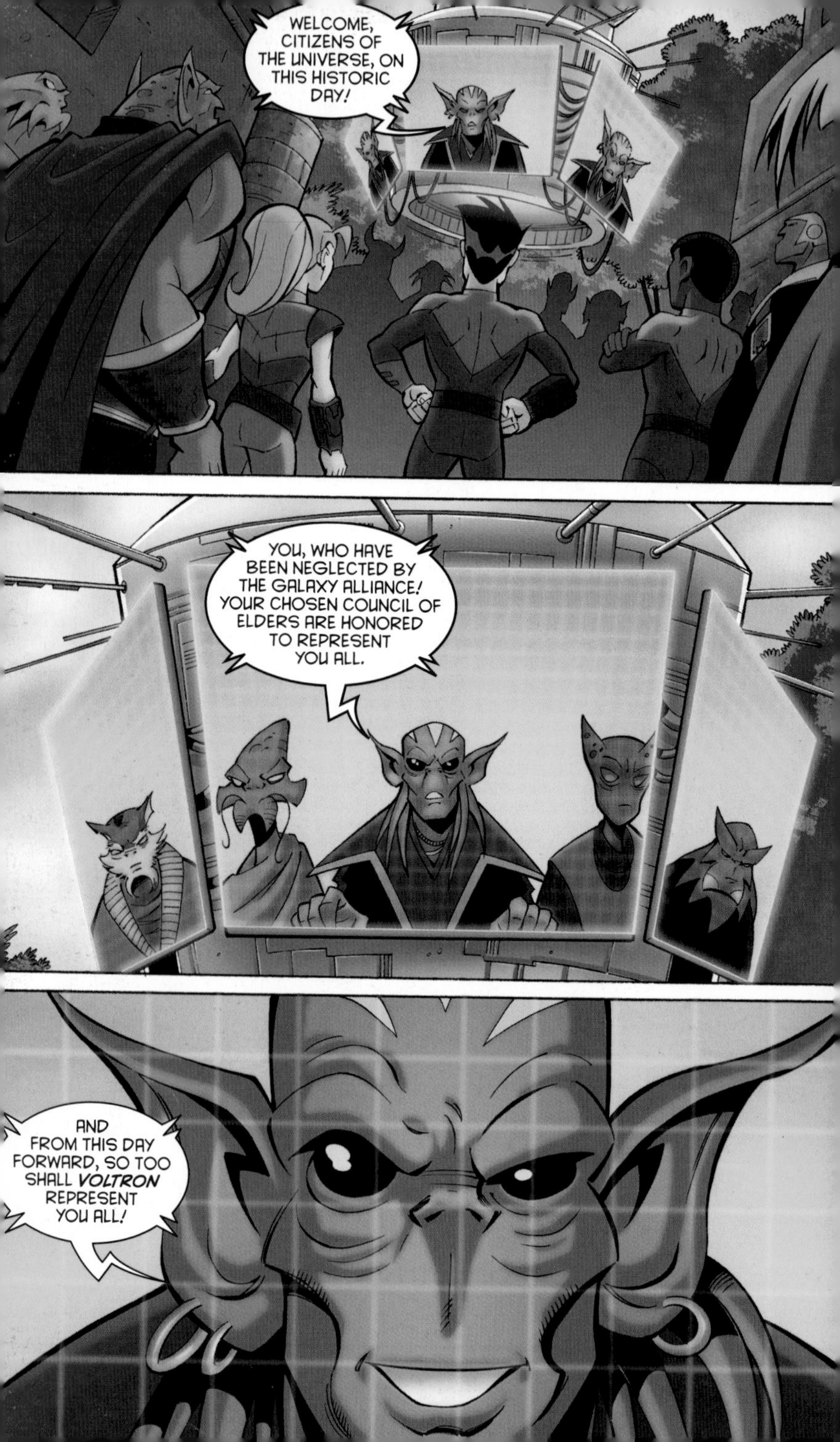
WELCOME, CITIZENS OF THE UNIVERSE, ON THIS HISTORIC DAY!
YOU, WHO HAVE BEEN NEGLECTED BY THE GALAXY ALLIANCE! YOUR CHOSEN COUNCIL OF ELDERS ARE HONORED TO REPRESENT YOU ALL.
AND FROM THIS DAY FORWARD, SO TOO SHALL *VOLTRON* REPRESENT YOU ALL!

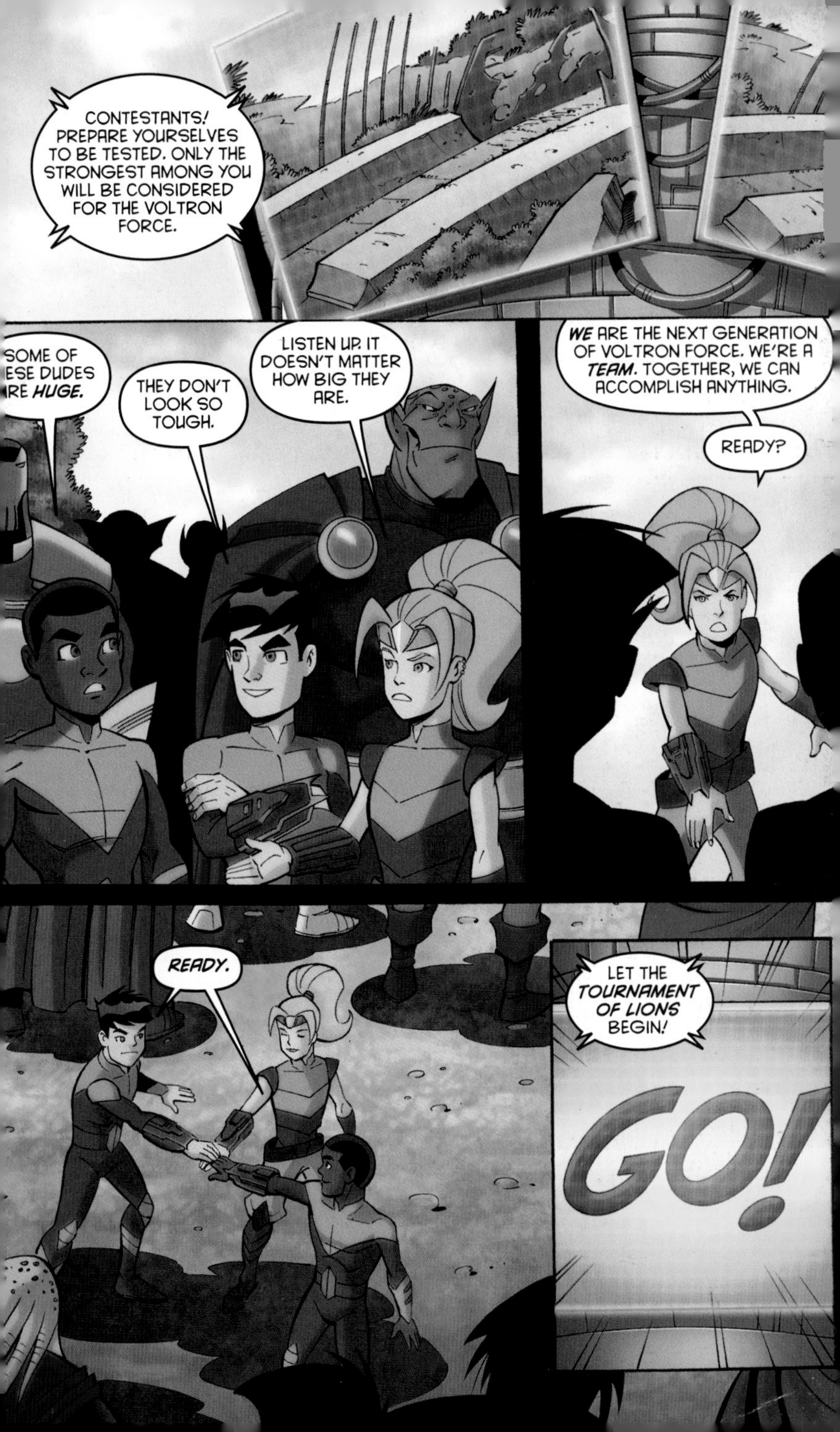
CONTESTANTS! PREPARE YOURSELVES TO BE TESTED. ONLY THE STRONGEST AMONG YOU WILL BE CONSIDERED FOR THE VOLTRON FORCE.
SOME OF ESE DUDES RE *HUGE.*
THEY DON'T LOOK SO TOUGH.
LISTEN UP. IT DOESN'T MATTER HOW BIG THEY ARE.
WE ARE THE NEXT GENERATION OF VOLTRON FORCE. WE'RE A *TEAM*. TOGETHER, WE CAN ACCOMPLISH ANYTHING.
READY?
READY.
LET THE *TOURNAMENT OF LIONS* BEGIN!
GO!

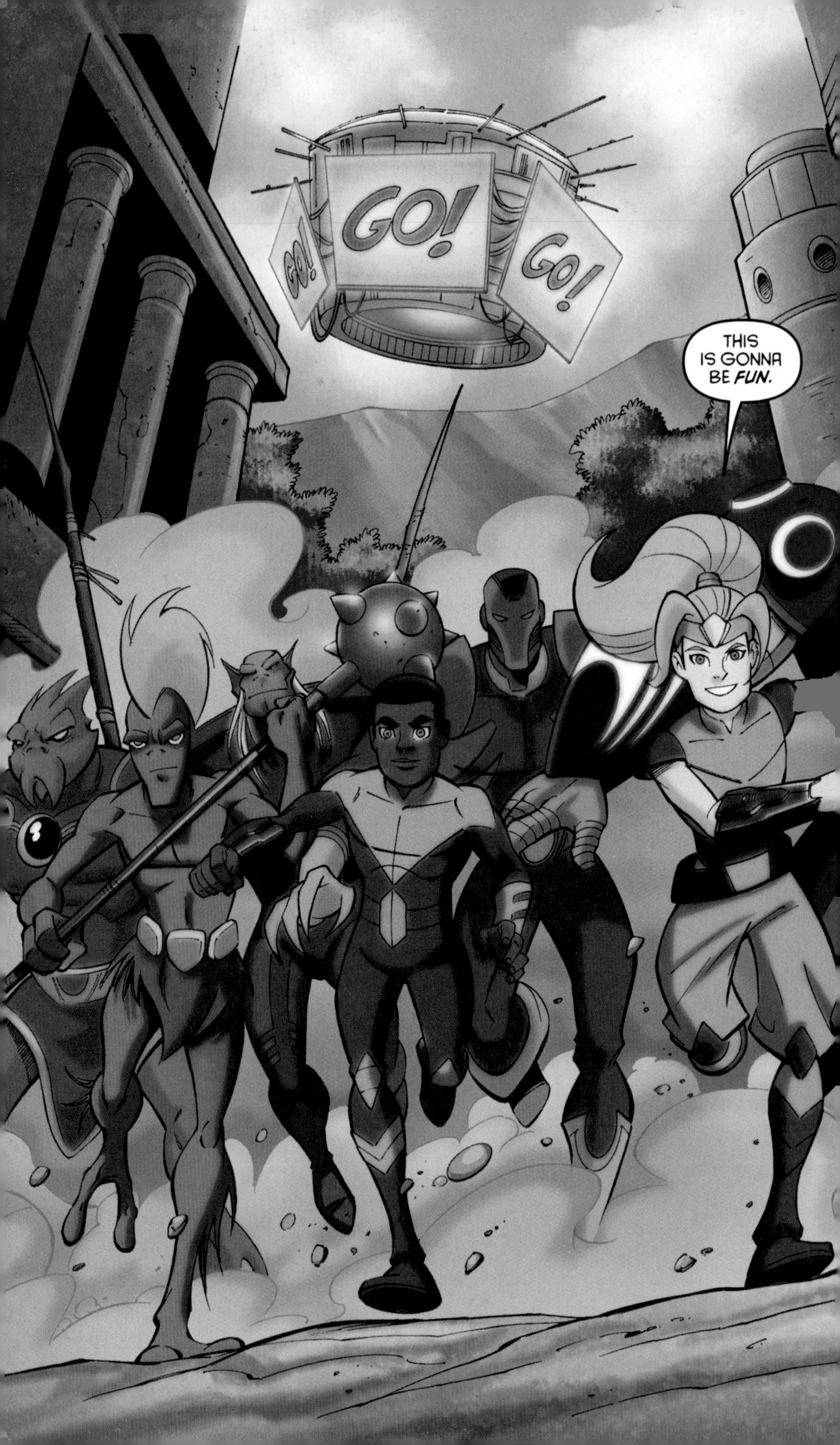
GO!
GO!
GO!
THIS IS GONNA BE *FUN*.

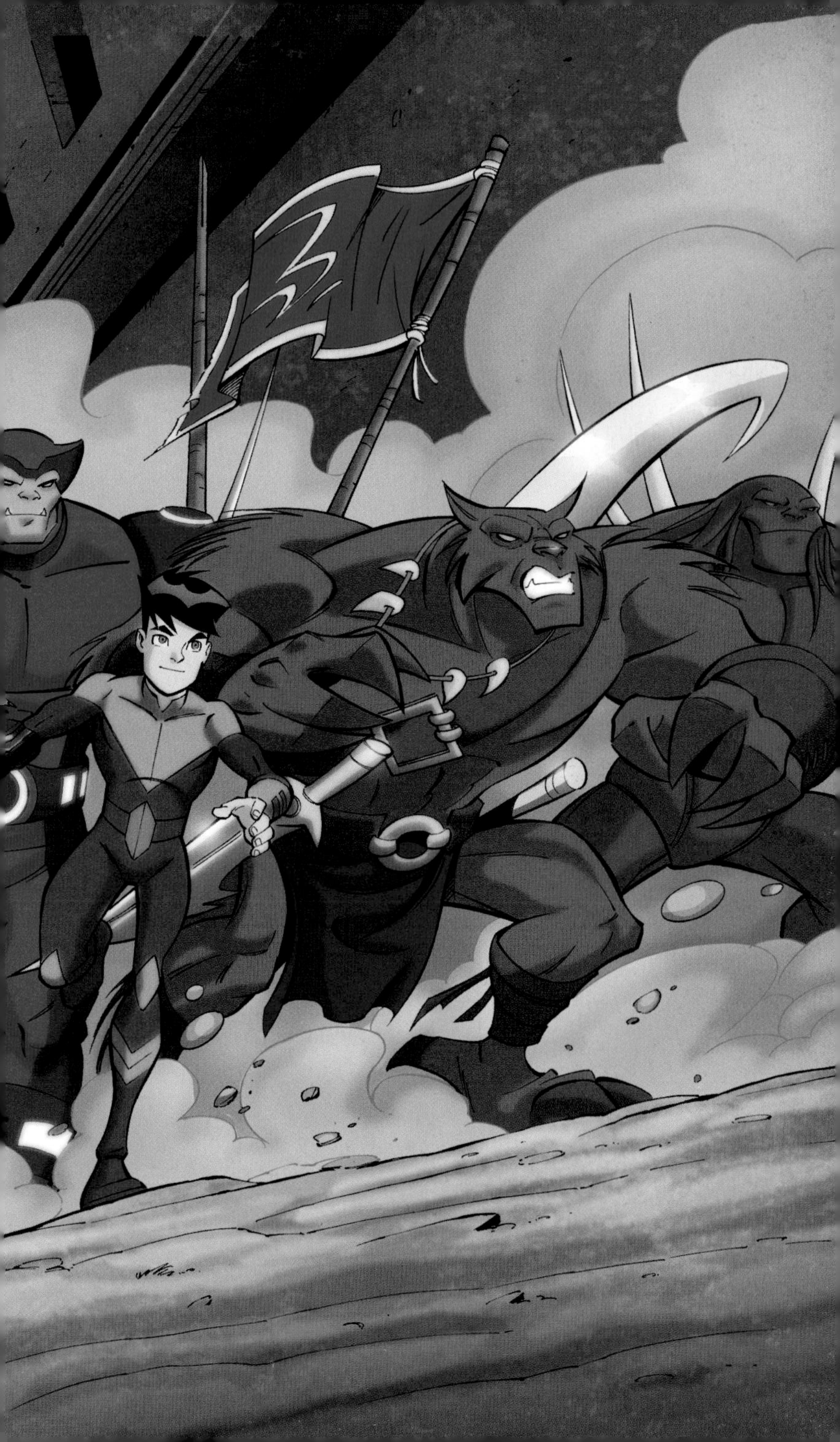

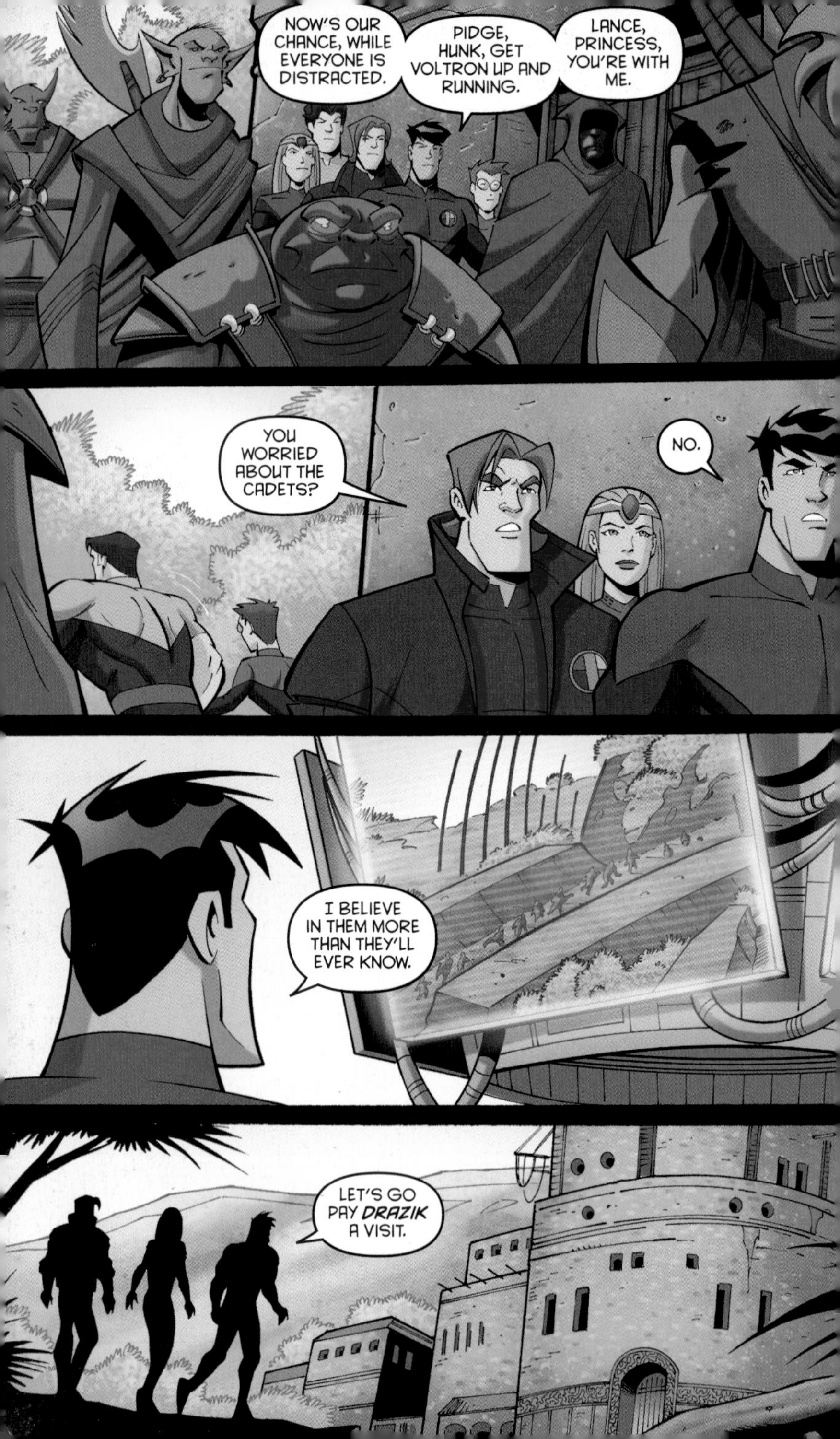
NOW'S OUR CHANCE, WHILE EVERYONE IS DISTRACTED.
PIDGE, HUNK, GET VOLTRON UP AND RUNNING.
LANCE, PRINCESS, YOU'RE WITH ME.
YOU WORRIED ABOUT THE CADETS?
NO.
I BELIEVE IN THEM MORE THAN THEY'LL EVER KNOW.
LET'S GO PAY *DRAZIK* A VISIT.

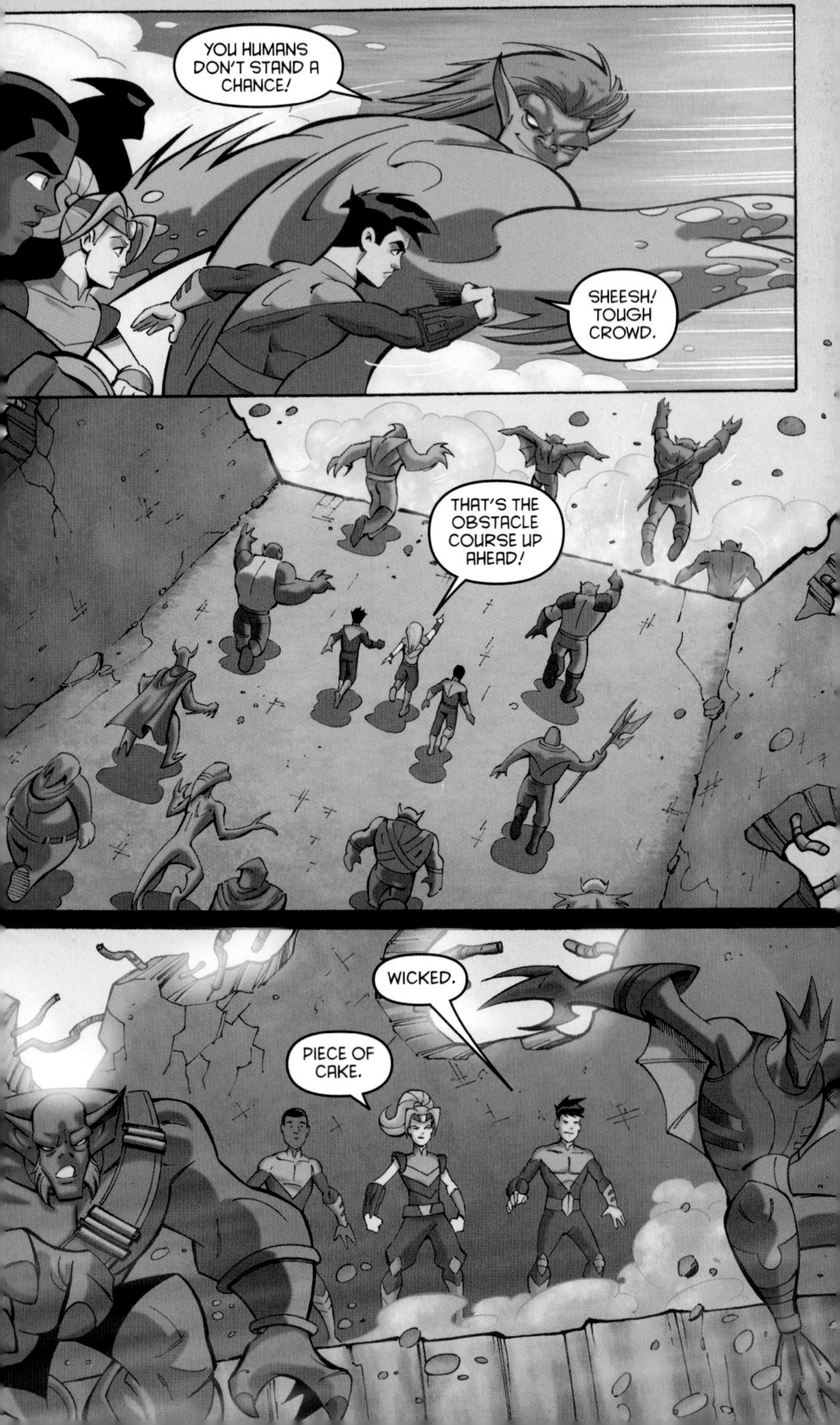
YOU HUMANS DON'T STAND A CHANCE!
SHEESH! TOUGH CROWD.
THAT'S THE OBSTACLE COURSE UP AHEAD!
WICKED.
PIECE OF CAKE.

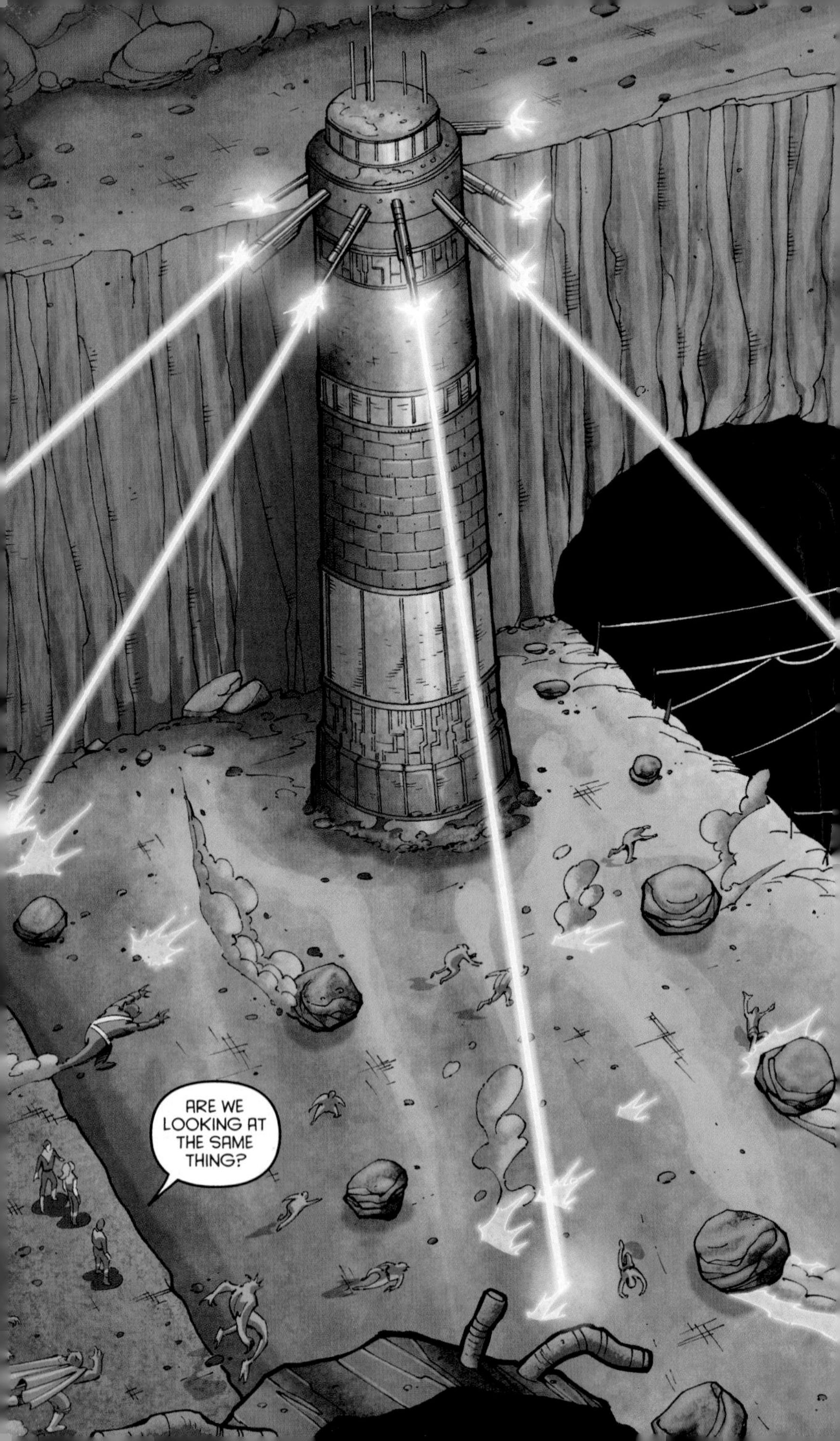
ARE WE LOOKING AT THE SAME THING?

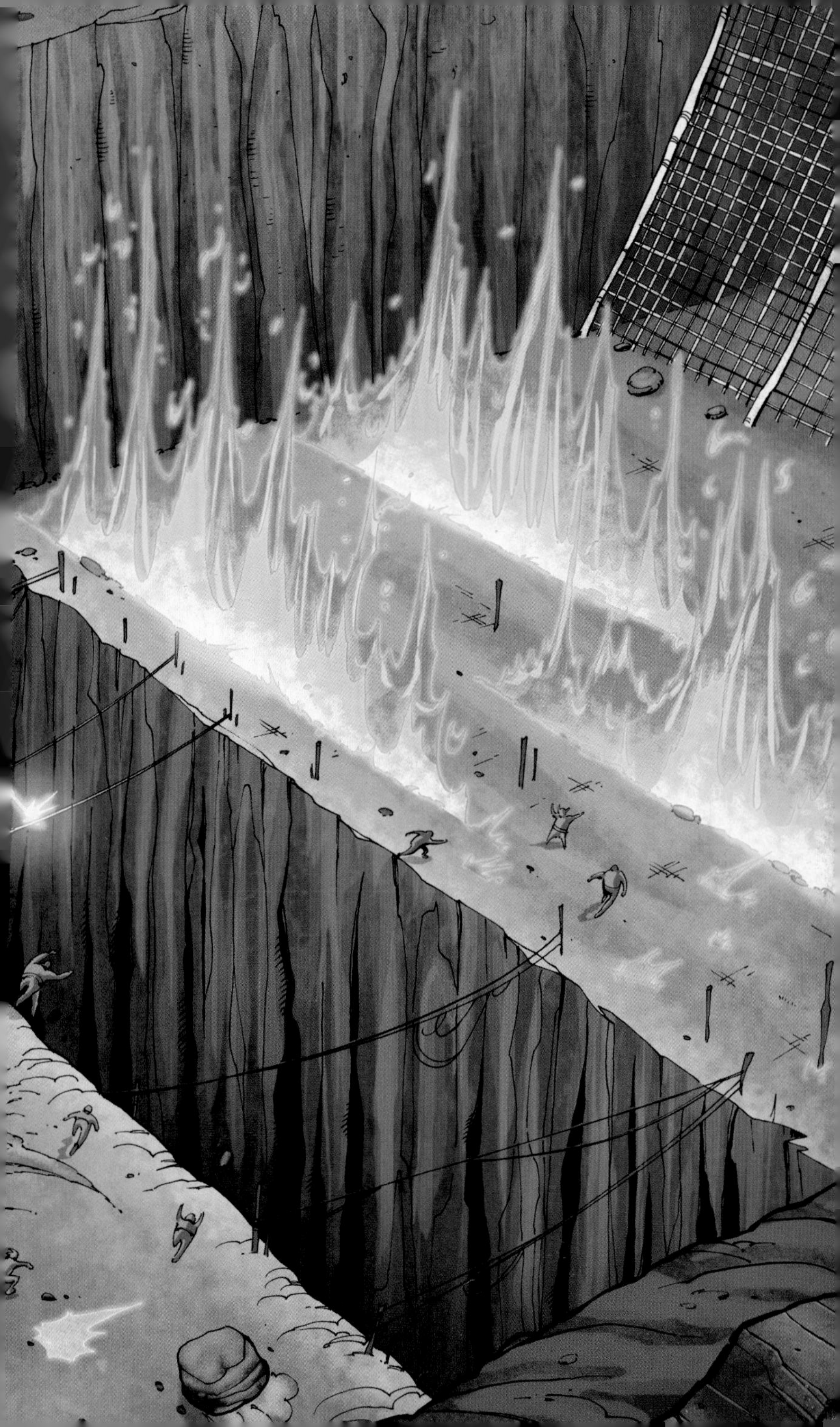

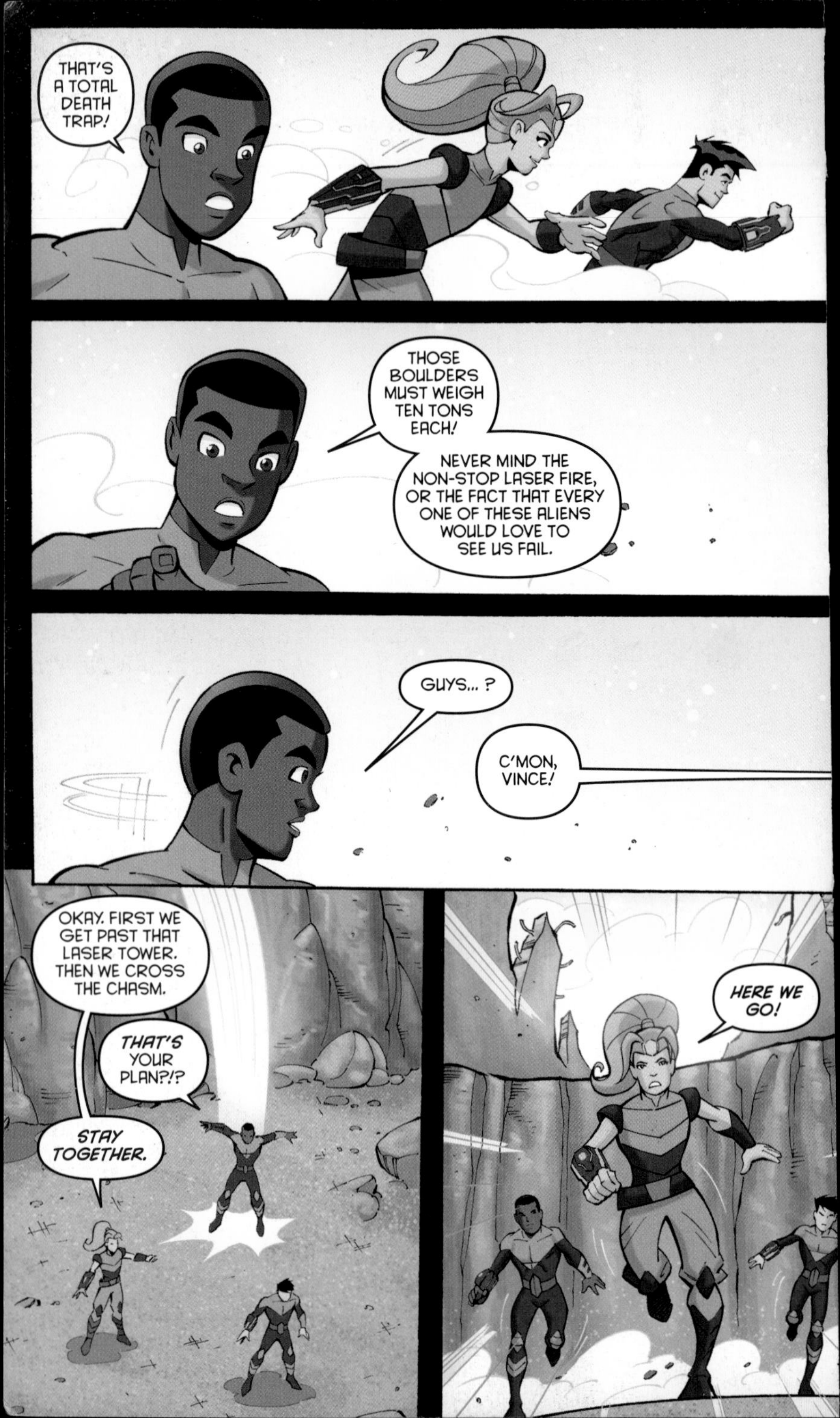
THAT'S A TOTAL DEATH TRAP!
THOSE BOULDERS MUST WEIGH TEN TONS EACH!
NEVER MIND THE NON-STOP LASER FIRE, OR THE FACT THAT EVERY ONE OF THESE ALIENS WOULD LOVE TO SEE US FAIL.
GUYS... ?
C'MON, VINCE!
OKAY. FIRST WE GET PAST THAT LASER TOWER. THEN WE CROSS THE CHASM.
THAT'S YOUR PLAN?!?
STAY TOGETHER.
HERE WE GO!

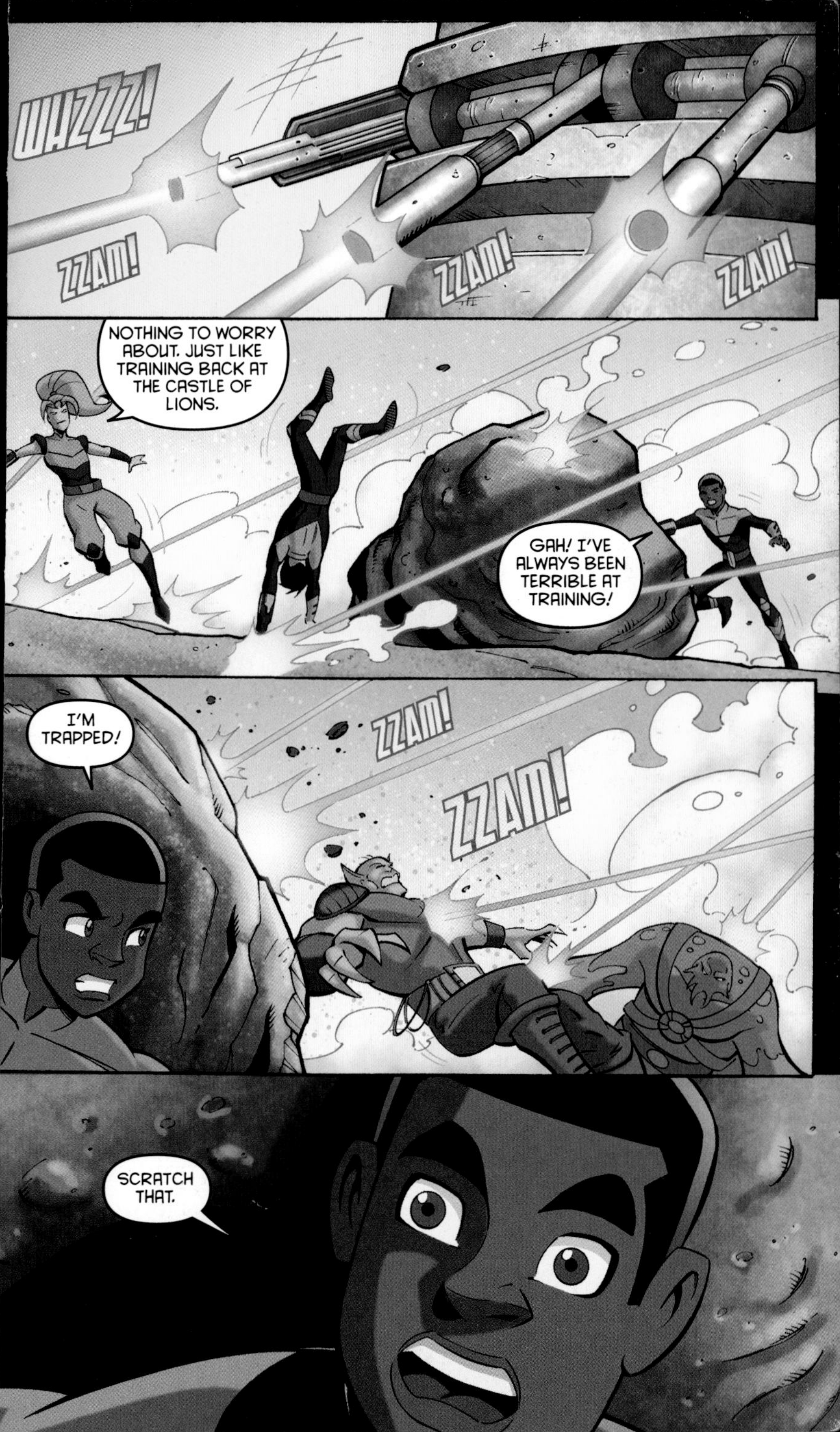
WHZZZ!
ZZAM!
ZZAM!
ZZAM!
NOTHING TO WORRY ABOUT. JUST LIKE TRAINING BACK AT THE CASTLE OF LIONS.
GAH! I'VE ALWAYS BEEN TERRIBLE AT TRAINING!
I'M TRAPPED!
ZZAM!
ZZAM!
SCRATCH THAT.

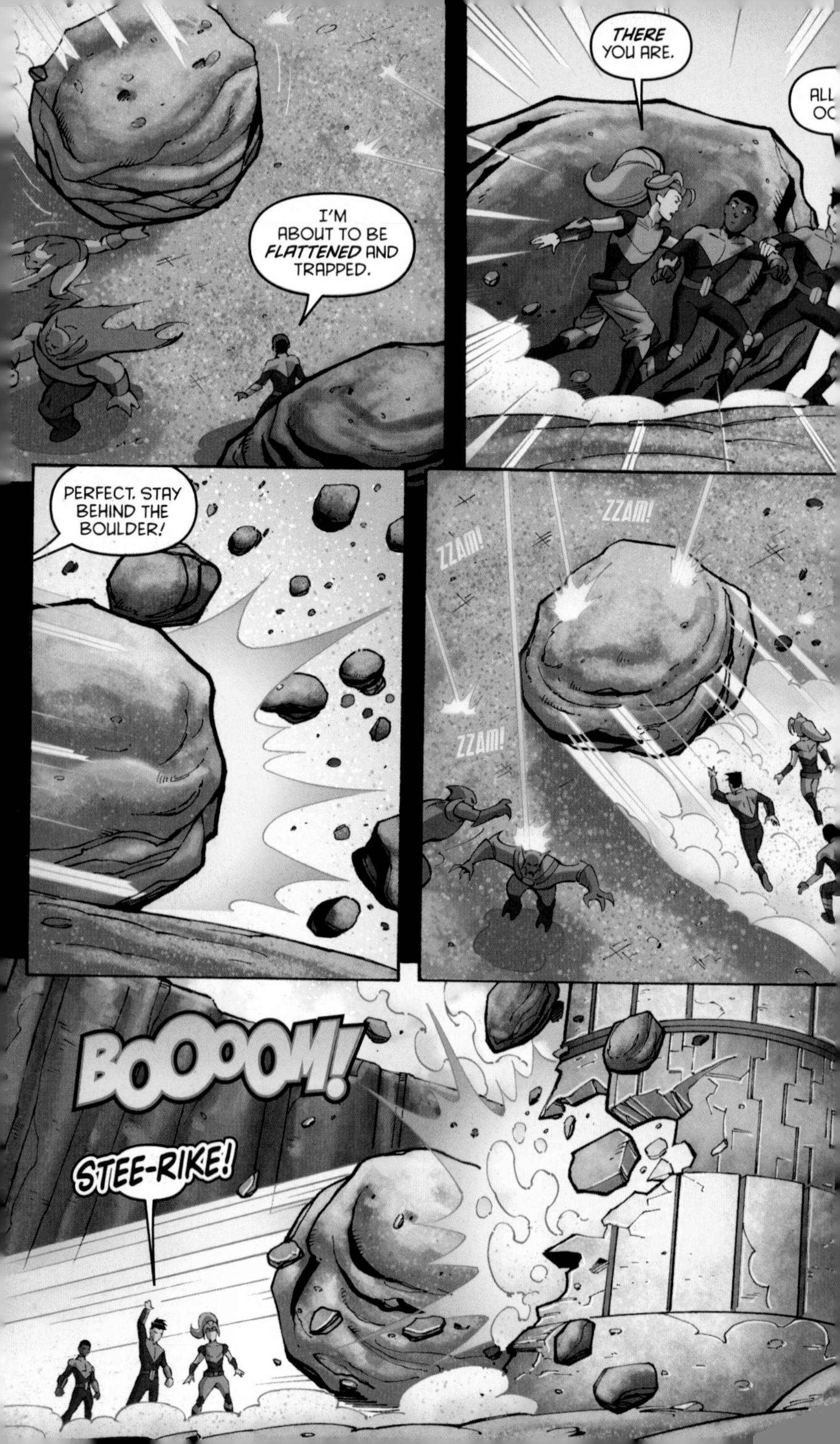
I'M ABOUT TO BE *FLATTENED* AND TRAPPED.
THERE YOU ARE.
ALL OC
PERFECT. STAY BEHIND THE BOULDER!
ZZAM!
ZZAM!
ZZAM!
BOOOOM!
STEE-RIKE!

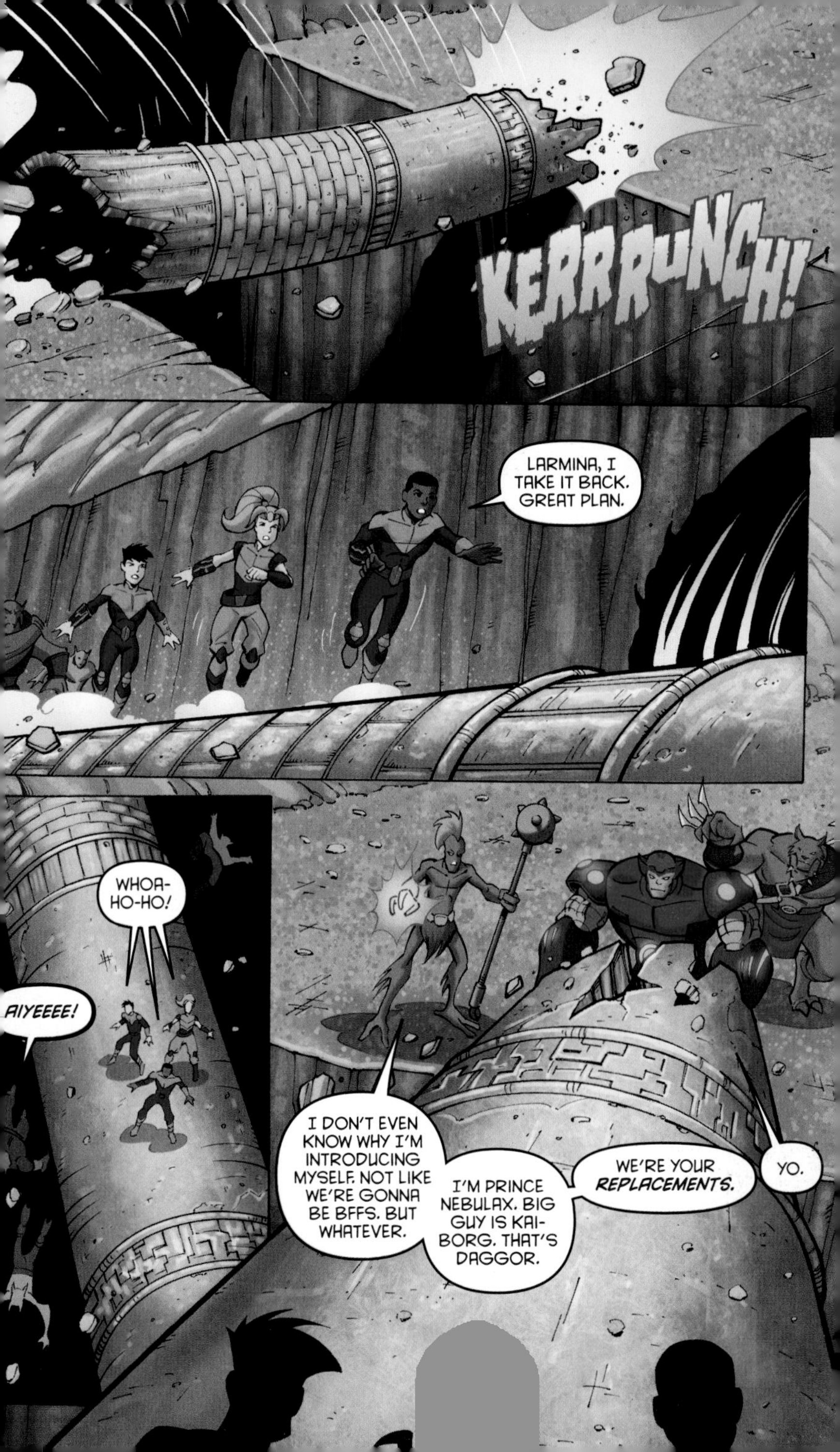
KERRRUNCH!
LARMINA, I TAKE IT BACK. GREAT PLAN.
WHOA-HO-HO!
AIYEEEE!
YO.
WE'RE YOUR REPLACEMENTS.
I'M PRINCE NEBULAX. BIG GUY IS KAI-BORG. THAT'S DAGGOR.
I DON'T EVEN KNOW WHY I'M INTRODUCING MYSELF. NOT LIKE WE'RE GONNA BE BFFS. BUT WHATEVER.

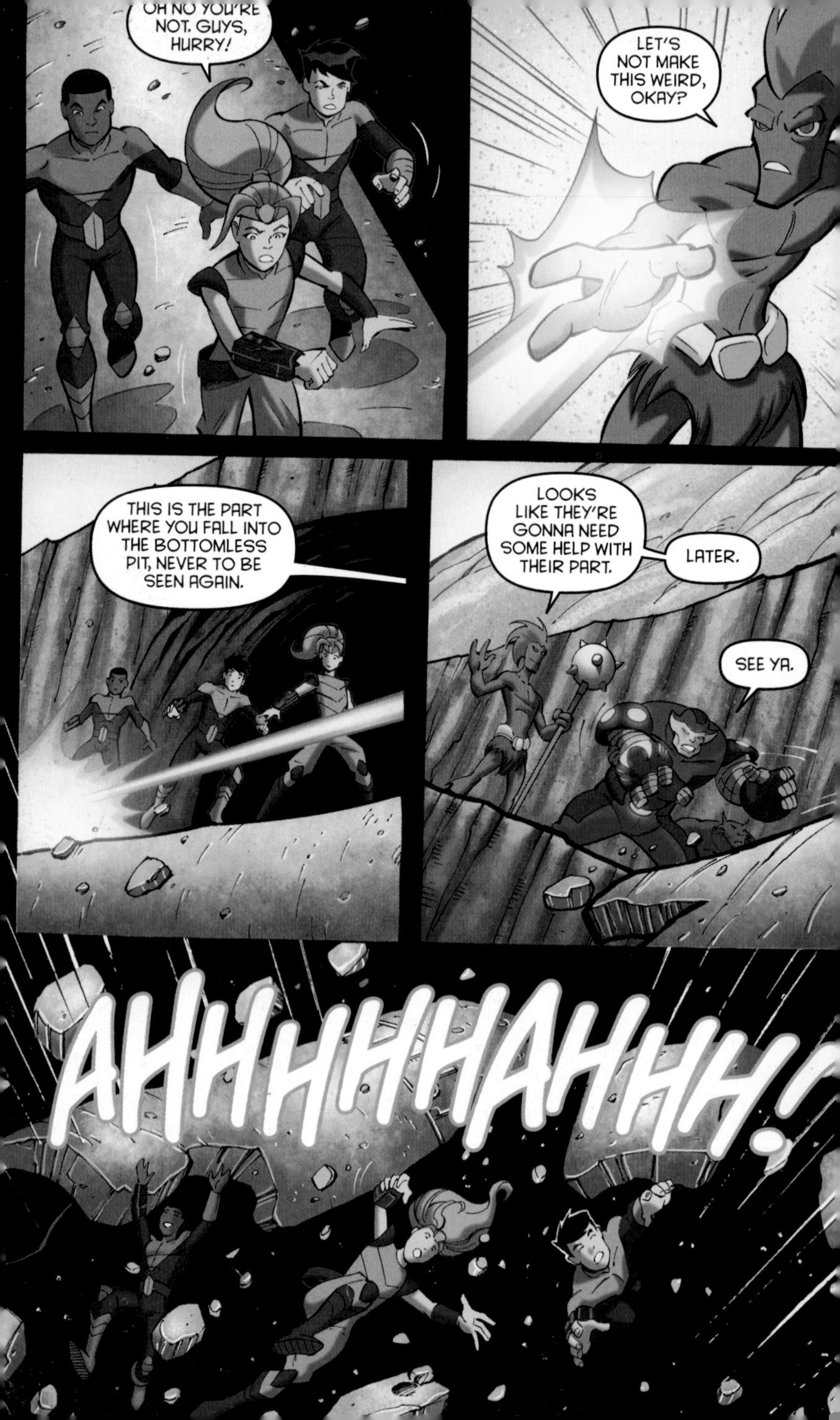
OH NO YOU'RE NOT. GUYS, HURRY!
LET'S NOT MAKE THIS WEIRD, OKAY?
THIS IS THE PART WHERE YOU FALL INTO THE BOTTOMLESS PIT, NEVER TO BE SEEN AGAIN.
LOOKS LIKE THEY'RE GONNA NEED SOME HELP WITH THEIR PART.
LATER.
SEE YA.
AHHHHHAHHH!

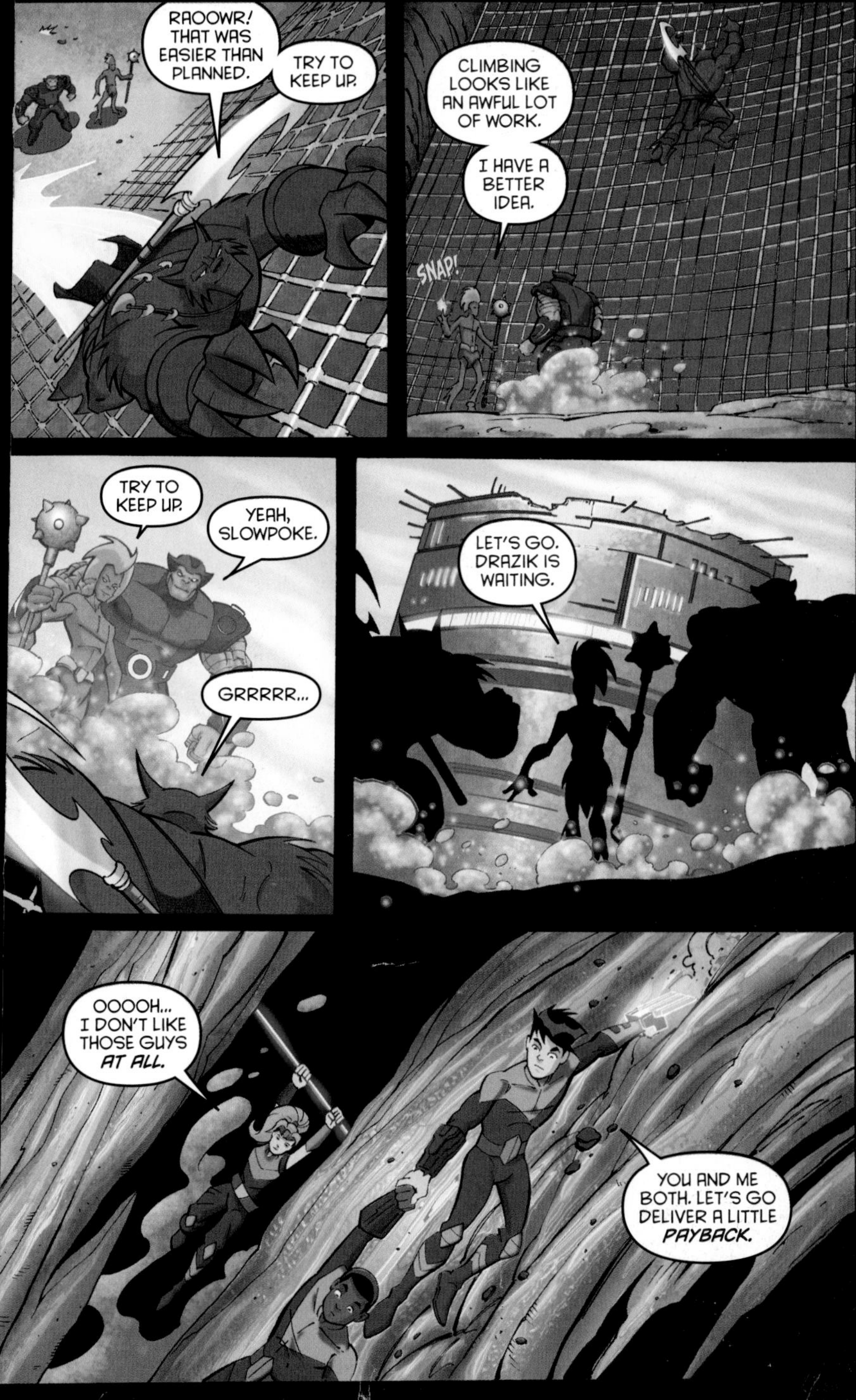
RAOOWR! THAT WAS EASIER THAN PLANNED.
TRY TO KEEP UP.
CLIMBING LOOKS LIKE AN AWFUL LOT OF WORK.
I HAVE A BETTER IDEA.
SNAP!
TRY TO KEEP UP.
YEAH, SLOWPOKE.
GRRRRR...
LET'S GO. DRAZIK IS WAITING.
OOOOH... I DON'T LIKE THOSE GUYS AT ALL.
YOU AND ME BOTH. LET'S GO DELIVER A LITTLE PAYBACK.

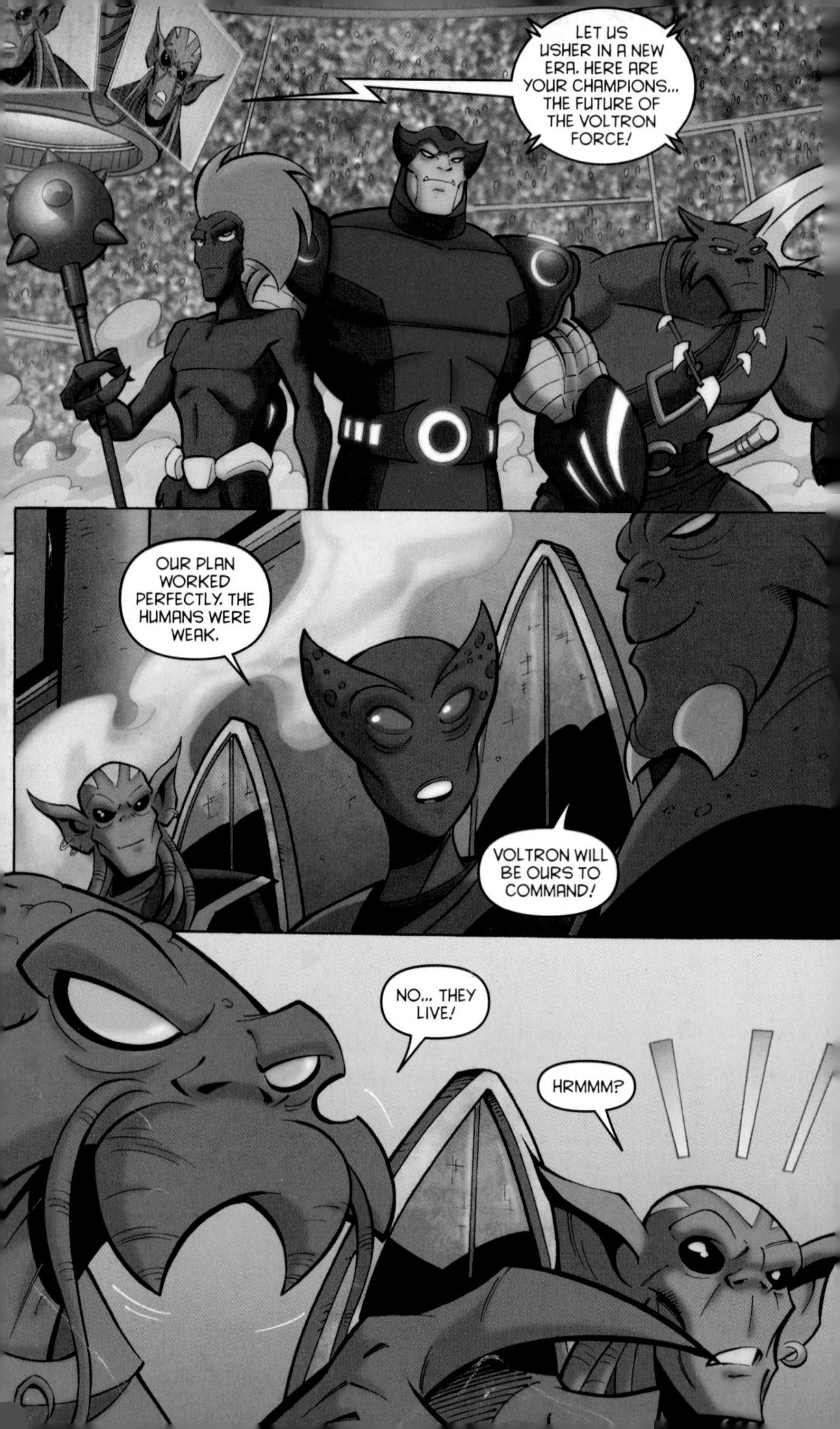
LET US USHER IN A NEW ERA. HERE ARE YOUR CHAMPIONS... THE FUTURE OF THE VOLTRON FORCE!
OUR PLAN WORKED PERFECTLY. THE HUMANS WERE WEAK.
VOLTRON WILL BE OURS TO COMMAND!
NO... THEY LIVE!
HRMMM?

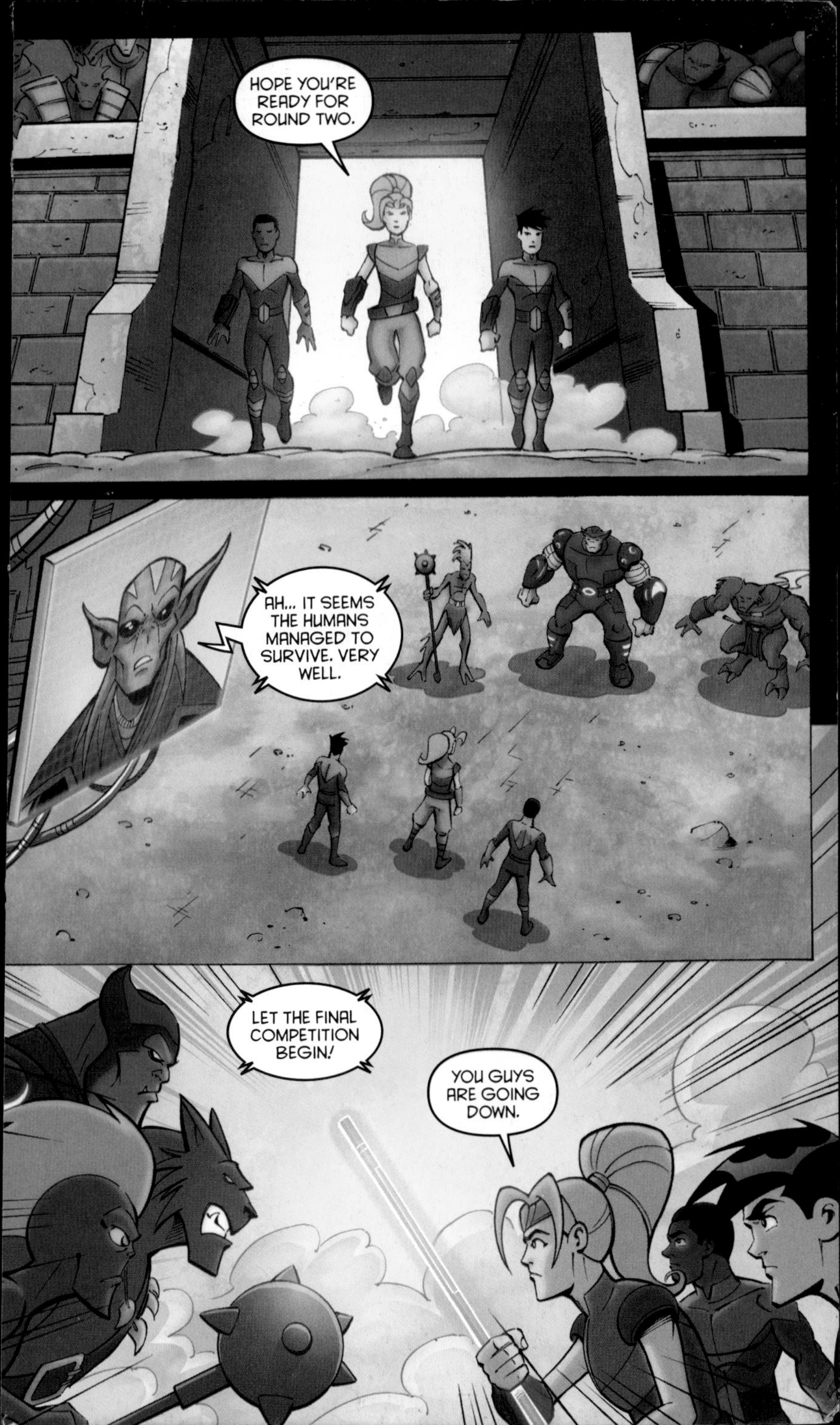
HOPE YOU'RE READY FOR ROUND TWO.
AH... IT SEEMS THE HUMANS MANAGED TO SURVIVE. VERY WELL.
LET THE FINAL COMPETITION BEGIN!
YOU GUYS ARE GOING DOWN.

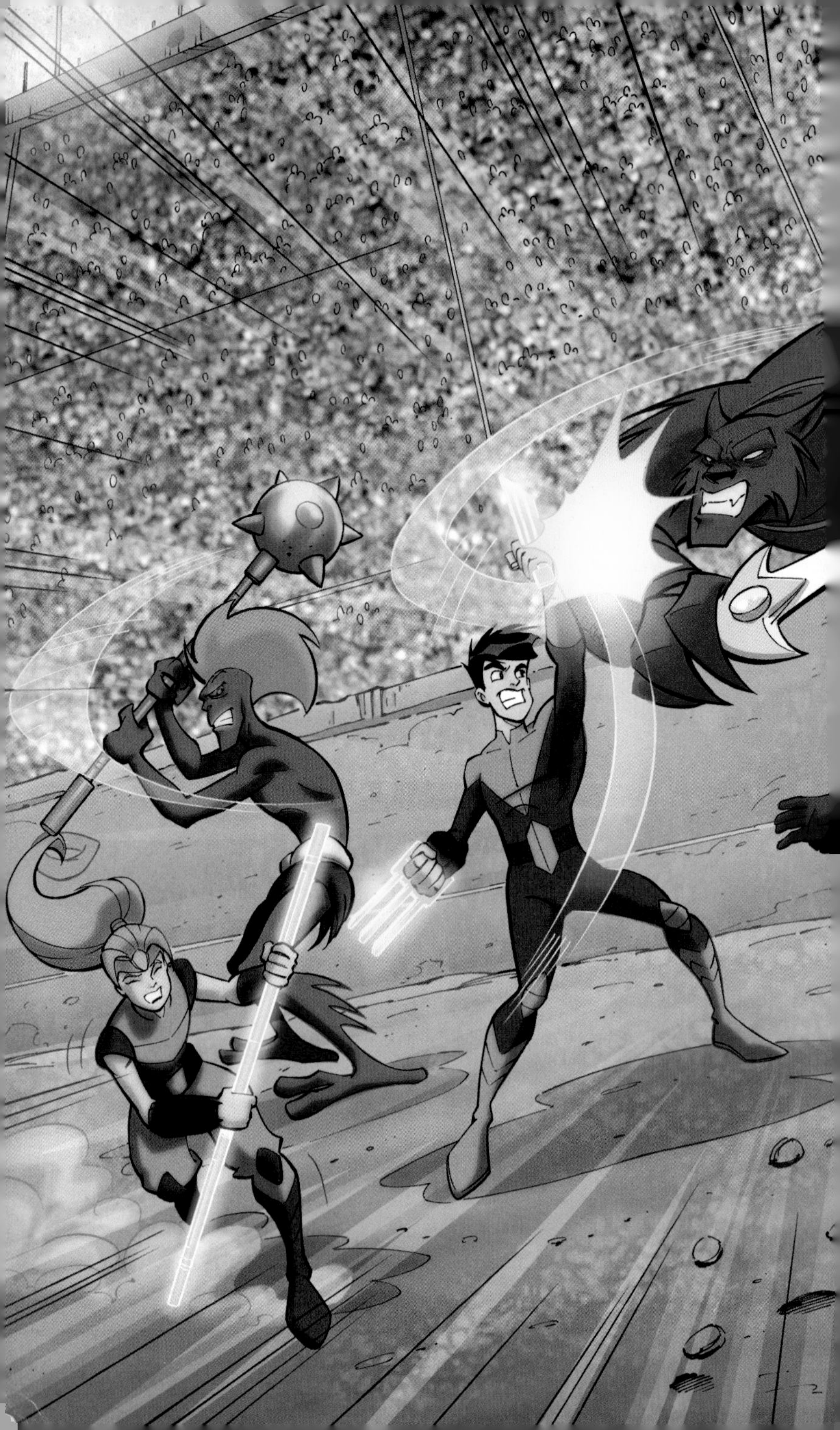

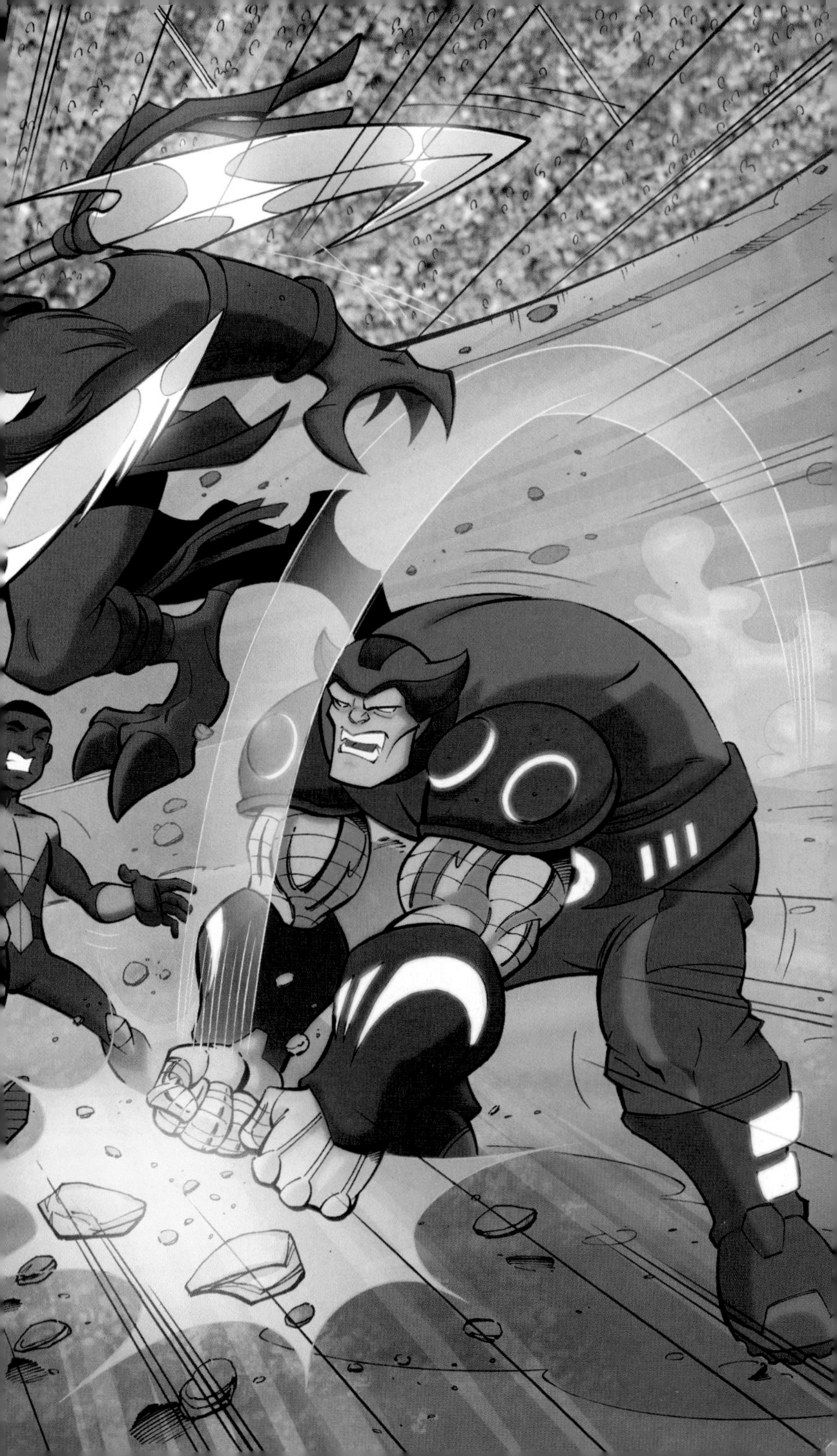

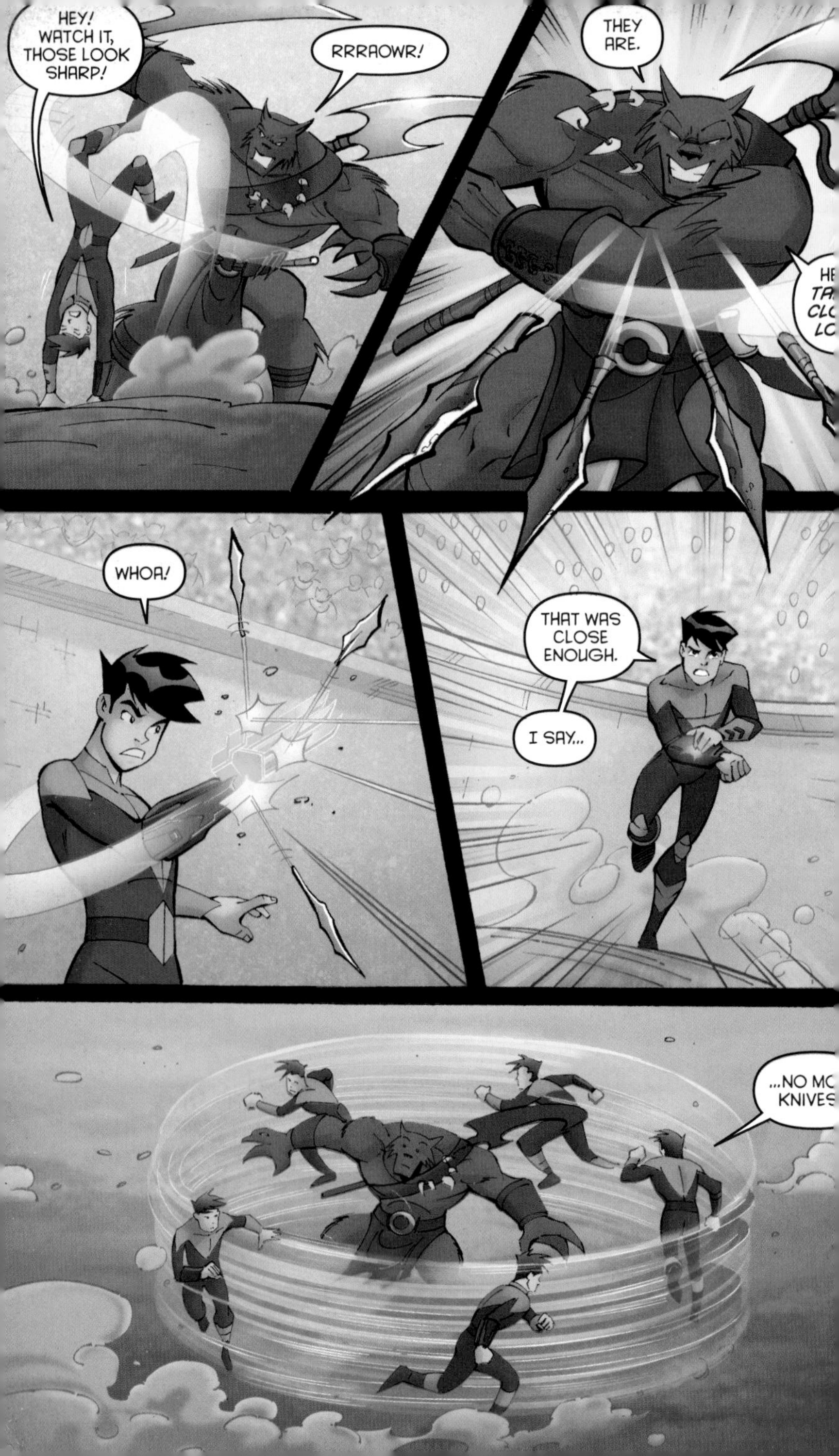
HEY! WATCH IT, THOSE LOOK SHARP!
RRRAOWR!
THEY ARE.
WHOA!
THAT WAS CLOSE ENOUGH.
I SAY...
...NO MO KNIVES

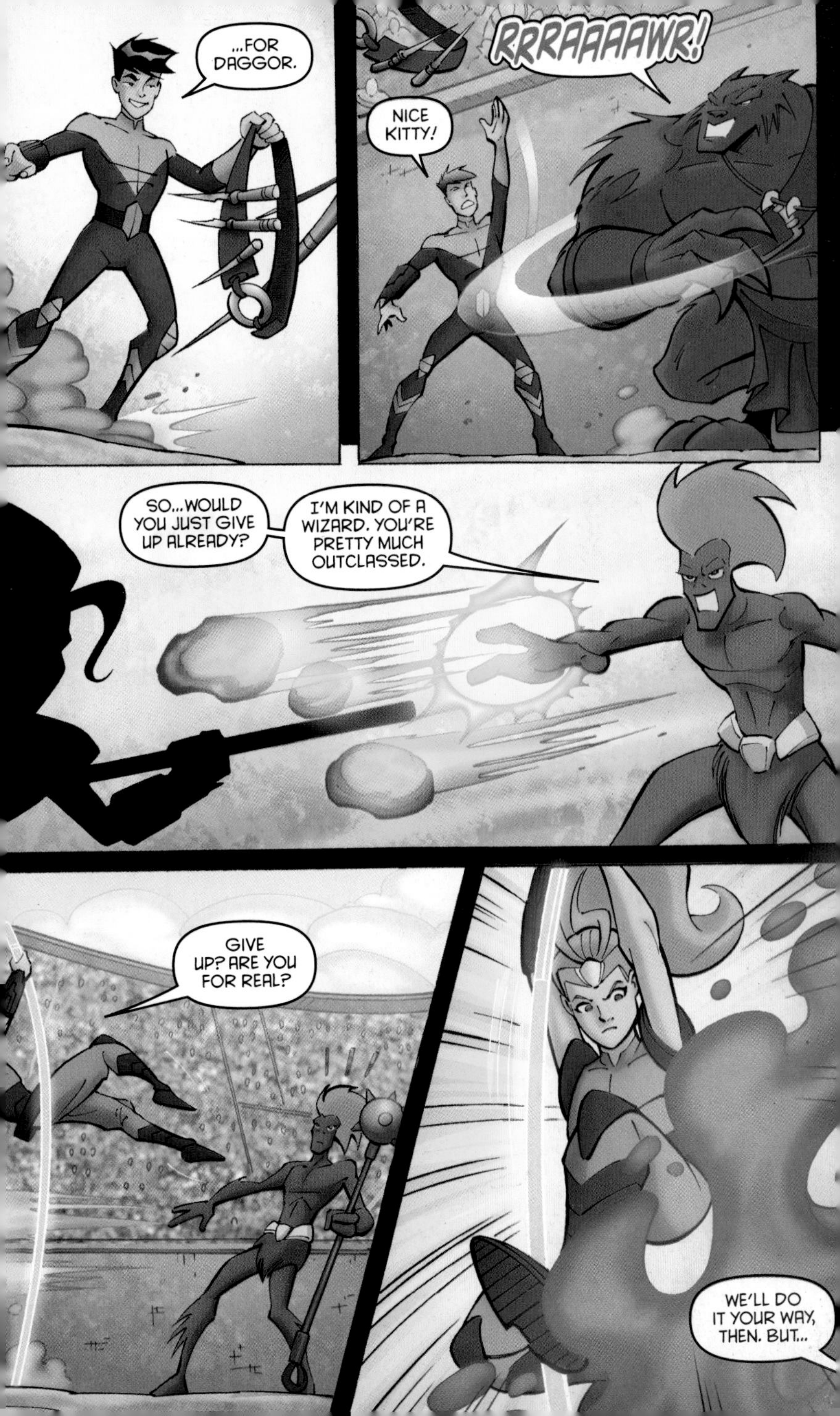

...FOR DAGGOR.
RRRAAAAAWR!
NICE KITTY!
SO...WOULD YOU JUST GIVE UP ALREADY?
I'M KIND OF A WIZARD. YOU'RE PRETTY MUCH OUTCLASSED.
GIVE UP? ARE YOU FOR REAL?
WE'LL DO IT YOUR WAY, THEN. BUT...

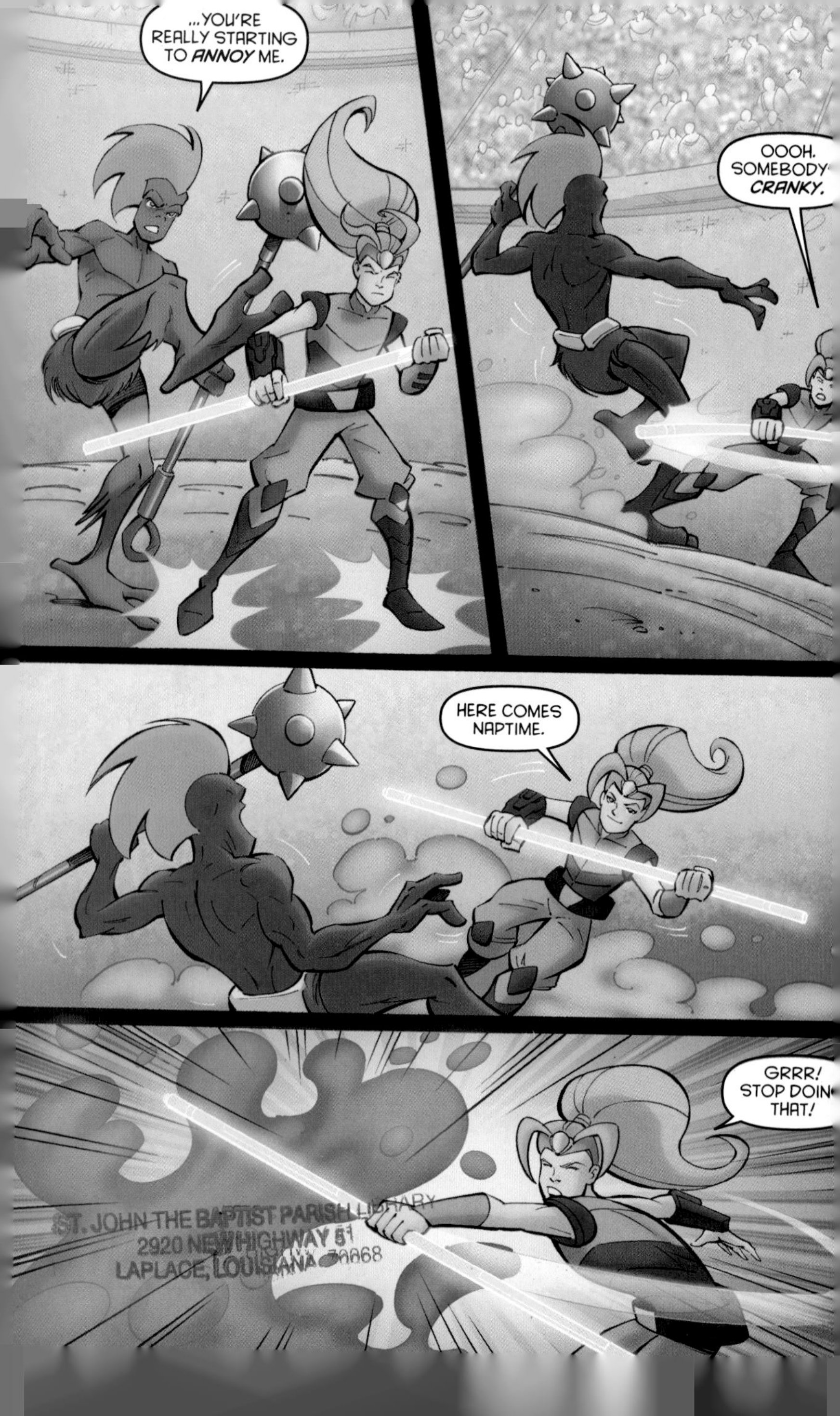
...YOU'RE REALLY STARTING TO *ANNOY* ME.
OOOH. SOMEBODY'S *CRANKY.*
HERE COMES NAPTIME.
GRRR! STOP DOING THAT!

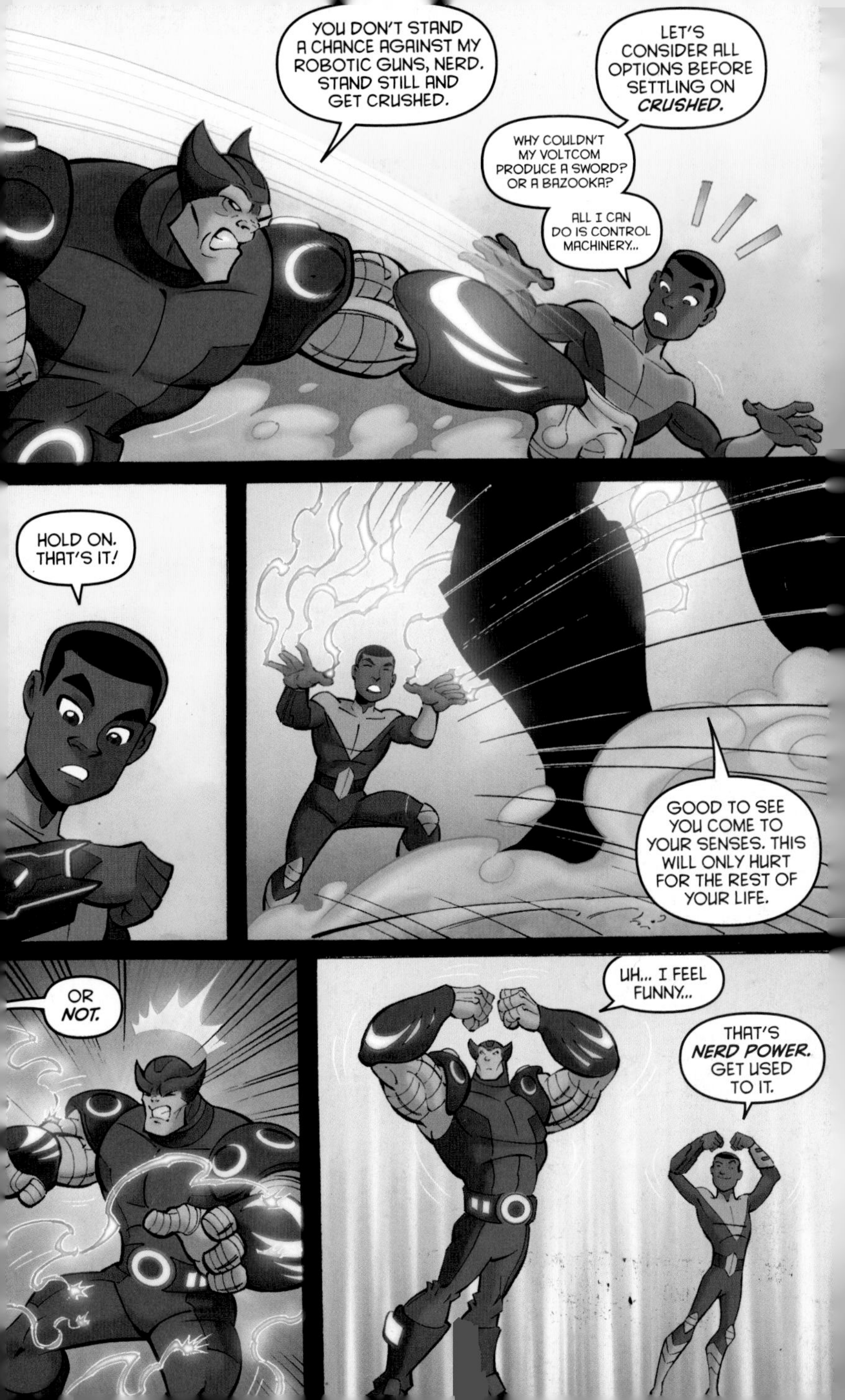
YOU DON'T STAND A CHANCE AGAINST MY ROBOTIC GUNS, NERD. STAND STILL AND GET CRUSHED.
LET'S CONSIDER ALL OPTIONS BEFORE SETTLING ON *CRUSHED.*
WHY COULDN'T MY VOLTCOM PRODUCE A SWORD? OR A BAZOOKA?
ALL I CAN DO IS CONTROL MACHINERY...
HOLD ON. THAT'S IT!
GOOD TO SEE YOU COME TO YOUR SENSES. THIS WILL ONLY HURT FOR THE REST OF YOUR LIFE.
OR *NOT.*
UH... I FEEL FUNNY...
THAT'S *NERD POWER.* GET USED TO IT.

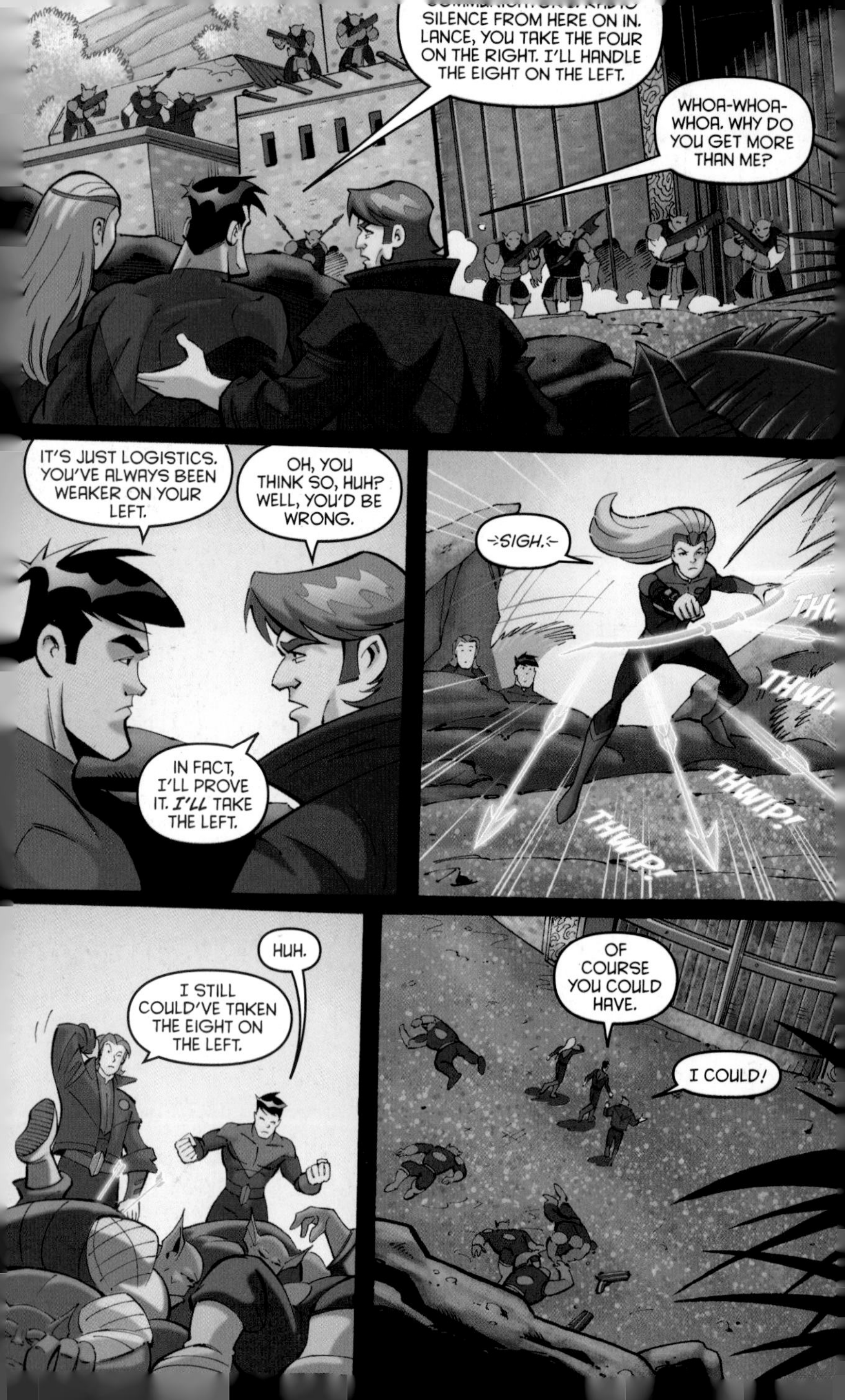

SILENCE FROM HERE ON IN. LANCE, YOU TAKE THE FOUR ON THE RIGHT. I'LL HANDLE THE EIGHT ON THE LEFT.
WHOA-WHOA-WHOA. WHY DO YOU GET MORE THAN ME?
IT'S JUST LOGISTICS. YOU'VE ALWAYS BEEN WEAKER ON YOUR LEFT.
OH, YOU THINK SO, HUH? WELL, YOU'D BE WRONG.
IN FACT, I'LL PROVE IT. *I'LL* TAKE THE LEFT.
-SIGH.-
THWIP!
THWIP!
HUH.
I STILL COULD'VE TAKEN THE EIGHT ON THE LEFT.
OF COURSE YOU COULD HAVE.
I COULD!

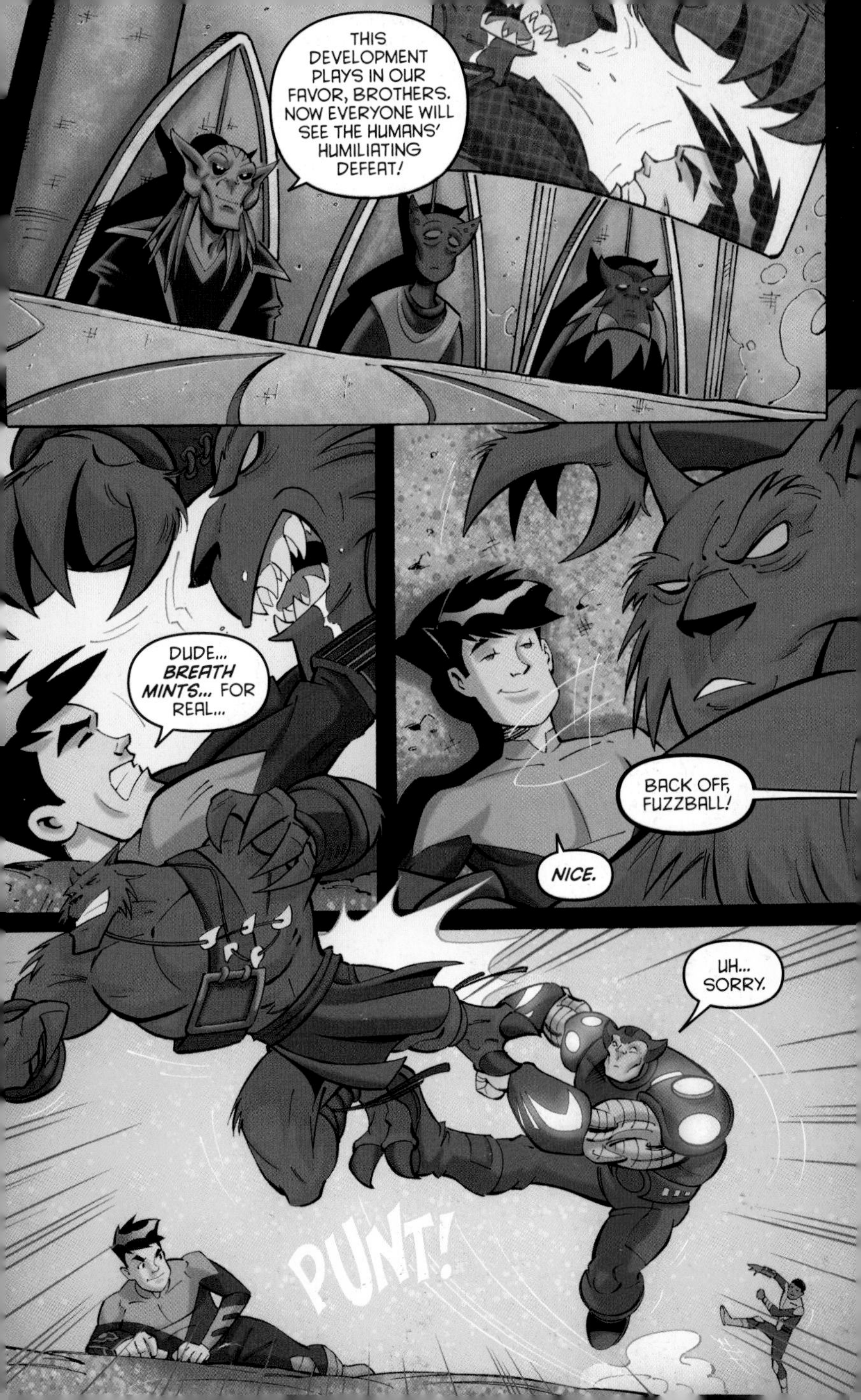
THIS DEVELOPMENT PLAYS IN OUR FAVOR, BROTHERS. NOW EVERYONE WILL SEE THE HUMANS' HUMILIATING DEFEAT!
DUDE... *BREATH MINTS...* FOR REAL...
BACK OFF, FUZZBALL!
NICE.
UH... SORRY.
PUNT!

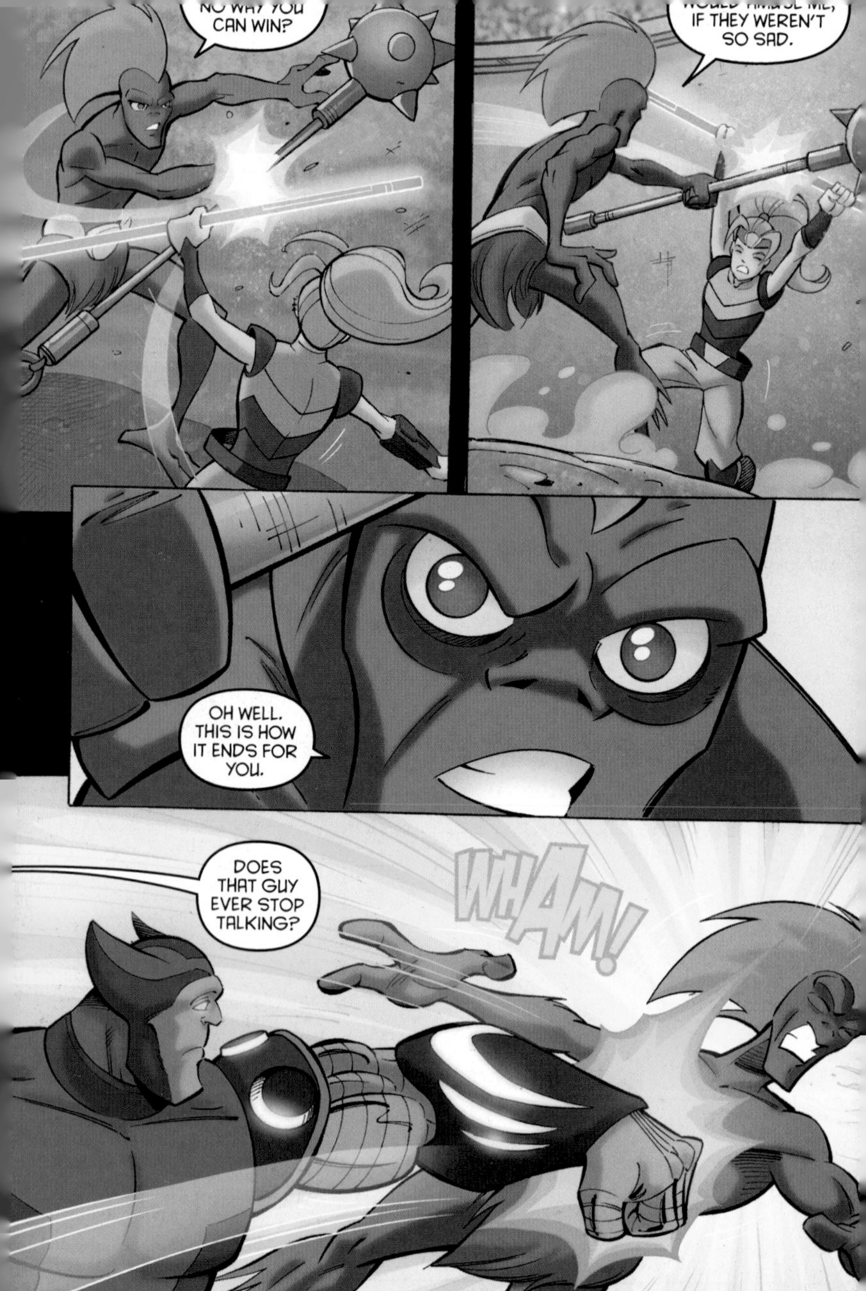
NO WAY YOU CAN WIN?
IF THEY WEREN'T SO SAD.
OH WELL. THIS IS HOW IT ENDS FOR YOU.
DOES THAT GUY EVER STOP TALKING?
WHAM!

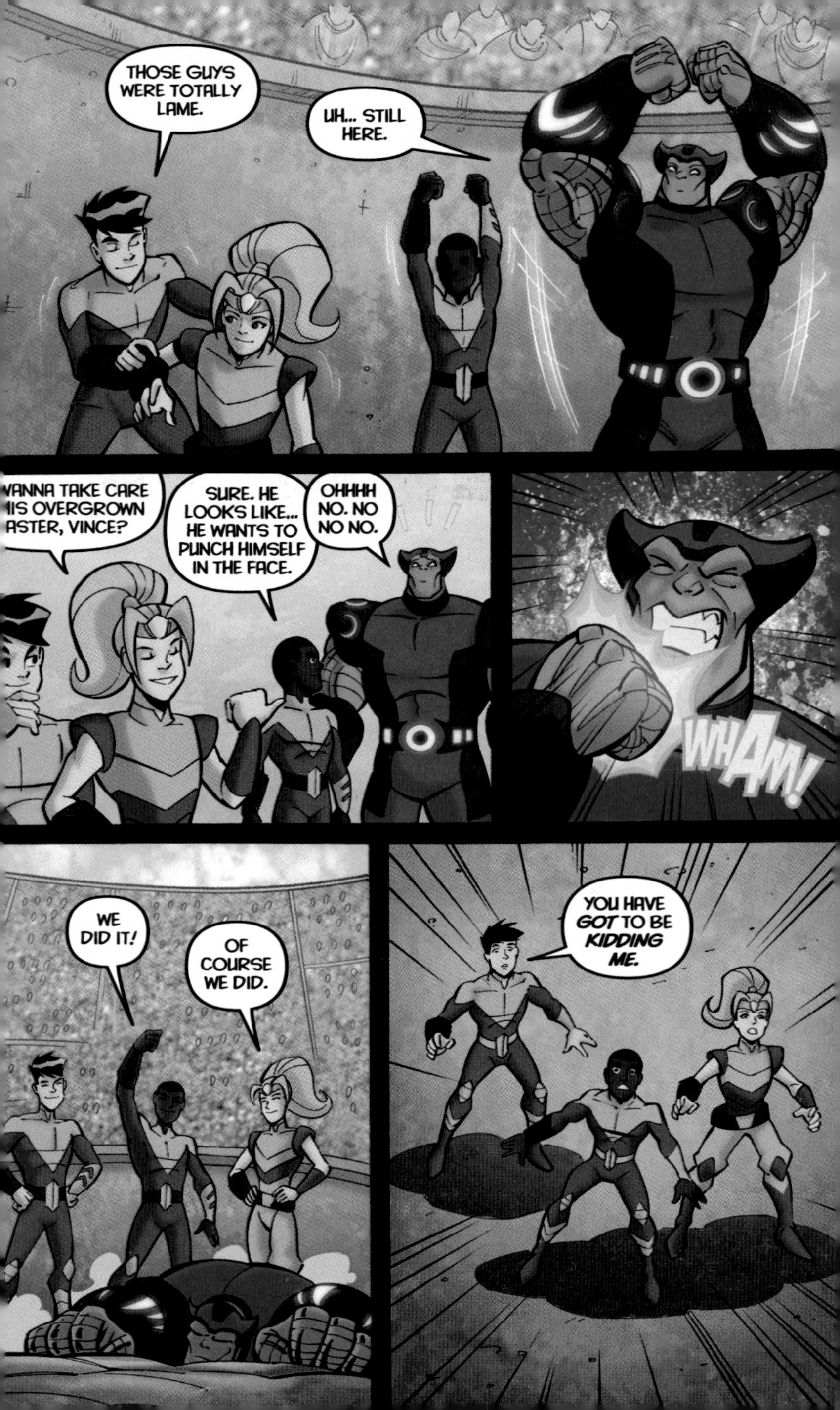

THOSE GUYS WERE TOTALLY LAME.
UH... STILL HERE.
WANNA TAKE CARE HIS OVERGROWN ASTER, VINCE?
SURE. HE LOOKS LIKE... HE WANTS TO PUNCH HIMSELF IN THE FACE.
OHHHH NO. NO NO NO.
WHAM!
WE DID IT!
OF COURSE WE DID.
YOU HAVE GOT TO BE KIDDING ME.

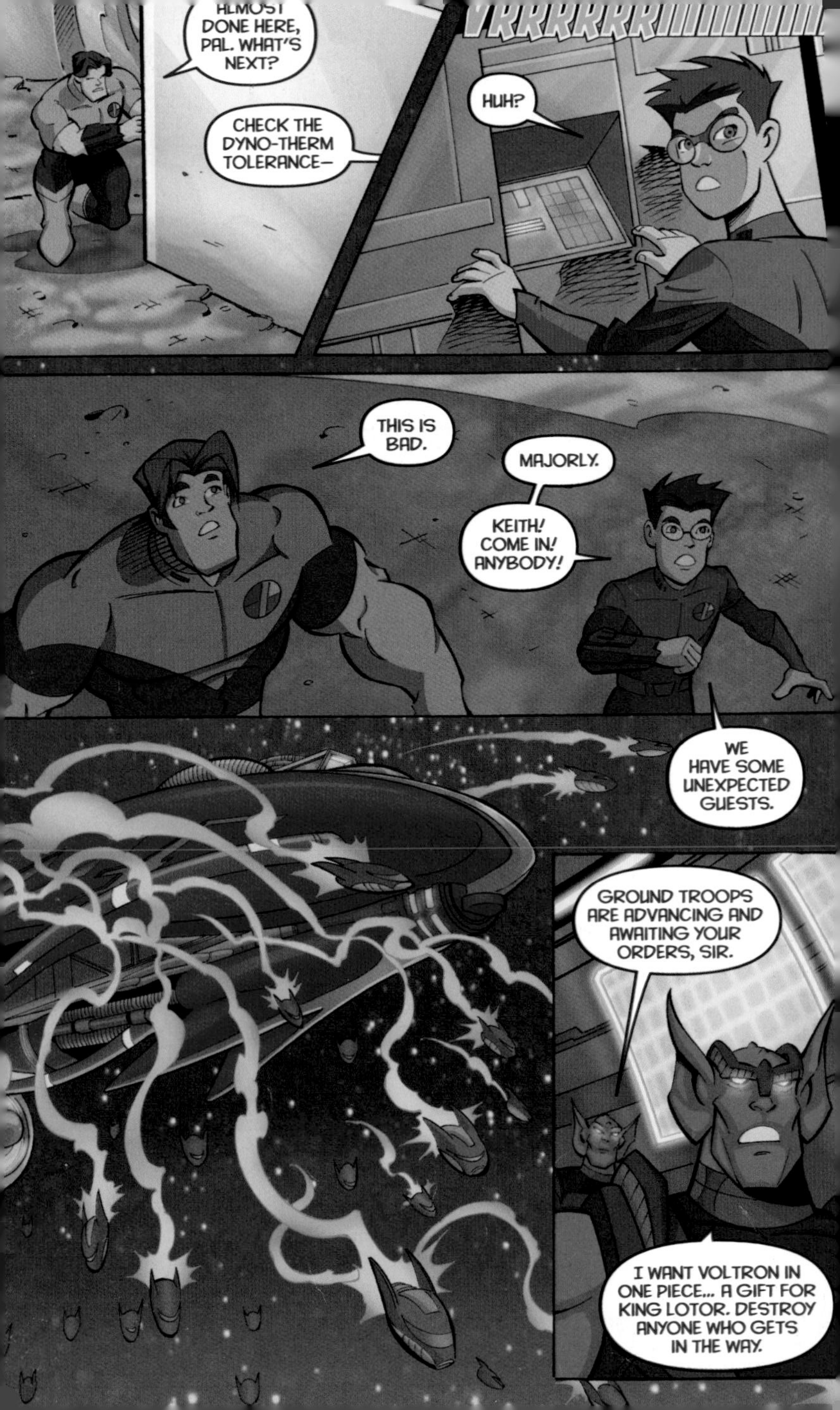
ALMOST DONE HERE, PAL. WHAT'S NEXT?
CHECK THE DYNO-THERM TOLERANCE—
VRRRRRRRIIIIIIIIIII
HUH?
THIS IS BAD.
MAJORLY.
KEITH! COME IN! ANYBODY!
WE HAVE SOME UNEXPECTED GUESTS.
GROUND TROOPS ARE ADVANCING AND AWAITING YOUR ORDERS, SIR.
I WANT VOLTRON IN ONE PIECE... A GIFT FOR KING LOTOR. DESTROY ANYONE WHO GETS IN THE WAY.

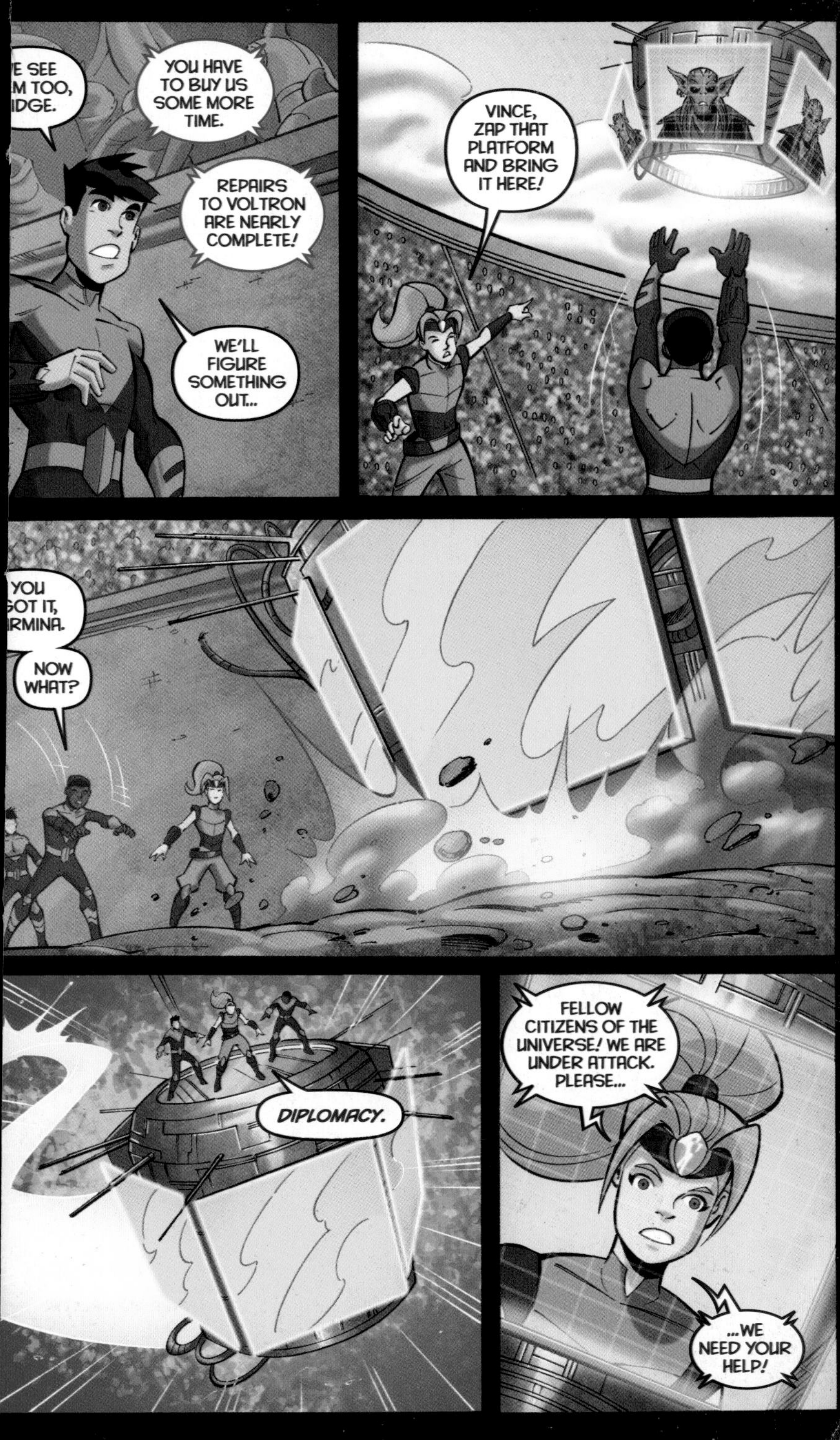
E SEE M TOO, IDGE.
YOU HAVE TO BUY US SOME MORE TIME.
REPAIRS TO VOLTRON ARE NEARLY COMPLETE!
WE'LL FIGURE SOMETHING OUT...
VINCE, ZAP THAT PLATFORM AND BRING IT HERE!
YOU GOT IT, RMINA.
NOW WHAT?
DIPLOMACY.
FELLOW CITIZENS OF THE UNIVERSE! WE ARE UNDER ATTACK. PLEASE...
...WE NEED YOUR HELP!

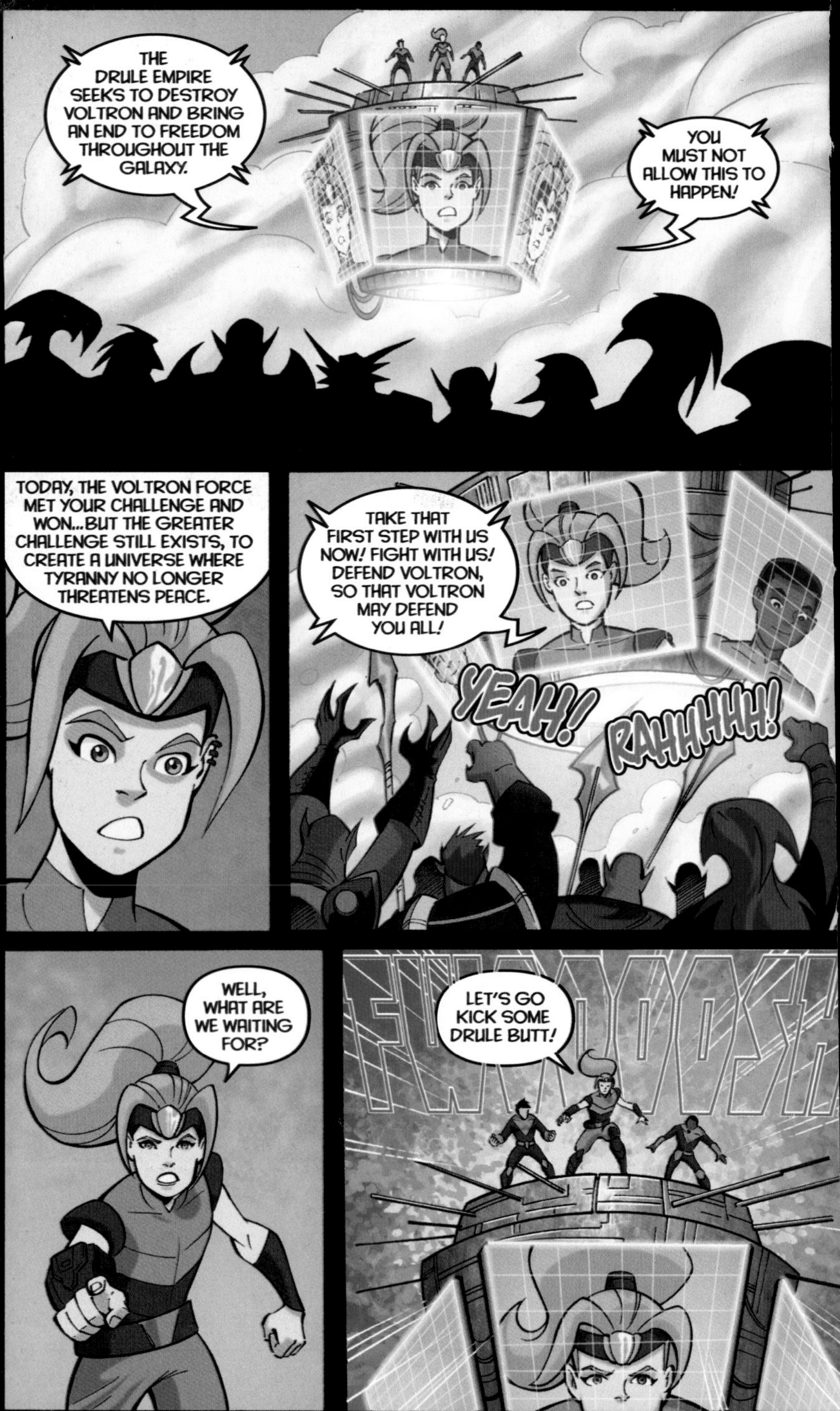
THE DRULE EMPIRE SEEKS TO DESTROY VOLTRON AND BRING AN END TO FREEDOM THROUGHOUT THE GALAXY.
YOU MUST NOT ALLOW THIS TO HAPPEN!
TODAY, THE VOLTRON FORCE MET YOUR CHALLENGE AND WON...BUT THE GREATER CHALLENGE STILL EXISTS, TO CREATE A UNIVERSE WHERE TYRANNY NO LONGER THREATENS PEACE.
TAKE THAT FIRST STEP WITH US NOW! FIGHT WITH US! DEFEND VOLTRON, SO THAT VOLTRON MAY DEFEND YOU ALL!
YEAH!
RAHHHHH!
WELL, WHAT ARE WE WAITING FOR?
LET'S GO KICK SOME DRULE BUTT!

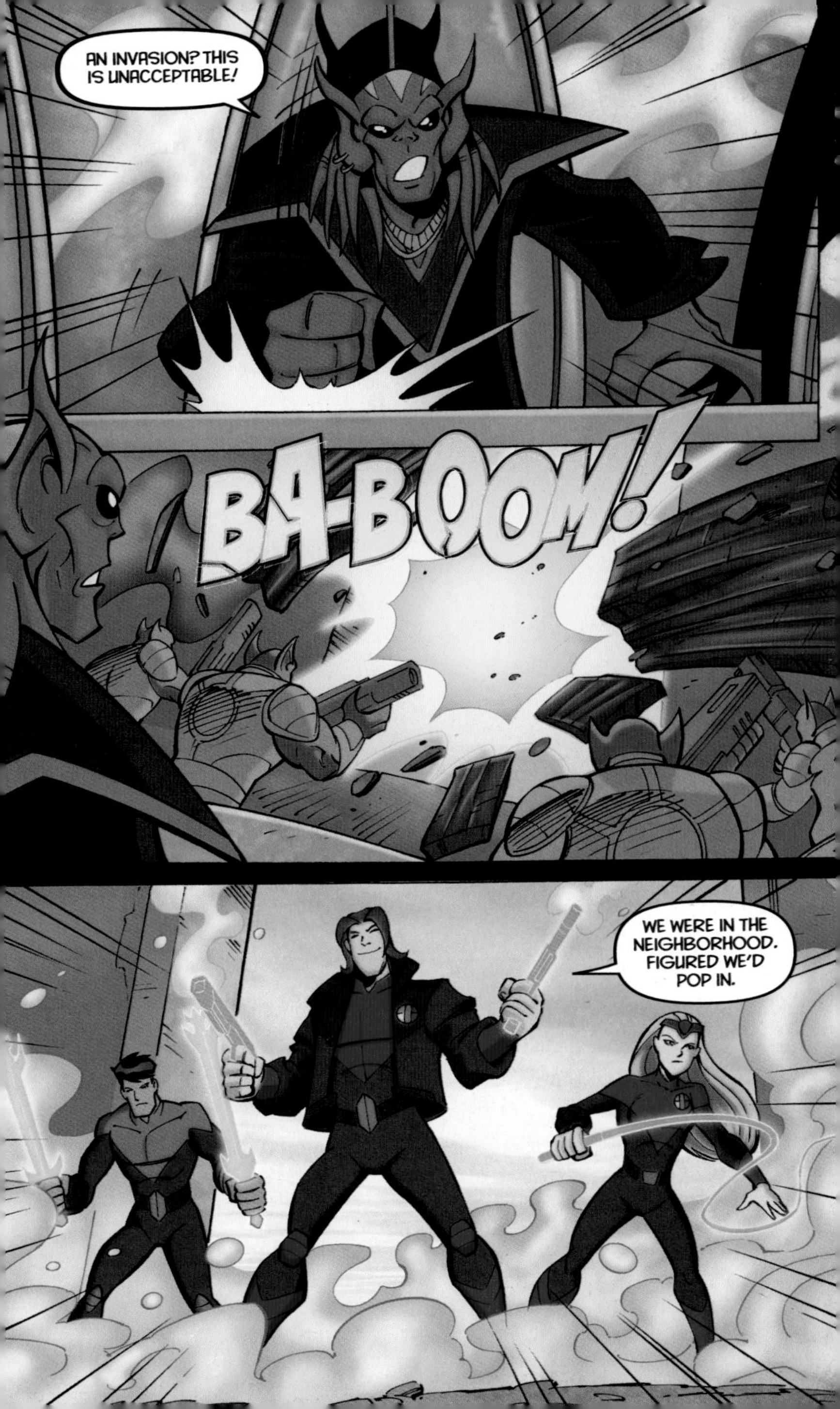
AN INVASION? THIS IS UNACCEPTABLE!
BA-BOOM!
WE WERE IN THE NEIGHBORHOOD. FIGURED WE'D POP IN.

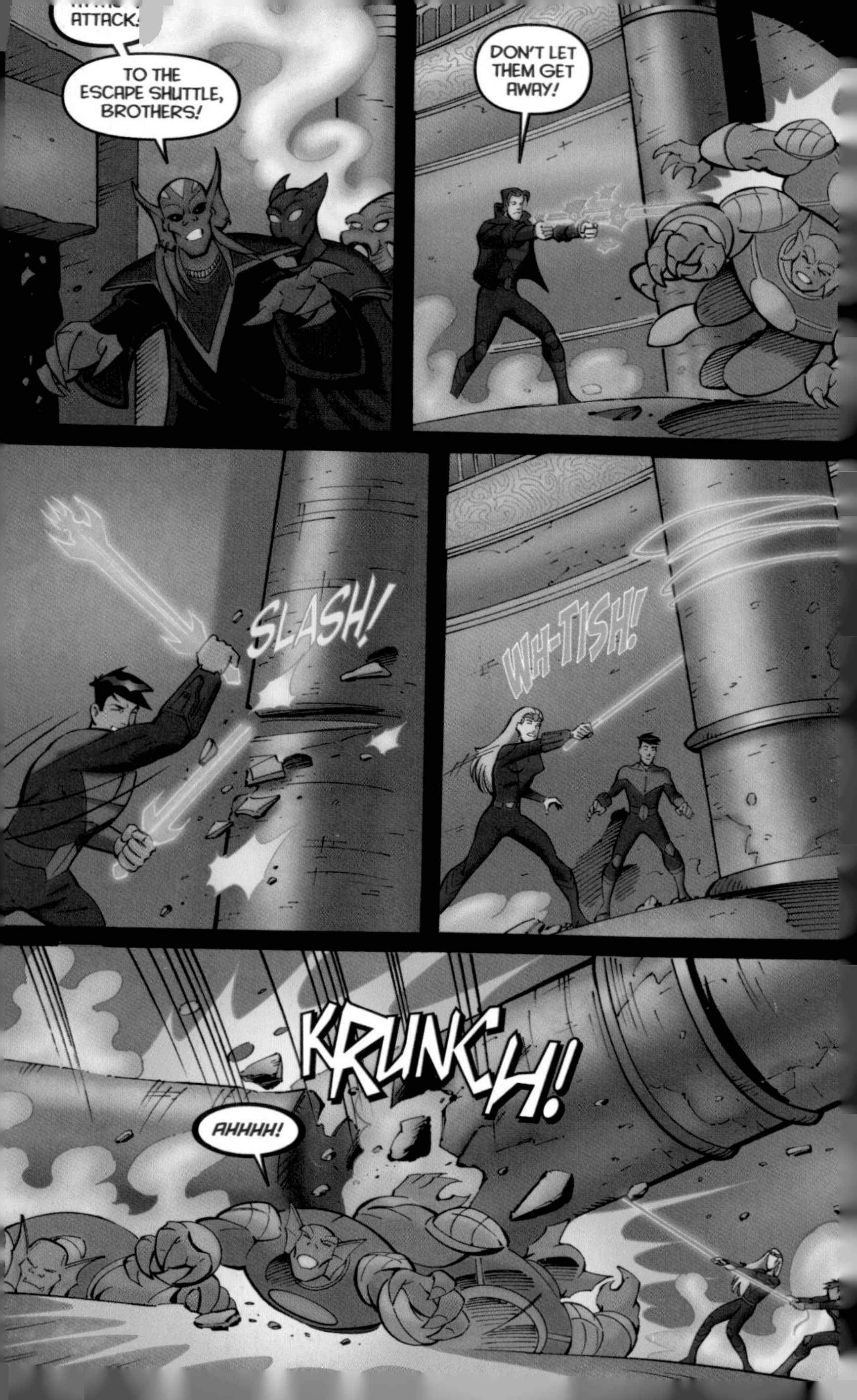

ATTACK!
TO THE ESCAPE SHUTTLE, BROTHERS!
DON'T LET THEM GET AWAY!
SLASH!
WH-TISH!
KRUNCH!
AHHHH!

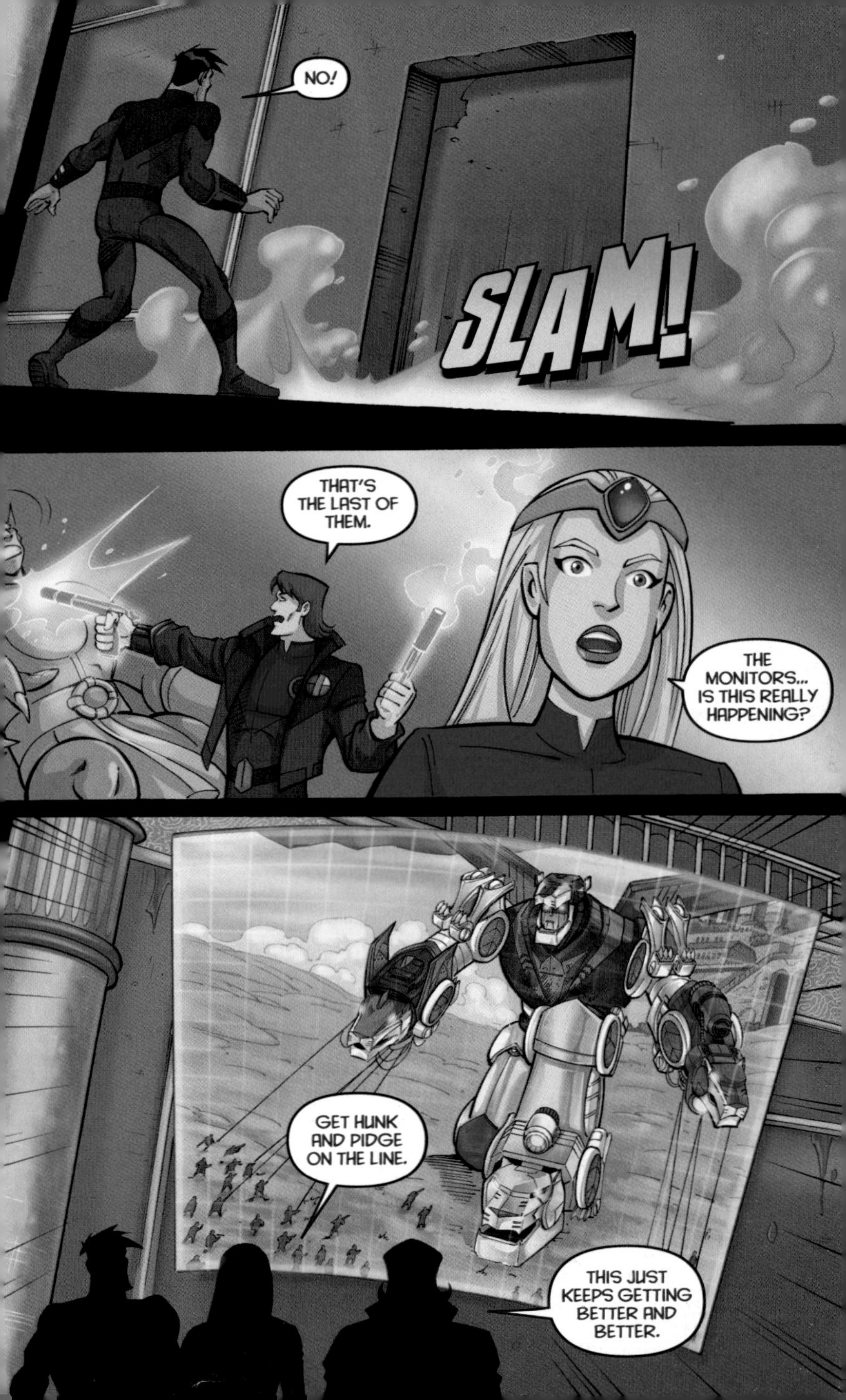
NO!
SLAM!
THAT'S THE LAST OF THEM.
THE MONITORS... IS THIS REALLY HAPPENING?
GET HUNK AND PIDGE ON THE LINE.
THIS JUST KEEPS GETTING BETTER AND BETTER.

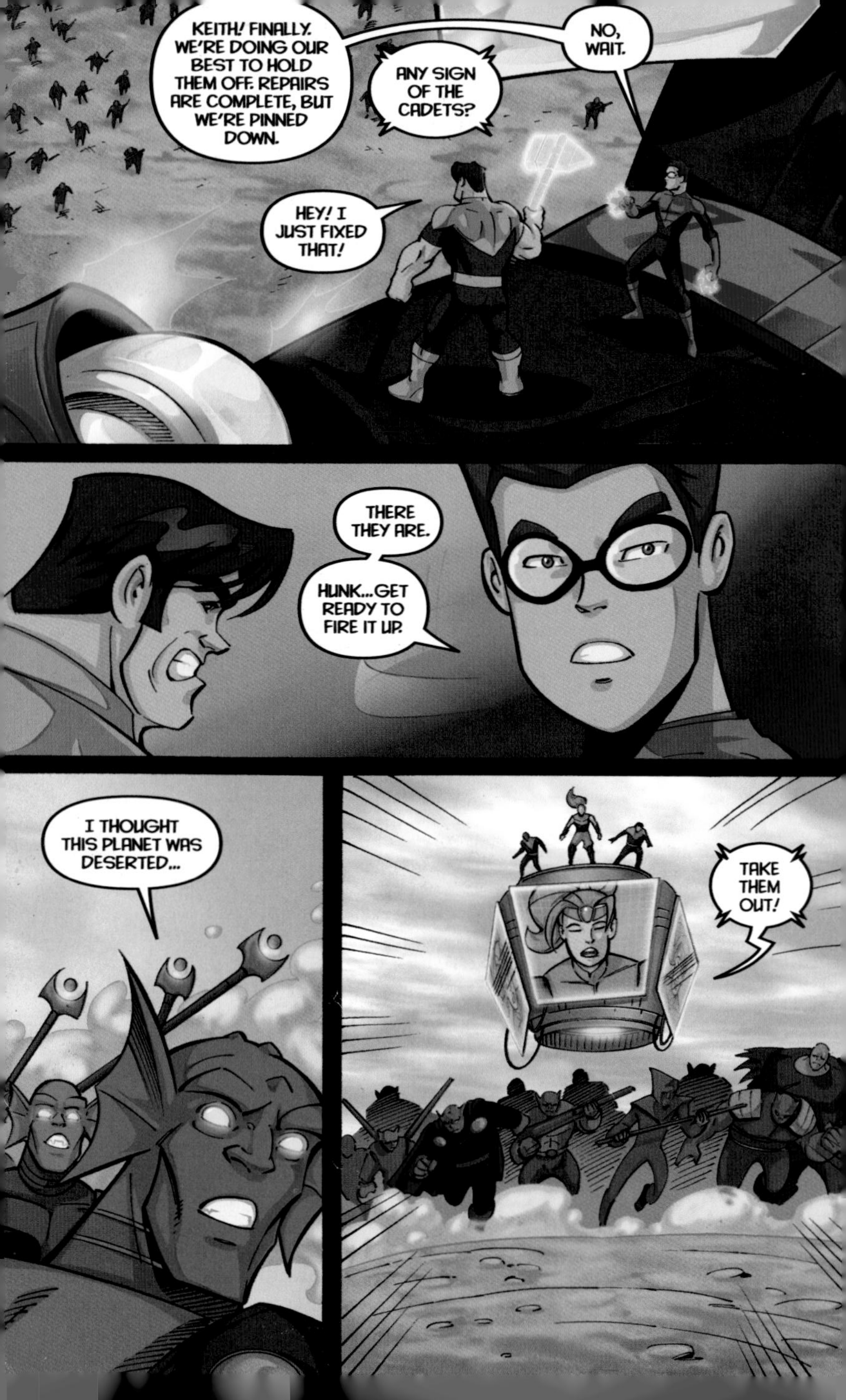
KEITH! FINALLY. WE'RE DOING OUR BEST TO HOLD THEM OFF. REPAIRS ARE COMPLETE, BUT WE'RE PINNED DOWN.
ANY SIGN OF THE CADETS?
NO, WAIT.
HEY! I JUST FIXED THAT!
THERE THEY ARE.
HUNK...GET READY TO FIRE IT UP.
I THOUGHT THIS PLANET WAS DESERTED...
TAKE THEM OUT!

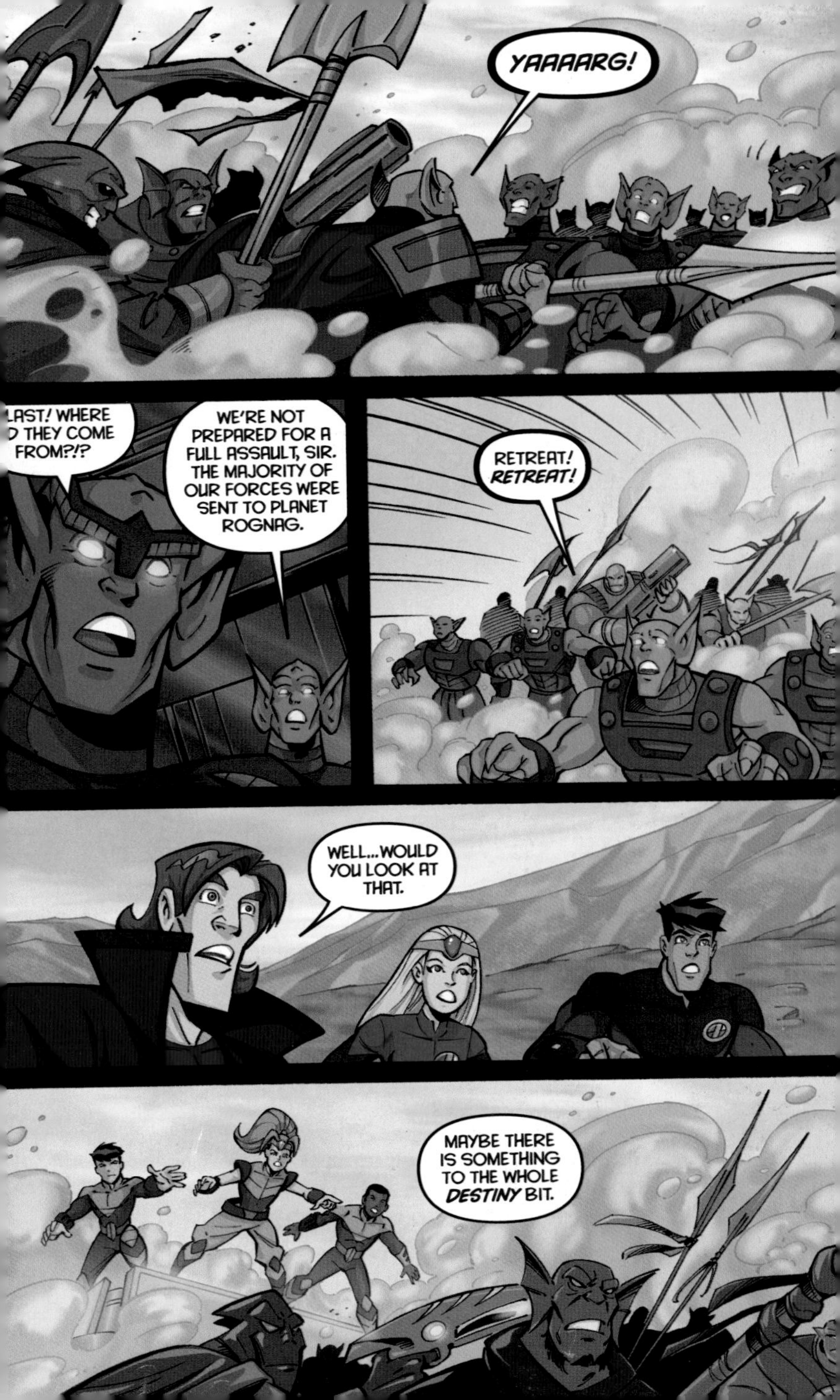
YAAAARG!
LAST! WHERE
D THEY COME
FROM?!?
WE'RE NOT PREPARED FOR A FULL ASSAULT, SIR. THE MAJORITY OF OUR FORCES WERE SENT TO PLANET ROGNAG.
RETREAT! *RETREAT!*
WELL...WOULD YOU LOOK AT THAT.
MAYBE THERE IS SOMETHING TO THE WHOLE *DESTINY* BIT.

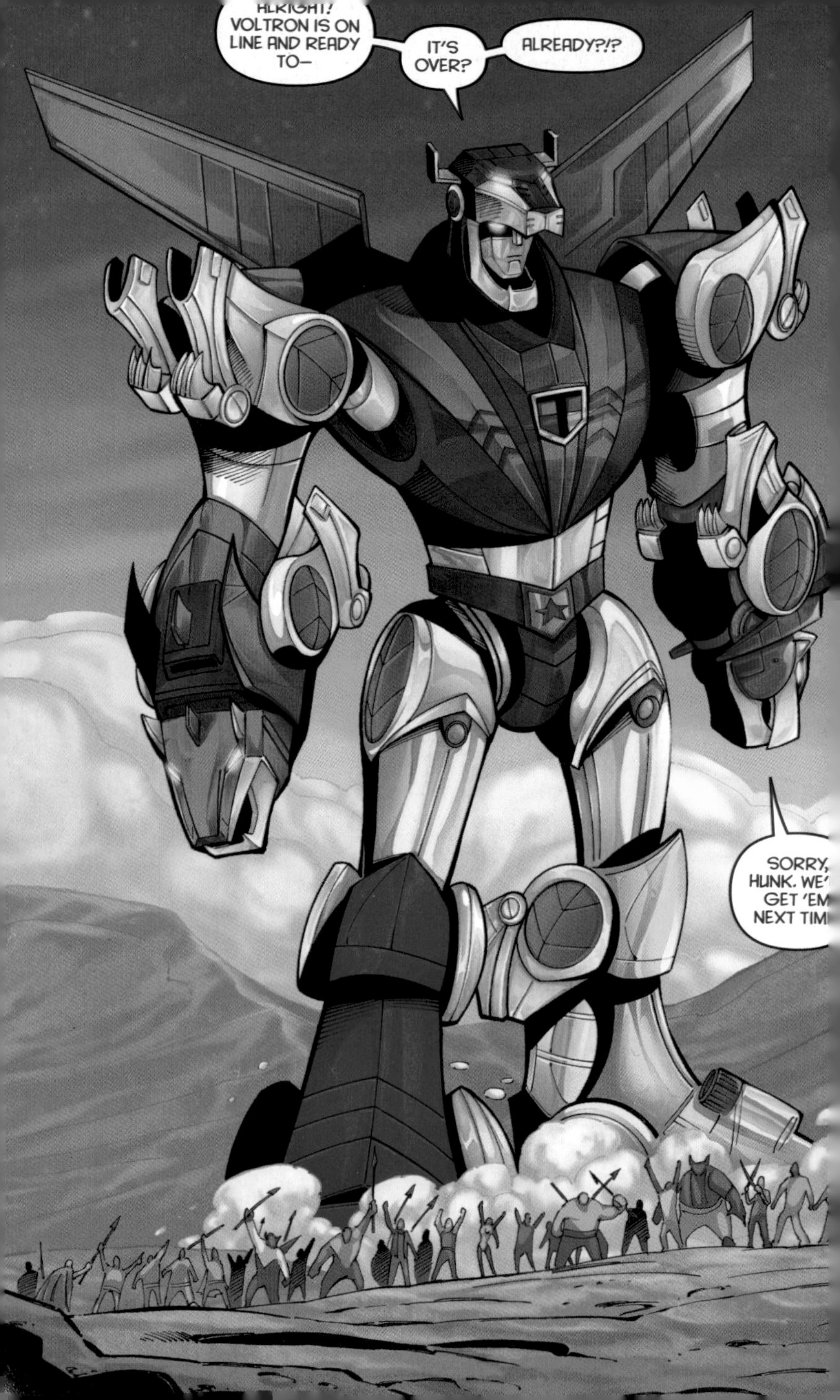
ALRIGHT! VOLTRON IS ON LINE AND READY TO—
IT'S OVER?
ALREADY?!?
SORRY, HUNK. WE' GET 'EM NEXT TIM

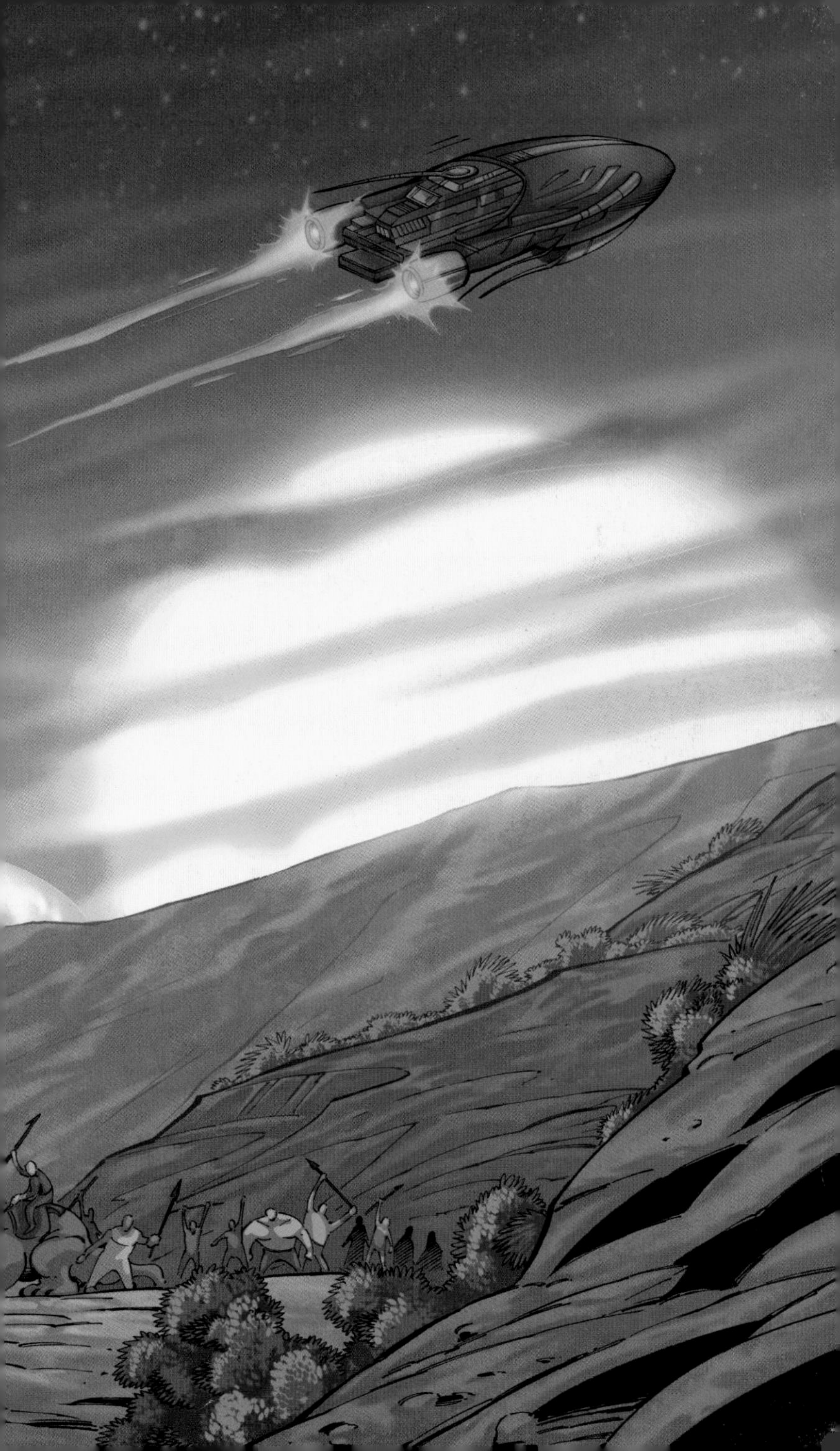

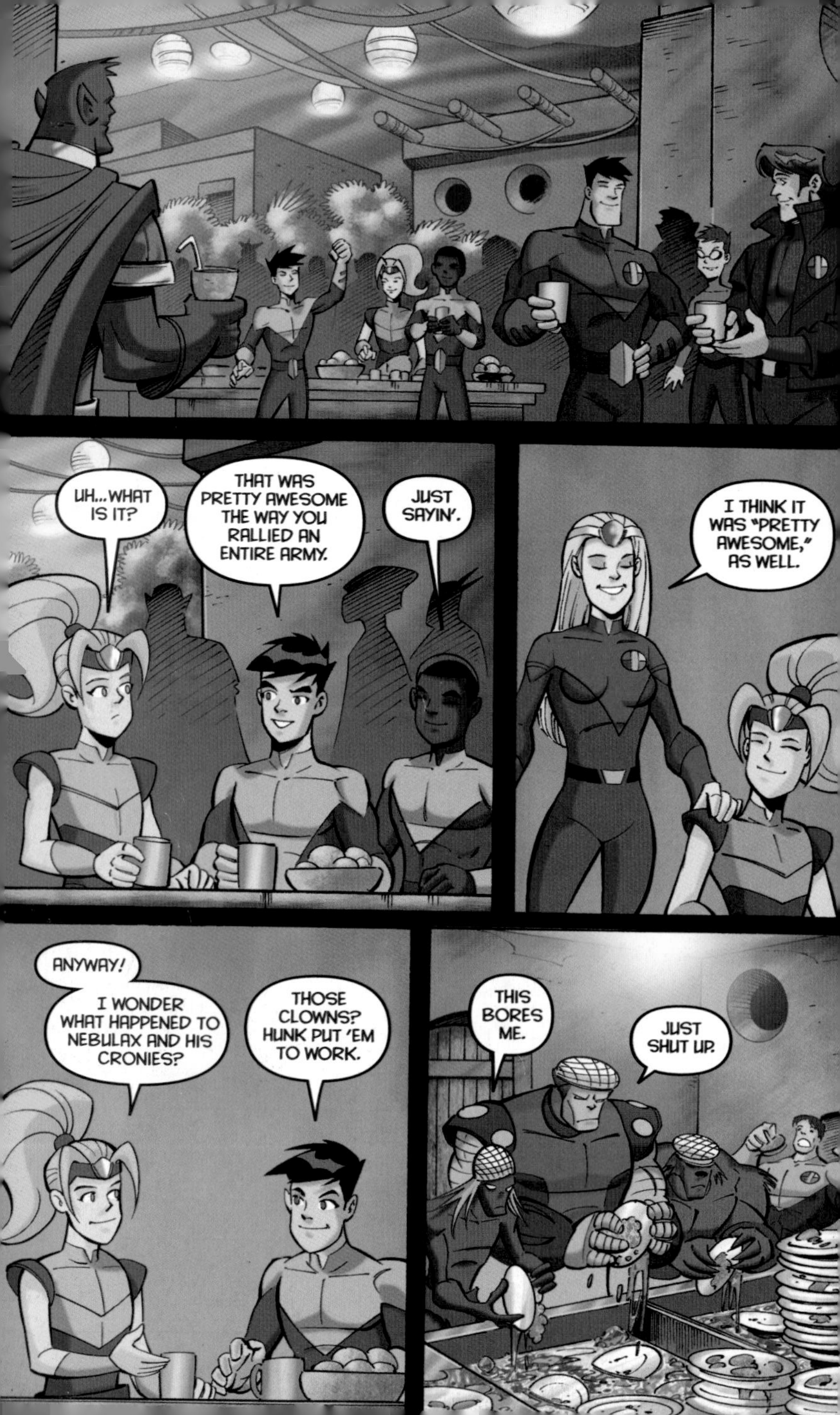
UH...WHAT IS IT?
THAT WAS PRETTY AWESOME THE WAY YOU RALLIED AN ENTIRE ARMY.
JUST SAYIN'.
I THINK IT WAS "PRETTY AWESOME," AS WELL.
ANYWAY!
I WONDER WHAT HAPPENED TO NEBULAX AND HIS CRONIES?
THOSE CLOWNS? HUNK PUT 'EM TO WORK.
THIS BORES ME.
JUST SHUT UP.

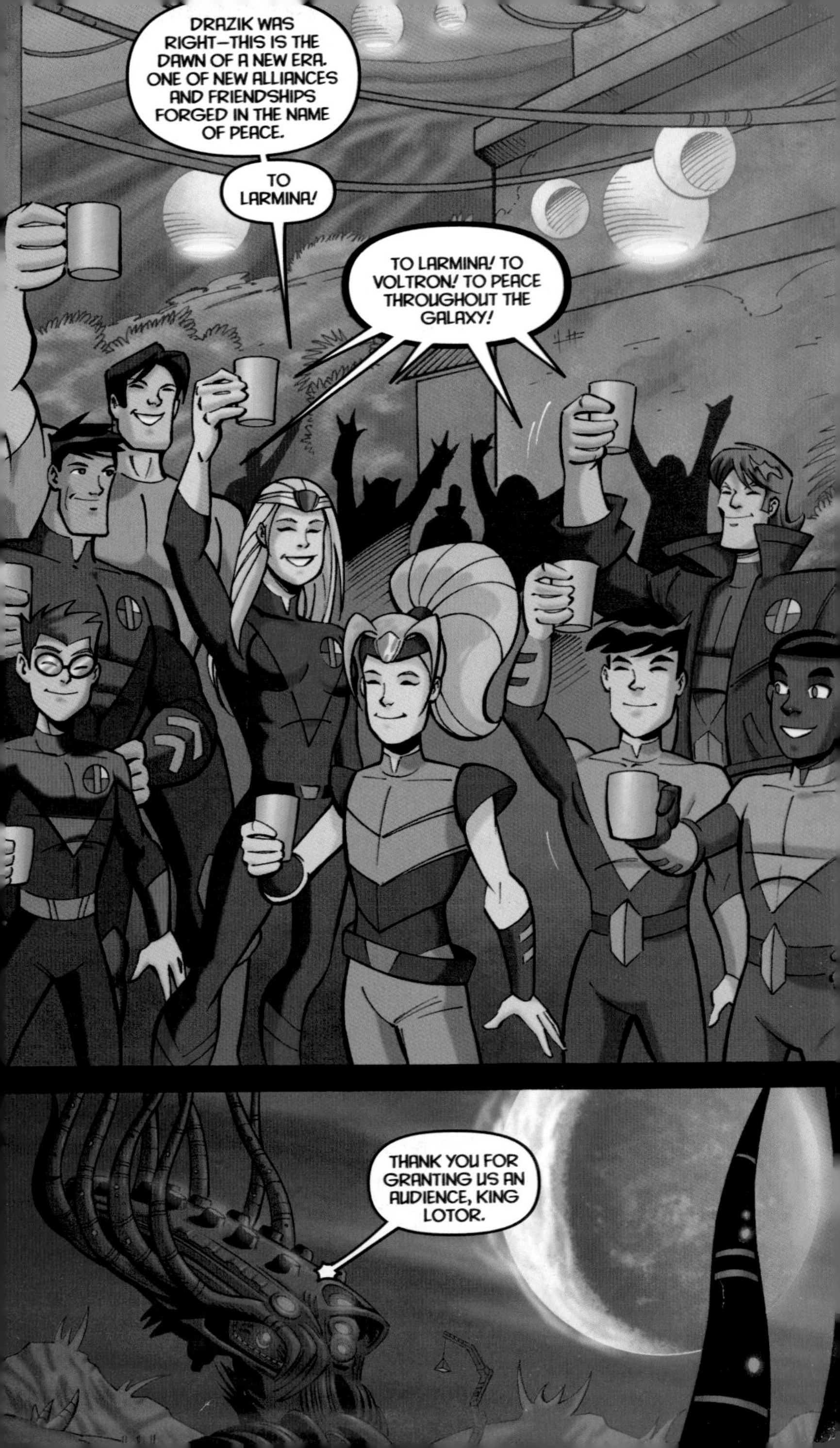
DRAZIK WAS RIGHT—THIS IS THE DAWN OF A NEW ERA. ONE OF NEW ALLIANCES AND FRIENDSHIPS FORGED IN THE NAME OF PEACE.
TO LARMINA!
TO LARMINA! TO VOLTRON! TO PEACE THROUGHOUT THE GALAXY!
THANK YOU FOR GRANTING US AN AUDIENCE, KING LOTOR.

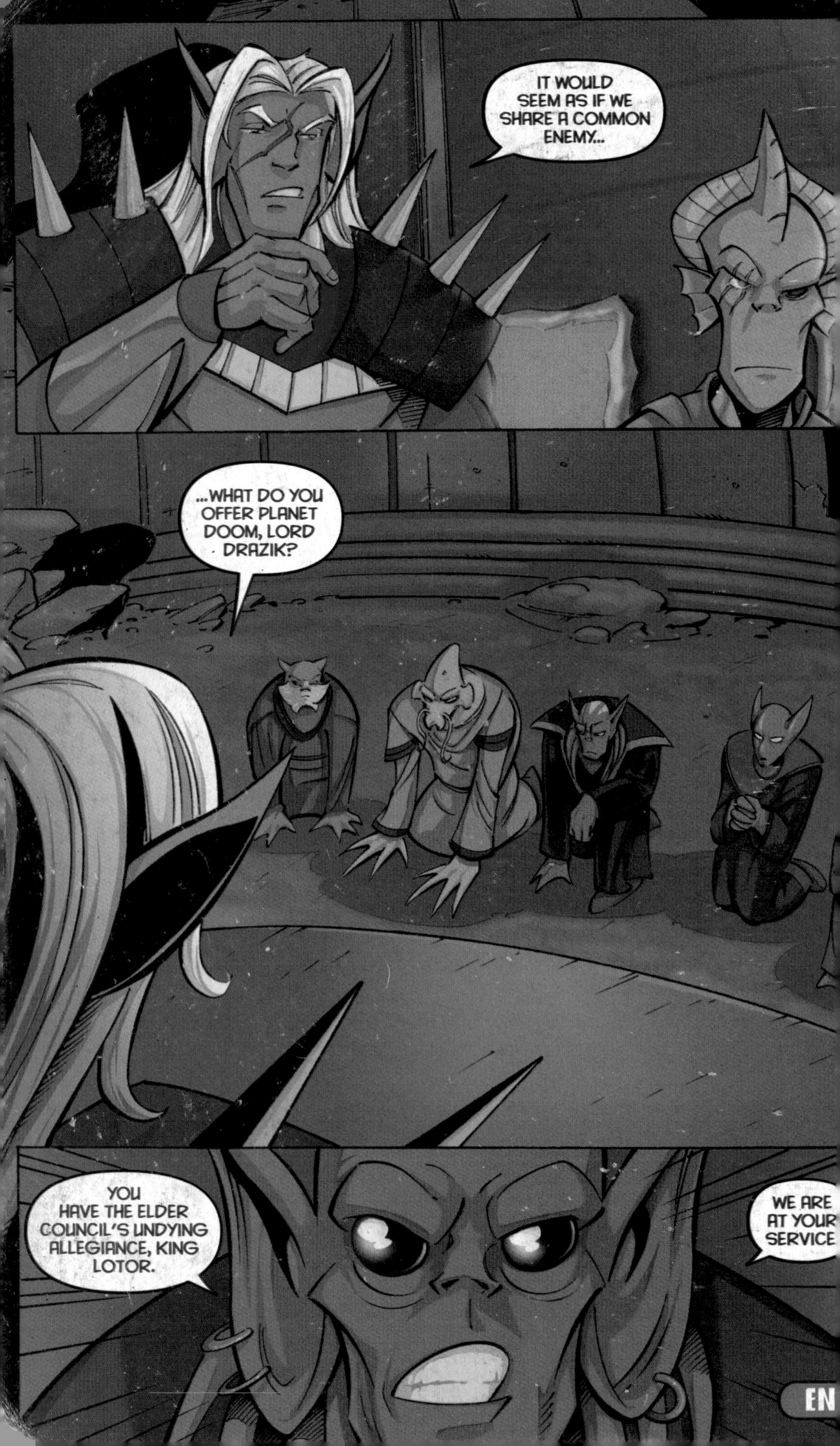
IT WOULD SEEM AS IF WE SHARE A COMMON ENEMY...
...WHAT DO YOU OFFER PLANET DOOM, LORD DRAZIK?
YOU HAVE THE ELDER COUNCIL'S UNDYING ALLEGIANCE, KING LOTOR.
WE ARE AT YOUR SERVICE

BRIAN SMITH Brian Smith is a former Marvel Comics editor. His credits include The *Ultimates*, *Ultimate Spider-Man*, *Iron Man*, *Captain America*, *The Incredible Hulk*, and dozens of other comics. Smith is the co-creator/writer behind the *New York Times* best-selling graphic novel *The Stuff of Legend*, and the writer/artist of the all-ages comic *The Intrepid EscapeGoat*. His writing credits include *Finding Nemo: Losing Dory* from BOOM! Studios and *SpongeBob Comics* from Bongo.

Smith is also the illustrator of *The Adventures of Daniel Boom AKA LOUDBOY!*, named one of The Top 10 Graphic Novels for Youths 2009 by Booklist Online. His illustration clients include *Time Out New York Magazine*, *Nickelodeon*, *MAD Kids Magazine*, Harper Collins, Bongo Comics, Grosset & Dunlap, and American Greetings.

DARIO BRIZUELA Dario Brizuela was born in Buenos Aires, Argentina, in 1977, and began his work in comics as assistant to Carlos Meglia at the age of 16, and has never stopped working on comics, animation, coloring and illustration. He broke into the U.S. market drawing *Star Wars* (Dark Horse), and has gone on to work for DC, Marvel, Mirage, IDW, and VIZ Media. Some of his titles include *Ninja Turtles*, *Ben 10*, *Justice League Unlimited*, *Transformers*, *Iron Man*, *Batman: The Brave and the Bold* and the *Green Lantern* animated series.

MARLO ALQUIZA Marlo Alquiza has been a lifelong comic fan and started his almost twenty-year career in the comic industry immediately after graduating from U.C. Berkeley with a degree in Fine Arts in 1993. He first worked for Image Comic's Extreme Studios and later moved on to work for Marvel, Top Cow, and with other Image Comics creators. From there, Marlo started a long run working for DC Comics that continues to this day. Past work includes *Avengelyne*, *Prophet*, *Darkchylde*, *Darkness*, *Witchblade*, *Tomb Raider*, *The Tenth*, *Spider-man*, *Catwoman*, *Superman*, *Teen Titans*, *Wonder Woman*, and *Green Lantern* to name a short few.

WALDEN WONG A veteran inker in the comics industry, Walden Wong has worked with DC Comics, Marvel Comics, Dark Horse Comics, Top Cow Comics, Disney Adventures, Image Comics, and more.

COMING SOON!

VOLTRON FORCE
TWIN TROUBLE
3
STORY BY BRIAN SMITH
ART BY HORACIO DOMINGUES AND PEDRO PABLO PEREZ VALIENTE

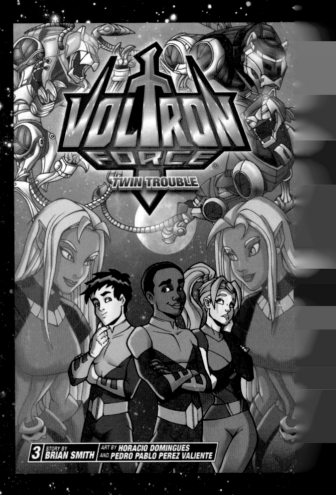

Now that Daniel's a Voltron Force cadet, he can't wait to sho
in front of his former Galaxy Alliance Flight Academy classm
He owns the skies in Black Lion, but not for long! Out of now
two unknown ships appear and put Daniel's flying to shame.
are these mysterious new pilots? And is their presence at the
academy an act of peace or an act of aggression?